The Gathering of the Court Cards
Scars and Stitches

Written by

Alexa Creed

Alexa Creed

Copyright © 2024 Alexa Creed

All Rights Reserved.

No Part of this book may be produced, stored in a retrieval system, or transmitted by any means without the written permission of the author.

ISBN: 978-1-962849-78-4

Case #: 1-13705950781

Dedication

To my grandmother Roberta McCrea, whose artistic inspiration and influence helped me discover my own medium in words being placed on paper.

Acknowledgment

To think this story began with my love for horror coming from both on the screen and the pages of books that are classics. I'd like to thank my grandmother Roberta who always had faith in me, even though there were times I doubted myself. Her words is what kept me going. If it wasn't for her, Scars and Stitches wouldn't exist. To think this story started when our family started working at a starter Renaissance Fair.

To my mother Cherie, who served as my motivation to keep moving forward even when times were tough. I wouldn't be the person that I am today because of her. Your support means the world to me.

I also like to thank Mary Shelley the author of Frankenstein. If it wasn't for her, Science Fiction wouldn't be what it is today, and have read Frankenstein two times in my lifetime.

And Oscar Wilde, who was an individual ahead of his time, whose novel The Picture of Dorian Gray taught me even the most beautiful things and places can be subjects of horror. And his plays showed me a glimpse of Victorian High Society in a humorous way with the 2002 movie adaptation of his play the Importance of Being Ernest being my favorite.

Overall, these aspects brought Scars and Stitches to life. Thank you.

Table Of Contents

Chapter One

The pain seared through my back as the scalpel sliced into my shoulder blades, a sharp and agonizing sensation. My screams of terror filled the room as the needle and suture thread sealed the wounds. "Think of it as a vaccination," the surgeon reassured me, though I could sense the falsehood in his words. Those were the only words I could recall from the nightmare that haunted my mind, the nightmare that had stolen my memories. I had been discovered by the family who ran the local bed and breakfast in the heart of the Garden District's southern sector. They had found me wandering the forest that marked the boundary between the slums and the nearest town in the dead of night, alone and barefoot.

As I lifted the covers from my bed, the realization washed over me—I wasn't in an operating room but in the welcoming embrace of the family who managed the bed and breakfast. Their kindness had allowed me to convalesce, saving me from the brink of death after my exposure to the elements. Despite the room's modest size, it exuded charm. Pastel purple adorned all the walls, while gilt molding elegantly traced the corners and edges. A white marble floor with a meandering blue mosaic path guided me to the centerpiece—a grand canopy bed.

A sigh escaped my lips. Ever since the chilling news of the Doll Killer had penetrated the slums, I'd been plagued by nightmares that were steadily wearing me down. It was a cruel twist of fate that I had no recollection of my former life, not since Sera and her parents discovered me, a lost soul, in the woods a week ago. They said I was fortunate not to have succumbed to a fever after enduring the frigid cold for who knew how many hours.

Regrettably, my memories remained elusive, shrouded in a thick fog. I couldn't conjure the faces of my parents or any family members; their names were empty blanks. The solitary remnant of my past was my name: Adelice. Alas, I had no inkling of my last name. The doctor who had examined me had explained that the journey to recovering my memories would be a lengthy one.

I had been convalescing at the bed and breakfast on the forest's edge for a week now, and still, no memories had emerged—not even a hint of a trigger.

The folks in the neighborhood showed remarkable kindness to me, even though I carried the label of a Halfling. Perhaps the true reason I hadn't been cast out by Sera and her parents lay in the discovery they made when they found me—a deck of tarot cards nestled in my coat's pocket. The memory of my most recent nightmare lingered so vividly that I couldn't bring myself to return to sleep, haunted by the sensation of the scalpel's sharp blade against my back.

Setting aside my residual dread, it seemed prudent to start preparing for the day. Today marked my final day of residence at the bed and breakfast. Sera's parents had taken the step of enrolling me in what they called "the System," a seemingly fancy term for foster care tailored to Halflings like me. Soon, I'd find myself under the care of a different family.

"Adelice, are you awake?" Sera's voice reached me from the other side of the door. "Yes, I'm up!" I replied. She had likely returned from purchasing groceries for the other guests who were staying at the bed and breakfast. It was a relief that I had regained enough strength to venture beyond this room. Today marked the commencement of the Doll Auction, an event hosted at the courthouse in the square.

"I've brought breakfast," Sera announced, gently guiding a small serving cart into the room. After the tray settled onto the bed, she made her way to the window and gracefully drew back the silk curtains. Sunlight cascaded in, accentuating the room's soothing blue and purple color palette. "You'll want to eat quickly if we're going to secure a good seat," Sera advised, handing me a set of clothes retrieved from the dark purple armoire.

At the sight of the light gray dress laid out on the bed, my lips curled into a sneer. "How delightful," I remarked dryly, popping a grape into my mouth. Sera's brow furrowed. "Adelice, it's imperative that we adhere to the specific colors and markings of the Elite we serve, in exchange for their protection."

"I apologize," I sighed, "I just didn't get much sleep last night." I confessed while taking a fortifying sip of the robust, budget-friendly coffee that Sera's parents provided to their guests. If I were to endure the day ahead, I'd need several more cups. I couldn't help but attribute these nightmares to the sensational tabloid stories about the Doll Killer.

I delved into the assortment of freshly cut fruit, buttery croissants, and delicate slices of cheddar cheese, washing it down with the last of the coffee from its metal pot. Now, it was time for a shower.

I turned my attention to the full-length mirror positioned by the vanity table. As I beheld my reflection, a gasp escaped my lips. The frail image that stared back at me featured a girl with pale olive skin, cornflower blue eyes, and cascading moonlit white hair. It was short at the back and graced with loose waves in the front.

The doctor who had examined me had been taken aback by the revelation of my natural hair color, and equally surprised by the thickness of my bangs. As I washed and scrubbed my body in the shower, my thoughts reluctantly returned to my recent nightmare—a grotesque rendition of a doctor's examination room. In that terrifying dream, I had been bound to the examination table. Despite its nightmarish nature, the experience had felt disconcertingly real.

One undeniable fact hung heavily in the air: there was a serial killer at large in the Empire of Alessia, a place that had once been two vast continents known as the Americas, though now largely forgotten by its citizens. When my shower concluded, I wrapped myself in a towel from the rack and dried off. Soon, I exchanged it for the light gray dress that Sera had selected for me to wear to the auction.

"You look adorable," Sera gushed upon seeing me. "I can't understand why I have to dress up," I groaned in response. So far, my deep aversion to dresses was the only fragment of my old life I could recall.

Regrettably, my memories remained clouded by the overwhelming trauma of my past, leaving only fragmented images of myself fleeing through the forest, desperately escaping from some ominous presence. Everything else had been locked away due to the shadow of PTSD, making the tarot deck the sole clue I possessed.

"We should head to the courthouse early and secure our seats," Sera suggested with enthusiasm.

I sighed, a growing awareness of the growing distance between us. Don't get me wrong; I liked Sera, but there was a reason for the segregation laws that kept Halflings apart from the Purebloods. It all revolved around the fact that my kind resided exclusively in the Grey Zone.

I spotted him at one of the tavern's corner tables—an older-looking Halfling boy, perhaps around fifteen years old. We shared a common identifier, the intricate filigree markings adorning the upper part of our left arms. These elegant swirls and patterns were unmistakable symbols of our Halfling heritage.

He was a tall lad with olive skin, dark brown hair, and captivating green eyes hidden behind thick, black-framed glasses. His attire, consisting of black jeans and a blue flannel shirt, gave him a nerdy yet rustic appearance. The laptop he carried only accentuated his nerdiness.

"Good morning," he greeted me. "Are you all set for the auction?"

I let out a sarcastic chuckle. "I suppose it won't be long until I'm handed off to my next host family. Today's my last day here, after all. What better way to celebrate than by attending the Doll Auction at the courthouse?"

The boy with the laptop nodded in understanding. We shared a solemn recognition of the harsh reality that came with being part of a host family—their temporary care extended only until the factions we were born into decided to claim us as their own.

"If you'd like," he offered, "I have some connections. I can give them a call and make arrangements for your next living accommodations."

I was aware of some of our kind who chose to reside in youth hostels to avoid being placed in the System. The drawback, of course, was having to share a bathroom with dozens of other kids.

I shook my head firmly. The idea of communal living already left a bad taste in my mouth. "I think I'll pass on that option."

Curious, I inquired about the boy's activities on his computer. He explained, "I'm scouring every article I can find about the Doll Killer. The stories in the major newspapers all have a common thread—victims' vital organs were harvested after their deaths. Unfortunately, that's where the trail goes cold. Gray claims the police have things under control, but I have my doubts." The name "Gray" struck a chord, but I wished I could access my memories to fully understand the significance.

Before long, Sera entered the tavern, her green eyes narrowing at the sight of the boy with the laptop. "Are you ready to go, Adelice?" she inquired.

The boy winked at me and rose from his seat. "I'll catch you at the auction," he said, then began to make his exit.

Sera's curiosity got the best of her as she prodded, "What on earth were you and Victor Frankenstein's son talking about?"

I offered a quick lie, not wanting her to report me for discussing the Doll Killer or for engaging in conversation with the offspring of a notorious scientist. It was a stark reminder of the paranoia that often gripped Purebloods. "Nothing," I replied.

Sera's sigh carried a heavy weight of guilt as she admitted, "I suppose I should come clean with you, Adelice. You won't be staying here after the auction." Her words landed like a blow, as I had assumed I'd have one more night.

"Do you know who my new host family is?" I inquired anxiously, needing to ascertain whether they were good or not. I believed I had the right to know.

Sera hesitated, then finally revealed, "You won't be with a family; it's a company called Marvelous Radiance." Disgust marred her features as she uttered the name.

The name Marvelous Radiance stirred memories of hushed conversations among the slum's residents during my recovery.

They spoke of a company fixated on perfecting the human image and social status. Whispers even suggested that the company's founder and CEO had made a Faustian bargain to retain eternal youth. Rumors swirled about Marvelous Radiance's involvement in shadowy dealings. The notion that such a multi-million dollar enterprise would take an interest in an amnesiac Halfling girl like me seemed inexplicable. Something didn't add up, and I thirsted for answers.

Chapter Two

The journey to the courthouse was a somber one. Time seemed to drag on, each minute stretching into an eternity, and each second feeling like an hour. Sera and I walked in silence, not exchanging a single word. We passed by the chattering debutantes, their excitement palpable as they eagerly discussed the forthcoming season. From the snippets I overheard, their enthusiasm revolved around personal preferences – from flower choices at the florist to the catered food and color schemes for various events. Unlike those around me, I couldn't muster any joy for the impending social gathering.

For the Halflings of the area, this was a rare opportunity to be visible in a world that often shunned us. My mind was still reeling from the revelation that the System had placed me under the care of Marvelous Radiance. I couldn't fathom what use such a company might have for someone like me.

I couldn't help but feel like a mere Halfling, burdened by the weight of my amnesia. The privileged elites seemed content in their obliviousness to the world beyond their social cocoon.

"You've been awfully quiet," Sera remarked, her gaze probing. "Not a word the entire walk."

I let out a heavy sigh. "Why would they choose me? I'm a nobody; I can't even remember my parents' faces." The bitterness clung to my words. I couldn't help but wonder why the System hadn't placed me elsewhere. When I got registered in their database, I hadn't anticipated such a sudden and unexpected turn of events.

Even though Sera's reassurance was kind, but it couldn't alleviate my sense of bewilderment. "I can't grasp why a dubious company fixated on vanity and perfection would have any interest in me," I mused aloud. Sera remained silent as we continued our journey to the courthouse.

"Maybe it's something about your hair?" she ventured.

I scoffed at the notion. "That would be a rather superficial reason to acquire someone."

I understood that Sera was doing her utmost to make my last day in the Slums more pleasant, but it couldn't alter the grim reality that awaited me—a future among shallow individuals. My gloomy thoughts began to dissipate as we arrived at the courthouse, where lush green lawns were teeming with people. It was a stark contrast to the solemn atmosphere, and I couldn't help but wonder about the twisted spectacle that was the Doll Auction, where an unfortunate girl was chosen to become a living toy, an entertainer, and a model for the wealthy.

It was like a Stepford Wife tradition, an unsettling display where hair texture and skin tone were manipulated to achieve a superficial perfection, all controlled by an eerie spell that reduced them to mindless automatons. As Sera and I approached the courthouse, we couldn't help but spot numerous Pureblood women dressed in their finest day gowns, adorned in pastel hues, while the men sported velvet frock coats in shades of olive green, brick red, navy blue, and jet black. Despite their exquisite appearance and flawless visages, a palpable aura of cruelty seemed to emanate from them.

"I never expected so many people to turn out," Sera remarked, her voice tinged with awe.

While Sera seemed enamored by their beauty, my perception cut deeper, revealing a dark undercurrent of malevolence and sinistral intentions. It was as though I could peer into the very souls of these people, unearthing the ugliness and sadism beneath their physical façades. Their actions confirmed my suspicions, and an ominous feeling settled in the pit of my stomach, foretelling impending disaster.

"You look like you're on the brink of a panic attack," Sera observed bluntly, her concern evident.

I rolled my eyes dismissively. "It's nothing," I lied, but she saw right through me.

"After the auction," Sera declared with surprising resolve, "I'm going to give you a head start to escape before the Social Worker comes for you."

Her words left me stunned. We had only known each other for a week, and yet she was willing to jeopardize her own safety to help me flee. I couldn't decide whether she was incredibly brave or unreasonably foolish.

Indeed, being entrusted to a bunch of shallow individuals was a fate no one should have to endure, particularly if it involved an infamous entity like Marvelous Radiance. I couldn't help but wonder who had stumbled upon my profile in the System's database. My best guess was someone with a penchant for Halflings bearing the most unusual traits, such as my ethereal, moonlit hair, so white it appeared to emit a faint glow in the darkness.

Just when I thought things couldn't deteriorate any further, my discomfort heightened as I noticed a plump woman with dark, beady eyes fixated on me.

The woman's presence bore an unsettling resemblance to Aunt Lydia from "The Handmaid's Tale," although lacking the brown attire and cattle prod. There was an eerie familiarity about her, but I couldn't quite place it.

Sera's hushed words broke the silence. "It's the social worker," she whispered. My heart skipped a beat in dread.

The question echoed in my mind: Why was a social worker attending a Doll Auction? My paranoia had momentarily overshadowed the fact that this was a public event.

Sera's determination shone through as she whispered, "I'll get you out, I promise." In the short time I had known her, I had come to realize that she was the kind of person who kept her word, especially with her claiming ceremony looming on the horizon. The elders would soon convene at the courthouse to determine which side, light or dark, she would align with.

As a Halfling, I was spared from the claiming ceremony, a ritual reserved for those on the cusp of choosing between the light and dark factions. My status as a "grey" marked me as a product of both sides, eternally bound by the intricate patterns adorning the top of my left arm—a symbol of perpetual ownership. Yet, I couldn't help but wonder what it would be like to experience true freedom, a dangerous question in the eyes of society.

Once Sera and I settled into our seats, I couldn't ignore the hostile glares from a few Purebloods. One of the cardinal rules for Halflings was to avoid being seen with Purebloods who weren't family members, and Sera didn't fall into that category.

Our scholars, our guides, had long clarified that we were beings of both light and dark, dwelling in a realm known as the Grey Zone.

This status bestowed upon us a unique gift—the ability to harness both white and black magic. We ceased aging between the tender ages of thirteen and nineteen, forever condemned to the facade of eternal teenagehood. It was a stark testament to our separation from the Purebloods, whether of the light or dark factions.

Just when I believed things couldn't grow any stranger, I caught sight of the boy with the laptop – Felix Frankenstein, to be precise – entering the courthouse. To my surprise, he settled into the seat right next to mine.

It was nothing short of astonishing to discover that the boy I had pegged as a self-proclaimed nerd, inseparable from his laptop, was actually the sole heir of a notorious mad scientist. Even stranger was the fact that he was a Halfling, just like me.

I began to grasp why he had been so cautious about revealing his identity during our tavern conversation. He clearly wished to avoid the unwanted attention that came with being the son of the infamous creator of a monstrous being. My amnesia might have obscured many memories, but I would never forget Felix's face.

He leaned in close, his words a breathy whisper, "Meet me in the forest after the auction." The clandestine nature of our meeting reflected the danger that loomed if we were overheard by the watchful Purebloods.

The meaningful exchange of glances between Felix and Sera conveyed all I needed to understand. She had undoubtedly approached him with the intention of securing my escape from the clutches of the looming social worker, who seemed determined to send me off to the unsettling individuals associated with the Marvelous Radiance Circle.

I was all too aware that their central headquarters lay in the New York Province, with a focus on the newly restored Manhattan, one of the most exorbitant cities to reside in—perfect for the founder and his cohorts.

An inexplicable longing tugged at my heart, urging me towards the Marvelous Radiance headquarters. There, I believed I might uncover the answers to my identity, a chance to reclaim the memories I had lost, and perhaps even reunite with my family.

The possibilities felt boundless, offering the tantalizing prospect of taking control of my own life, no longer tethered to the whims of the enigmatic agents who governed the System.

A hushed anticipation swept through the audience as the host made his entrance onto the stage, signaling the imminent start of the show. All eyes and cameras converged on him as he greeted the assembled crowd.

"Good morning, ladies and gentlemen, children of all ages," he announced, his voice projected through the venue and transmitted to countless television screens across the vast Empire. "I am deeply honored to be your host for today's Doll Auction. Imagine my astonishment when I received a call from the Emperor himself to preside over a tradition that has been an integral part of Alessia since its inception."

The grim reality of the situation settled over me, dispelling any inclination to laugh. Becoming a Doll was a fate marred by servitude and prostitution, a life predetermined for the girls chosen by the Committee, while boys became Jesters. It was a cruel display of the Emperor's absolute power and dominion over humans, magic users, immortals, and supernatural beings alike.

"Now, onto the first Doll," the host announced, his voice laden with malevolence as he began to unveil the name enclosed in the dark red envelope. A sinister grin stretched across his face as he declared, "Faith Peters!" The reaction was immediate, with uncontrollable wails and sobs erupting from the girl seated next to Sera and me. It was clear that chaos was on the brink of breaking loose.

Chapter Three

Faith Peters' scream tore through the air, an otherworldly wail that seemed more like the cry of a banshee than a human being. It sent shivers down our spines. Even the boy seated beside her, likely her boyfriend, appeared dumbfounded, as if he believed this was some heartless prank played on him. The already chaotic scene escalated when Faith abruptly shot out of her seat and sprinted down the aisles of the courthouse, her movements wild and unbridled.

"Stop her!" a Pureblood man barked, his voice ringing with authority as panic rippled through the crowd.

"Allow me," a dark-haired young man offered, his words cool and detached. He removed his black gloves, unveiling long, razor-sharp nails adorned in a deep shade of purple. The entire audience's attention was riveted on him as he raised his ungloved hand aloft, slowly curling his fingers downward until they pointed directly at Faith. It was then that her worst nightmare came true: her body froze, eyes widening in terror as she realized she couldn't move. This young man possessed the chilling power to control people with a mere flick of his fingers.

The audience remained silent, captivated by the spectacle, as the young man slowly approached Faith's immobilized figure. With a commanding gesture, he pointed towards the stage, and she began to move as if controlled by invisible strings, her steps marred by heart-wrenching sobs. The young man couldn't resist a mocking comment as he watched her obey his command. "Now, that wasn't so difficult, was it?" he taunted cruelly. "It's a pity we must transform you into such an ugly duckling."

With his dark eyes fixed upon the host, the young man relinquished control. "She's all yours," he stated, retaking his seat. The host nodded in gratitude to the enigmatic nobleman who had aligned himself with the dark faction. Amusement glimmered in the host's eyes as he comprehended the rare opportunity he had been granted—to publicly humiliate Faith before the entire audience. The indifferent expressions worn by those present made it painfully clear that none among them harbored any intention of coming to her aid.

"There's a penalty for running away, darling," the host taunted with a sardonic smile, his once warm, dark brown eyes now appearing cold and lifeless from afar. His tone took on a twisted affection as he continued, "Such a pretty face, I wonder what will happen if we add a few flaws to it? Bring me a scalpel!" he thundered, his command echoing through the hall.

Without delay, a servant emerged onto the stage, bearing a white satin pillow upon which rested a gleaming scalpel. Faith's piercing screams tore through the air as the host wielded the blade, cruelly marring her face. It was the ultimate punishment for those who dared to defy the Empire's laws, and a malevolent satisfaction emanated from the host as he gazed upon the now-bloodied scalpel.

The Pureblood girl crumpled to her knees, her anguished whimpering a testament to the excruciating pain now etched upon her scarred face. The physical wounds were gruesome, but the emotional scars she would carry with her for a lifetime were far more profound.

"Now the swan is an ugly duckling," the host enthused, placing the scalpel back on the pillow. Faith's agonized scream of, "How could you do this?" was met with a harsh slap from the host. "You shouldn't have run away," he declared with a chilling coldness. "Things could have been different if you hadn't run. You should have felt honored. You were chosen. Not every girl is afforded this opportunity."

"You're a sick bastard," Faith spat defiantly, her words earning her another stinging slap. "Not only have you insulted me, but you've also insulted the Emperor. Your lack of respect for our illustrious ruler has sealed your fate as his human pet." A gasp escaped me, realizing that becoming a pet was a fate even grimmer than becoming a doll.

I watched in horror as the security personnel ushered Faith off the stage and out of the courthouse, a stark indication that the harrowing auction had come to a dreadful end.

As we distanced ourselves from the courthouse, a deep sense of unease settled over me. Sera clung to my hand tightly, offering a source of solace as we made our way back to the bed and breakfast. Though I had never known Faith, a profound sympathy welled within me for the dreadful fate she had endured.

To compound the mounting distress, I noticed a sleek limousine parked in front of the bed and breakfast. In the distance, I could see Sera's parents engaged in conversation with the plump woman I had previously observed at the courthouse.

Still reeling from the tormenting spectacle of Faith Peters' fate, I had momentarily forgotten the impending arrival of the social worker tasked with ushering me into my new "home." Sera's urgent guidance brought me back to the present.

We hastened to the rear of the house and followed a path that led us to an abandoned windmill, a location infamous for its haunted reputation. Beyond that, lay another trail, delving deep into the forest, serving as the starting point for my escape route. Sera remained outside the mill, patiently waiting as I hurriedly changed into a pair of loose jeans, a neon green shirt, and a pair of running sneakers from the small duffel bag she had thoughtfully prepared for me. Relief washed over me as I realized it wasn't the tattered coat and pajama set I had been discovered in just a week ago. It all felt surreal, the only memory I possessed was that of fleeing from an unknown terror.

A week had passed, and while I still lacked my memories, at least now I knew who or what it was I was running from. As Sera handed me the duffel bag, she shared, "There are more clothes in the bag, along with all our savings."

Baffled by her unwavering support, I questioned, "Why are you helping me?"

Sera's eyes bore a profound conviction as she replied, "Crazy as it may sound, Adelice, I have this inexplicable feeling that something greater is at work here. I sensed you were special when my parents found you. A Halfling like you should not be taken in by Gray's company. I've witnessed firsthand what they are capable of. They're monsters, every last one of them."

With a basket of food for the journey into the forest, Sera continued to provide for my escape. "This should sustain you and Felix until you reach the next town after crossing the border," she informed me.

I nodded in gratitude, deeply moved by her willingness to risk her life for my sake. Her actions were a testament that not all Purebloods were hostile towards us, that some could indeed be trusted. For Sera, this was her opportunity to undertake a noble act before the Committee decided which of the two sides she would align with.

With the basket and duffel bag in each hand, I followed Sera down the trail that led to the forest's entrance. A swirl of emotions welled within me, a mixture of fear and excitement, as I ventured into an uncertain future.

I was relieved to find that I wouldn't be embarking on this journey alone; Felix stood near the forest's entrance, clutching a backpack and a tote bag in his hands. It seemed fitting that Sera would provide him with the remaining supplies for our escape. Notably, the social worker had arrived not just to collect me, but Felix as well, likely to return him to his father.

The gravity of Sera's involvement struck me even more profoundly; she was putting her life in severe jeopardy by assisting two Halflings in escaping from the clutches of the System.

Sera provided us with crucial guidance, assuring us, "Once you're out of the forest, you'll be able to cross the border and reach the next town without getting caught." Her explanation was cut short as the sound of her mother's voice calling her name echoed through the air. Her parents and the social worker had yet to realize that we were not inside.

Recognizing the urgency of the situation, Sera pressed us to leave. I nodded in acknowledgment, knowing that this would likely be our final farewell. "This is goodbye. Take care of each other, and promise to watch over one another," she urged with a sense of urgency and finality in her voice.

"We will," Felix confirmed, his vivid green eyes flicking towards me. "Ready, partner?" he inquired, casting a hopeful glance in my direction.

I felt a sense of camaraderie in that moment, the beginning of what promised to be a profound friendship. "I'm ready," I affirmed with determination. With that, the two of us darted into the woods, our future uncertain as we approached the border, but unwavering in our belief that whatever lay ahead would be worth the risk.

Chapter Four

I couldn't determine how long Felix and I had been running. By this point, it was certain that Sera's parents and the social worker had discovered our escape into the forest. It was highly probable that a bounty had been placed on our heads as we dared to defy the Purebloods. Marvelous Radiance had even offered a reward for anyone who could betray me. I couldn't help but smirk as I envisioned the rage of those who had acquired my information from the System's database.

I harbored no desire to let either faction dictate the course of my life. "I believe it's safe for us to halt here," Felix remarked, his smile faint but reassuring. Undoubtedly, the relentless running had taken its toll on him, much as it had on me. It was almost surreal to think that such a kind-hearted individual was the offspring of a mad scientist who had brought a creature to life through the most unorthodox means, defying all divine norms. Despite his unconventional lineage, I placed my trust in him, recognizing that both of us relied on each other for survival.

"By now, we're officially fugitives," he said with a hint of humor. Both of us were acutely aware of the gravity of our situation and the perils that accompanied it.

"You don't seem troubled by it," I remarked bluntly.

"No, I'm not," Felix confessed.

"So, who exactly was it that procured you from the System's database?" he inquired, his curiosity genuine.

"I'm not certain; all I can say is that they're affiliated with Marvelous Radiance."

"Well, that's disheartening," Felix shook his head, his disgust aimed not at me, but at the individuals who had acquired me.

"This whole situation is baffling. Why would a company catering to purebloods be interested in you?"

"I wish I had an answer, but I don't."

"This smells like Gray's handiwork," Felix added, and for some reason, the name Gray struck a chord of familiarity in me.

"Sera mentioned your amnesia, so I'll give you the essentials. Dorian Gray is the founder and CEO of Marvelous Radiance, the company your patrons are affiliated with. Among all my father's associates, he's the most sinister of the lot."

"In what way is he a threat?" I inquired.

"Well, let's just say he pulled off some pretty insane stunts back when Emperor Seneca was just an heir apparent, and that's what they call 'spares' – those in line for the throne after the main contenders. He's a threat because he plays a crucial role in keeping the nobility subordinate to the immortals."

"I'll bear that in mind," I replied with a nod. Felix had given me a comprehensive overview of the company's founder, whose enterprise revolved around the ideals of perfection, image, and the relentless pursuit of pleasure and desire, manifesting in forms such as sex and entertainment.

Felix recounted Gray's origin story—a tale of a naive young man who had traded his soul to retain perpetual youth while his portrait aged, a path fraught with tragedy, all to safeguard his vanity. Yet, it was revealed that he had fallen under the sway of a corrupt noble. What struck me as the most unsettling aspect of his narrative was Gray's passionate love affair with a captivating young actress employed in a run-down London theater. He had been so enamored that he wished to make her his wife. However, he abruptly abandoned her when she chose to forsake her acting career in pursuit of genuine love, a decision that tragically led her to take her own life by poison.

Felix proceeded with his narrative. "Following her demise, he descended into a life of debauchery, frequenting brothels and opium dens, indulging in drugs, and engaging in countless liaisons with women throughout the East End of London. Astonishingly, he even resorted to murdering the artist responsible for crafting the portrait that revealed the grotesque truth of his inner self."

After Felix concluded the account of the company's founder, I interjected, "Yet, it still doesn't clarify why his company has an interest in me."

"I'm not entirely certain," Felix admitted. "But whatever Gray desires from you, it's unlikely to bode well. He's ruthless, and it's quite astounding that someone of his nature managed to establish a domestic life."

I was taken aback. "Wait, he has a wife?" I asked, clearly surprised.

"Yes, but she remains out of the public eye, as she belongs to the category of socialites who experienced a sheltered upbringing."

"It's a rather disheartening tale," I remarked, shaking my head in disdain.

"Well, there's not much we can change about it," Felix replied with a resigned shrug.

As Felix and I ventured further into the woods, we stumbled upon a small clearing just as the sun started its descent. It dawned on me that evening was approaching rapidly. "Nightfall is upon us. We ought to establish our camp for the night and aim to reach the border come morning," I proposed.

Felix nodded in concurrence, immediately setting about collecting wood for a fire. While he toiled, my gaze was drawn to a stunning rosebush nearby, adorned with pastel purple and ice blue roses in full bloom. As I observed these delicate blossoms, a dormant memory stirred within me. Slowly, I began to recollect a woman with creamy blonde hair, her locks cascading in gentle waves, although her visage remained elusive in my mind's eye. Alongside her, another image emerged—a man with long, dark hair fashioned into a ponytail, bound by a violet ribbon. Though the features of his countenance remained somewhat blurred, I couldn't help but sense a profound familiarity and a comforting warmth in his presence.

Lost in my reverie, I suddenly became aware of Felix's voice, pulling me back to the present moment. "Adelice, are you alright?" he inquired, genuine concern evident in his eyes.

I blinked and shook my head, attempting to regain my focus. "Yes, I'm alright. It's just... I believe I had a fleeting memory. It's rather peculiar, but I saw a woman with blonde hair and a man with dark hair tied back with a ribbon. They felt significant somehow."

Felix's expression turned one of genuine intrigue. "Perhaps it's a fragment of your past resurfacing. We can make an effort to piece together the puzzle as we continue."

With a small, grateful smile, I joined Felix in preparing our campsite and tending to the fire. As the flames danced and the night enveloped us, my thoughts couldn't help but dwell on the significance of those elusive memories and what they might unveil about my true identity.

Beneath the crackling of the fire and the warm glow it cast over our makeshift camp, I found solace in Felix's words. The mere glimpse of my parents, even in an incomplete recollection, offered a glimmer of hope, a reassurance that I wasn't alone in this vast world. I understood that the quest to find them and unearth my past would be an arduous one, but I harbored a renewed sense of determination to see it through.

Felix's unwavering presence by my side was a source of great comfort. In this perilous and uncertain journey, he had transformed into a true friend and companion. His kindness and support held an immeasurable significance that words could scarcely convey. I turned my gaze once more to the pastel purple and ice blue roses, their petals touched by the gentle caress of frost, and felt an inexplicable bond with them. Somehow, these delicate blooms had acted as a catalyst, evoking a fleeting glimpse of my forgotten memories, serving as a sign that there was more to uncover.

As I closed my eyes, surrendering to the gradual embrace of sleep, I couldn't help but contemplate the day's whirlwind of experiences. From the distressing scenes at the Doll Auction to the serenity of the forest and the rekindling of memories about my parents, it had been an emotional rollercoaster. I clung to the image of those pastel roses—a symbol of love and connection—as I drifted into a deep and undisturbed slumber.

Chapter Five

The following morning, we arrived at the border. Felix and I managed to secure a ride in the back of an aged pickup truck, laden with crates brimming with apples. After roughly twenty minutes, our journey halted in a quaint town, its heart adorned with vintage shops and cozy cafes enveloping the central square. "You can't help but appreciate the charm of small towns," Felix remarked with a grin as we strolled into the closest coffee shop. The potent aroma of freshly ground coffee greeted us, jolting my senses and adding an extra layer of alertness to my already awakened state.

My eyes fell upon a table conveniently situated beside one of the televisions strategically placed around the serving area. A surge of excitement washed over me, for this marked my inaugural encounter with a television. However, my laughter swiftly ebbed away as the screen flickered to life, displaying the unmistakable Marvelous Radiance logo. An inexplicable unease tightened my stomach as the image of Dorian Gray, the company's founder, materialized on the screen. Memories of overhearing Sera's parents discussing the astounding extent of his power while I convalesced in my room at the bed and breakfast flooded my mind.

The sight of Gray on the television screen served as a stark reminder of the narrow-mindedness that often plagued the Purebloods when it came to the Empire's rigid caste system. It provided a glaring illustration of their yearning to break free from the constraints of their birth-given castes. As I scrutinized Gray's image, an unsettling feeling gnawed at me. There was an inexplicable discord about him, extending beyond his outward appearance—from his impeccably long, dark, wavy hair to the flawless violet suit he adorned. It became increasingly apparent to me that there was an underlying malevolence beneath his facade.

"Enjoy every inch of me while it lasts," Gray's voice chimed, his smile directed right into the camera. I couldn't suppress a groan, as I could almost hear the chorus of women in the background, clamoring to catch a glimpse of the self-absorbed CEO. It was not beyond the realm of possibility that some would go to extremes, even resorting to harming one another, for a chance to be near him.

Felix placed our breakfast on the table, consisting of two croissants filled with roasted potatoes and two generous mocha latte mugs. "So, you've had your first encounter with the adversary," he observed.

It seemed that coffee would become a frequent companion on our journey, as Felix and I had now officially become fugitives, fleeing from the Empire's watchful authorities. I took a sip of the mocha latte, fortifying myself for the challenges ahead.

"So, what exactly makes Gray our adversary?" I inquired, my curiosity piqued.

"It's because of him that there's been no official investigation into the Doll Killer murders. I'm still baffled by how he managed to keep the press at bay," Felix explained.

"Could he be hiding something?" I probed.

Felix pondered for a moment before responding, "I don't just think it, I feel it. And, to be frank, Adelice, I'm wrestling with uncertainty myself. But what matters above all else is uncovering the truth." We lapsed into a silence, our focus returning to our meal. Discovering the identity of the Doll Killer marked the inception of a perilous adventure.

Upon departing the coffee shop, it was time to resume our journey. Consulting the map Sera had provided, we discovered a network of trails that would guide us to the docks. The ferry represented our swiftest route out of the Province, an opportunity I had longed for, as traveling by ship was the predominant means of transit when journeying between Provinces along the East Coast.

As we made our way to the next town on foot, I took the opportunity to review all the articles about the Doll Killer that Felix had gathered from the black market. Among the materials were chilling crime scene photographs depicting the lifeless bodies of several young women, each arranged in a unique pose. The most unsettling detail was the presence of surgical incisions carefully sewn shut, suggesting that the killer had extracted vital organs with a disturbing proficiency in anatomy, reminiscent of the notorious Jack the Ripper.

It had become evident that the perpetrator of these gruesome murders was not of human origin but rather a supernatural entity. As Felix and I treaded along the rugged path of the trail, an unsettling sensation swept over me—an unshakable awareness that someone or something trailed behind us. It certainly wasn't a common thief.

"I believe we're being pursued," I whispered to Felix. He nodded, sharing my unease.

"We're aware you're tailing us, so there's no need for concealment!" I called out, only to receive a mocking response. "You're in for a rough time, girl," a sarcastic voice taunted from behind a tree on the roadside.

To my astonishment, the voice belonged to a tall young man with a deep complexion, clad in a black jacket. He emerged from his hiding spot with a sneer on his lips, his pumpkin orange eyes providing a stark contrast to his appearance. Panic surged within me. Felix and I had been fugitives for only a day, and we had already encountered adversity. It was becoming evident that we were in for a world of trouble, and there seemed to be no way out.

Chapter Six

Finding the Doll Killer isn't going to help you crawl out of the pit run by the System. Hate to break it to you and your boyfriend," the young man in the leather jacket declared, his words carrying the authority of a gang leader. It was becoming evident that he harbored an agenda concerning Felix and me, leaving us to ponder why he had been shadowing us along the trail leading to the docks.

I chose a more diplomatic approach. "Clearly, you have something in mind for my bespectacled friend and me. So, state your terms, and we'll be on our way," I suggested.

"It's not what I want; it's what my twin sister desires. Isn't that right, Halle?" The figure concealed behind the tree sighed and stepped forward, revealing a girl with curly black hair and mocha brown skin. Her pumpkin orange eyes matched those of her brother, and she was dressed in jeans and a slim-fitting white long-sleeve blouse.

My eyes widened as I noticed the intricate filigree markings on their arms, identical to the ones that Felix and I bore. The marks, coupled with their close height and striking resemblance, made it evident that they were Halflings who happened to be twins.

I shifted my attention to Halle. "So, what is it that you and your brother seek from my friend— who's not my boyfriend— and me?" I inquired, my curiosity piqued.

"We wish to join you on your quest to uncover the truth behind the Doll Killer," she replied. Her unexpected request left me astounded. "As unconventional as it may sound, Trey and I believe that it's in our best interest, as Halflings, to travel together. We're convinced that there's something much larger at play than just those murders."

Halle went on to provide further context, "Scavenger Season in the Central Park District is about to commence, and those in possession of tarot decks are eligible to participate. Competitors take on challenges to collect items symbolizing the lower court cards of the Minor Arcana. This year's Scavenger is being hosted by Gray."

My gaze shifted to Felix, and he nodded in agreement, signaling our willingness to accept the twins as companions on our journey.

"I'm Halle, and this is my twin brother Trey. Together, we are the Crane Twins," Halle introduced themselves.

"I'm Felix Frankenstein," Felix responded.

"And I'm Adelice. I don't recall my last name due to amnesia," I explained, wanting to be transparent. "She's telling the truth, just so you guys don't jump to the conclusion that she's trying to be cute," Felix added.

"We understand," both twins chimed in unison.

In the span of just one day, our party had grown by two new members, both resolute in their determination to pursue the Doll Killer. It was becoming increasingly clear that our group was on the brink of expansion, particularly as we realized that Felix and I weren't the sole Halflings en route to the Central Park District.

As evening descended, marking the end of another full day of trekking, we collectively decided it was prudent to halt and establish our camp for the night. As darkness settled in, Halle embarked on instructing me in the rudiments of card reading, utilizing the deck I possessed. Meanwhile, Trey and Felix skillfully prepared the two rabbits they had ensnared using traps that the twins had brought along from the town they had fled.

Halle took a moment to reassure me about our camping situation. "This is just a temporary arrangement," she said.

Curiosity gnawed at me as I asked, "Do you have any idea how long it will take us to reach the docks?"

Halle shrugged, her expression uncertain. "Your guess is as good as mine; it could take us a whole week if we continue on foot." My sense of urgency to distance myself from the social worker and Marvelous Radiance intensified with every passing moment.

"I can't fathom why the cards in my deck appear so… uninspiring," I confessed in frustration. "I had hoped they would serve as a key to unlocking my identity and restoring my lost memories."

Halle offered reassurance, her voice soothing. "Patience, Adelice. It will come to you, not all at once, but bit by bit."

I let out a sigh of resignation. "My main hope right now is to find my mother once we reach the Central Park District. So far, knowing I have parents is the only remnant from my past life that I can recall."

"Have you uncovered any hints as to why Marvelous Radiance acquired you from the System's database?" Halle inquired. I shook my head, my resolve unwavering. "No, and I have no intention of allowing them to take me."

Halle offered words of encouragement. "You're a courageous individual, Adelice. If anyone can confront Gray, it's you." Her statement resonated with me. I harbored no fear of the conceited CEO whose company had claimed me. I had reached a juncture in my life where I was prepared to wage a battle for my own future.

Chapter Seven

Trouble descended upon us as we arrived in the subsequent town. It all commenced when we emerged from a nearby convenience store, laden with additional supplies, courtesy of the funds Sera had provided us. I couldn't pinpoint how long they had been lurking, but their intent was unmistakable—they were tailing us. This peculiar trio constituted triplets, encompassing two girls and one boy, each adorned with dark hair, pale skin, and almond-shaped eyes, reminiscent of Geisha's narrowed gazes.

One of the female triplets possessed hair as sleek and smooth as silk, while the other's locks tumbled in graceful curls. Their brother, in contrast, sported short, wavy hair. What caught my immediate attention, however, were the unmistakable filigree markings adorning their skin—symbols that marked them as Halflings, akin to Felix and me.

It was evident that the trio shared a similar heritage, with one parent likely of Asian descent and the other of European origin. Yet, the perplexing question that loomed over us was why they were shadowing our every move. It was a question that remained unanswered as the situation took a sudden and chaotic turn.

My heart sank as I spotted a plump woman engaged in conversation with one of the townsfolk in the bustling square. It was the social worker. Panic surged through me; how had she managed to track us down so swiftly? We needed to vacate the area before she laid eyes on us. In just a matter of days, the bounty on our heads had escalated, and our situation had grown even more precarious.

Halle sensed my distress and inquired, "What's wrong?"

"The social worker," were the only words that escaped my trembling lips.

"Damn it, how did she locate us?" Felix muttered, his face contorted with concern.

"It doesn't matter now; we need to leave before she spots us!" Trey urged with a sense of urgency that resonated with all of us.

As if synchronized, one of the triplets made a discreet hand signal, beckoning us to trail after them. Trey voiced his uncertainty, asking, "Do you believe we can trust them?" I nodded resolutely. "They represent our sole opportunity for escape." It was a perilous gamble, but we found ourselves with no alternative. And so, we followed the triplets, descending into a narrow alley so obscure that it swallowed us in darkness, rendering us utterly blind to our surroundings.

"Follow us," one of the triplets directed as we veered to the left within the alley. Once my eyes acclimated to the dim surroundings, I recognized that we had entered a multi-level parking garage, replete with an array of parked vehicles. "This way," another triplet indicated, motioning toward a substantial black van, its door already ajar. They must have pilfered the keys from its owner.

"Seems like we're taking a ride to the docks," Felix remarked, grinning. Both of us were acutely aware that the trails were no longer a safe option for our journey.

"Anyone have the skills to drive this thing?" the male triplet inquired, a note of uncertainty in his voice.

"I'll take the wheel," Trey declared as he inserted the key into the ignition.

I couldn't help but express my skepticism. "You know how to drive?"

He responded confidently, "No, but I've spent a lot of my free time studying driving manuals." It wasn't an ideal situation, but at least Trey possessed a theoretical understanding of the fundamentals.

We were fortunate to discover a road that led us straight to the freeway. I cast a glance toward the triplets, who had positioned themselves in the rear of the van. "Thank you," I offered gratefully.

Although none of them uttered a word, it was evident that all three were blushing.

"Well, we've got to stick together," stated the female triplet with straight black hair.

"The only ones we can truly trust are our own kind," chimed in the other triplet with curly brown hair.

Halle, taking the initiative, suggested, "You might as well share your names. It's the least you can do, considering you saved us from falling into the social worker's clutches. If you still wish to accompany us."

"Do you mean that?" queried the male triplet, his dark eyes sparkling with anticipation.

"You've certainly made a persuasive argument," Felix quipped with a grin. "Thank you for your help. My sisters and I would be honored to join your group as fellow travelers," the male triplet declared, acknowledging our agreement with a brief nod.

"Now that we're all bound for the Central Park District, perhaps it's time we share our names," Halle suggested.

The triplet with the straight dark hair introduced herself first. "I'm Isabelle."

The one with curly hair followed, saying, "I'm Lily."

Lastly, the male triplet responded in a somewhat reserved manner, "I'm Elliot." It was apparent that he wasn't accustomed to conversing with individuals outside of his sisters.

Halle extended a warm introduction, "I'm Halle, and this is my twin brother, Trey."

"What's up?" Trey called from the driver's seat, eliciting laughter from all of us.

"I'm Adelice, and this is Felix," I replied, formally introducing ourselves to our newfound companions.

"You're the girl who holds the top spot on the bounty list," Lily murmured, her voice tinged with awe. I remained silent, the realization settling in that my buyers had already escalated the reward for anyone who could apprehend me.

Elliot inquired further, "Do you have any idea why Gray's company is pursuing you?" I shook my head, my expression reflecting my frustration. "I wish I knew," I admitted somberly. "The truth is, I don't even know who I am because I've lost my memories. My hope is that I'll uncover some clues about my past, especially about my mother, once we reach the Central Park District."

"But that's where he resides," Elliot pointed out, a sober reminder for all of us. We were fully cognizant of the individual he was alluding to—Dorian Gray, as the Central Park District served as the headquarters for Marvelous Radiance. Venturing into that sector of Alessia amounted to infiltrating enemy territory, rendering it an expedient way for the social worker to capture me and deliver me directly into the clutches of both Gray and my buyers.

Despite the perils and uncertainties that lay ahead, I held steadfast in my conviction that my family was actively searching for me. Seeking confirmation, I inquired of Lily, "Am I indeed the most sought-after target on the bounty list?" Her enthusiastic nod served as the definitive answer I needed.

"Does the prospect of what Gray might inflict upon you upon capture terrify you?" the curly-haired triplet inquired, her voice laced with concern.

I released a weary sigh. "Would I be deceiving you if I said I wasn't apprehensive about what he and his associates might subject me to if such an outcome does transpire?"

"At least you're candid about the gravity of your predicament," Lily acknowledged sympathetically.

Following this exchange, a somber hush settled over the van. It was Lily who eventually broached the topic that had propelled her and her siblings toward the Central Park District. Much like the twins, they were also in pursuit of the enigmatic Doll Killer.

"He's essentially the Empire's rendition of Jack the Ripper, but with a macabre twist. Instead of harvesting female body parts, he's extracting vital organs—the lungs, liver, kidneys, and even the heart. These organs command a substantial price on the black market, and what's most disconcerting is that they serve as trophies for his gruesome deeds," Lily elucidated.

Felix offered a thoughtful response, "It's possible we're dealing with a copycat." We found common ground in the belief that the perpetrator might be a human with an extensive knowledge of anatomy, which would account for the precise and clean extraction of the organs, leaving behind minimal mess.

Felix took his turn at the wheel, and much like Trey, he had committed the driving fundamentals to memory, transforming into a proficient driver. As dusk encroached upon us, the pressing need arose to locate a suitable resting place for the night.

Elliot, wielding his expertise as a master hacker, managed to breach the System's database and validate the veracity of Lily's assertion. It was undeniable; I occupied the topmost position on the bounty list. The revelation evoked a blend of fear and exhilaration. Regrettably, the database yielded no information regarding the identity of the individuals offering the substantial reward for my capture.

"Private individuals, most likely, given the correlation between wealth and privacy," Elliot deduced.

I couldn't help but express my longing. "I wish I could uncover their identities and steer clear of them entirely."

Elliot offered a perceptive observation, "One thing's for certain— they're doing their utmost to keep your escape from the Slums village under wraps."

In response, I rebutted, "I didn't merely vanish; I made a conscious decision to flee."

"They're merely framing it that way to avert a potential scandal that the tabloids would undoubtedly seize upon," Isabelle interjected. "Scandals have a tendency to find their way to the front page."

"We will uncover the identities of the individuals who purchased you and ensure your safety," Lily vowed with determination.

As six hours of driving elapsed, night descended upon us. Gazing at my image within the database, I was inundated with a mixture of emotions. The conspicuous abundance of zeros in the reward sum served as a stark testament to the extraordinary wealth possessed by those responsible for my purchase.

Nonetheless, the spark of hope that I clung to remained unextinguished—I still held onto the belief that I could reunite with my mother.

The frustration of being unable to remember my mother's face weighed heavily on me. Lost in my contemplations, I failed to notice the gradual onset of darkness within the confines of the van.

"We should seek out a place to spend the night," Halle asserted resolutely. She was absolutely correct; the hour was growing late, and we all required shelter. The anticipation of several more days of travel to reach the docks loomed before us.

Trey presented a practical suggestion, "Perhaps our best option is to locate the most budget-friendly motel we can find."

Alternatively, Lily put forth an alternative, gesturing toward a large stone building on the left. The desolation of the parking lot suggested we might have stumbled upon a suitable place to rest for the night.

This marked our inaugural experience of sleeping indoors since our escape began. "Any idea what this place is?" Felix inquired. I offered a nonchalant shrug. "I haven't the foggiest, but there's only one way to find out." After all, what would be the point of refraining from exploration?

Chapter Eight

We not only had a place to stay but also a spot to replenish our clothing. "I'm in heaven," Lily exclaimed, her eyes fixed on the array of dresses adorning the racks. They were all stunning, ranging from hand-painted silks to velvety textures, and encompassing a spectrum of solid colors in satin and taffeta.

Despite my wonder, I couldn't shake the feeling of being an intruder. We shouldn't have been there, after all. Nevertheless, the dresses held a captivating allure. I suspected they were crafted by talented seamstresses capable of turning custom-made dresses into genuine works of art.

"What's troubling you?" Halle inquired.

"My mom used to wear dresses like these," I replied, a faint smile gracing my lips. It was another fragment from my past that was slowly returning to me.

"Perhaps we should seek something a bit more casual," Felix suggested.

I nodded, falling in step behind him as we ascended the stairs to the second floor of the warehouse. It was like hitting the jackpot. I'd never felt happier as we browsed the diverse array of clothing on display. For once, I could look forward to wearing something different each day until we reached the docks.

I chose a variety of colors, with my current favorite being a dark purple shirt, complemented by a black coat, a medium blue jean skirt, and a pair of green tennis shoes.

"Hey, everyone, they've got showers!" Elliot called out.

Each of us took turns scrubbing away the grime accumulated from nights spent sleeping outdoors. While I used the soap to cleanse myself, my thoughts centered on Sera. By now, the social worker must have deduced that she was the one who aided Felix and me in our escape. I couldn't help but fear that Gray's enforcers were exacting retribution on her.

The most dreaded punishment for defying the Empire was to endure the cruel swipe of a scalpel, leaving a permanent scar on one's face. Alternatively, they might have hastened her claiming ceremony, compelling her to pick a side before the other pureblood kids of her age, all against her will.

Once I finished my shower, I donned the clothes I had chosen earlier.

"That color suits you perfectly," Lily beamed, her dark eyes fixed on the purple shirt adorning me. "Did you know that purple is associated with royalty?" she inquired. "In the past, it was such a rare and costly color that only those of royal lineage could afford to wear it."

"No, I didn't," I shook my head.

"Well, now you do," Lily replied with a grin as she stepped into the shower stall.

As I walked past the room with the stunning display of dresses, one in particular caught my eye. It was crafted from silk and organza, an empire-waist gown featuring short sleeves and a ruffled skirt adorned with meticulously hand-sewn silver swirls and patterns. It must have taken the seamstress hours of meticulous work to create such a masterpiece.

The colors themselves blended harmoniously, a fusion of orange and yellow that evoked memories of the sunsets I used to admire in my grandmother's studio paintings.

"Grandma's studio," I murmured, as fragments of memories flashed before me. It was a recollection of myself seated in her studio, observing her as she painted on the canvas. The intricate blending of colors on the dress before me must have consumed days to achieve.

In that moment, I realized that not only did I have a mother, but I also cherished memories of a grandmother with whom I had lovingly spent time in her studio.

The studio was one of the rare places that had always felt like home, where I truly belonged. A deep, unsettling feeling gnawed at me, suggesting that something had gone disastrously wrong at my parents' house. Something so harrowing that it had compelled me to escape, seeking solace in the refuge of my dimly lit bedroom.

But the question remained: What had transpired to make me run away from home?

Once we were all cleaned up, we made our way to the breakroom to satisfy our hunger. Munching on candy bars, potato chips, and popcorn from the vending machines felt like a taste of paradise. We also enjoyed the bite-sized sandwich wraps, cheese cubes, and cookies neatly stocked in the fridge. To top it off, we discovered a television that provided us with entertainment, sharing laughs as we watched reruns of old sitcoms from the time before the Empire's founding.

Just as we were about to settle in for a movie on FX, Felix stumbled upon a news channel airing a talk show. "Why not see what's happening?" Elliot suggested, curiosity piqued. However, his expression quickly shifted to one of alarm when the anchorwoman, blonde-haired and clad in a purple dress, announced the evening's guest.

"Good evening, everyone. Tonight, we are honored to have the founder and CEO of Marvelous Radiance, Mr. Dorian Gray!" The announcement on the talk show stirred strong reactions among us.

"Ugh!" Isabelle groaned in sheer disgust. "Let's change the channel on his ass!" Trey chimed in, reaching for the remote. However, Halle intervened, her tone serious. "Wait, this could be important," she urged.

I seized the opportunity to lay eyes on the man behind the company that had placed a bounty on me. While I had glimpsed Gray on TV during my time at the coffee shop, this was my first chance to scrutinize his appearance in greater detail. Like most purebloods, he stood tall and slender, attired in a dark violet suit accompanied by a matching waistcoat adorned with brass buttons. To add to the intrigue, he wore black silk gloves that concealed his hands, as if harboring a secret.

His countenance possessed a striking, almost ethereal beauty, undoubtedly explaining why so many women fell under his spell. Long, wavy dark hair, secured in a ponytail by a deep purple satin ribbon, cascaded down his back. Yet, it was his eyes that held a peculiar magnetism - almond-shaped and adorned with irises of cornflower blue. There was an undeniable familiarity about him, a nagging sensation that I had encountered him before, but the memory eluded me.

My trance was broken when I noticed an intriguing detail: Gray sported a gold-framed monocle that concealed his left eye, adding an air of mystery to his already enigmatic presence.

"Greetings, everyone," Gray greeted the audience with a smile that sent the women into a swooning frenzy. His voice had an intoxicating quality that drew you in. "It's delightful to be here; it seems people just can't get enough of me." His self-assuredness was enough to make me and the others nauseous.

"Mr. Gray, is it true that you're hosting this year's Scavenger for the artifacts of the Minor Arcana's lower court cards?" the anchorwoman inquired, her unwavering gaze locked onto Gray, evidently another admirer.

Gray chuckled. "I won't deny that my company is indeed hosting this year's Scavenger. An event exclusively open to those who draw their magic from the tarot." Suddenly, my attention was fully captured. We all possessed tarot decks, which meant we could potentially participate in the Scavenger.

"He's definitely plotting something," Felix commented. "But what could he possibly gain from hosting the Scavenger for the lower court cards?"

"I wish I knew," Halle responded, shaking her head. "For all we know, he might be using the Scavenger to lure Adelice to him and the people who purchased her."

"By entering the Scavenger, we'd have to complete all eight tasks to reach the Edge," Elliot added. "This might be our best shot at locating and exposing the Doll Killer."

"The Scavenger represents my only hope of finding my family," I pointed out.

"We won't let Gray intimidate us," Trey declared.

"Count us in!" Isabelle beamed, her siblings nodding in unison.

"It's bound to be perilous, but it'll all be worth it," Halle affirmed.

With everyone committed to participating in the Scavenger, I felt one step closer to uncovering my true identity.

Chapter Nine

To register for the Scavenger, we had to make our way to the closest Doll Factory, the very same places where Dolls were reprogrammed and modified to cater to the whims of wealthy clients. These artificial beings were among Marvelous Radiance's top-selling products, highly sought after by the nobility of the Elite.

Halle took a trip to the nearest Walmart and purchased a baseball hat along with pitch-black sunglasses. The presence of major chain stores in proximity to the factory struck me as odd. Still, I hoped this simple disguise would suffice to deceive the doctors in charge of the facility.

"Of all the places to register for the Scavenger, it had to be the very site where they transform girls into living dolls," Isabelle remarked, her disgust evident.

"I'm hoping for a miracle that no one recognizes us," Lily expressed her concerns.

"Especially Kathy Ann, who's searching for us," Elliot added.

"Kathy Ann?" I inquired, puzzled.

"That's the name of the social worker who's on the hunt for you," Halle clarified.

"She's like the Aunt Lydia of our kind," Trey remarked as he drove us to the factory the next morning. I never would have imagined that Social Workers had names, given that they all seemed like indistinguishable drones to us.

I felt a sense of confusion. Why did I remember reading "The Handmaid's Tale" by Margaret Atwood in my previous life? My grandmother had adored that book, drawing parallels between the Dome Colonies and Gilead, both being cults that condemned art and science and preached hatred against the supernatural and magic users who chose to reside in the Empire. If Kathy Ann was akin to Aunt Lydia, I fervently hoped I would never have to cross paths with her.

"We'll be okay," Felix reassured me, but the reality was that all of us were battling anxiety.

We were about to step into a facility owned by Gray's company. For all I knew, the doctors responsible for the Dolls might have received word about the bounty on my head. The tension was palpable as we approached the Doll Factory.

"Alright, let's stick to the plan, everyone," Trey instructed. The plan was straightforward: get in, register, and get out. It was a formula we had to execute flawlessly.

Chills ran down my spine as we passed through the Iron Gate surrounding the building. Trey drove the van into the large parking garage adjacent to the main facility, where we were fortunate to find a parking spot on the first floor.

With the van parked, the rest of us entered the elevator. As soon as the button was pressed, the operation was underway. The sound of Frank Sinatra's voice filled the elevator, enveloping us as we waited for it to reach the main floor. The lobby resembled a scene from a sci-fi movie, all stark white and futuristic, with the only bursts of color coming from the posters featuring Dolls whose images had graced past tabloid covers.

It was a challenge to discern whether the Dolls were real or not, given their flawless skin and lifelike hair texture. "Stay close, everyone," Felix cautioned, sensing the arrival of one of the doctors responsible for the Doll transformations in the lobby. He was a middle-aged pureblood man with salt and pepper hair, dressed in a pristine white lab coat.

"Hello," the doctor greeted us warmly, his demeanor friendly. "Are you lovely children here to register for the Scavenger?"

"Yes," Halle replied, and the doctor nodded, jotting down notes onto the clipboard he clutched tightly in his hands. "Follow me; I'll take you to the registration rooms," he instructed as he led us to a door that led to the labs. As we walked down the narrow hallway, I couldn't help but notice several cryogenic capsules lining both sides of the walls.

Each capsule cradled a girl, completely unclothed, slumbering in oblivion as the world continued around her. They were encased in clear blue liquid, designed to both preserve their bodies and supply the necessary nutrients.

"This is where we keep the dolls until they're ready for preparation," the doctor elucidated when he noticed my lingering gaze upon one of the frozen figures.

The sight of those frozen girls stirred a profound sense of discomfort within me. It felt like I was witnessing the dehumanization of individuals, reducing them to mere commodities for the affluent elite to acquire.

The doctor's evasive reply only deepened my suspicions regarding the ominous activities that could be transpiring within the confines of this facility.

As we proceeded down the hallway, my thoughts raced with inquiries regarding the ethical quandaries of these practices. Were these girls willing participants, or were they abducted and coerced into this destiny? Did their families have knowledge of their fates? An increasing anger and resolve welled up within me as I was determined to unearth the truth about the Doll Factory and its ties to Gray's empire.

The stark contrast between the sterile, high-tech laboratory and the disconcerting reality of the frozen girls within the capsules was jarring. It presented a striking juxtaposition of scientific advancement and moral ambiguity. As we moved through the lab, I couldn't escape the nagging curiosity about the nature of experiments and procedures conducted in this place. It served as a stark reminder of the grim underbelly that often hid beneath the veneer of ostensibly advanced and sophisticated institutions.

My mind raced with questions and concerns, but I recognized that this wasn't the moment to voice them. Our purpose here was to register for the Scavenger, collect information, and maintain a low profile. As much as I yearned to unearth the truth, I had to exercise patience and prudence in this perilous setting.

My mind raced with questions and concerns, but I recognized that this wasn't the moment to voice them. Our purpose here was to register for the Scavenger, collect information, and maintain a low profile. As much as I yearned to unearth the truth, I had to exercise patience and prudence in this perilous setting.

The registration room presented a stark contrast to the laboratories we had traversed earlier. It was well-lit and decorated with banners advertising the upcoming Scavenger event. Rows of desks were neatly arranged, each manned by a staff member ready to aid the participants. The doctor handed us each a registration form and a pen.

As I diligently filled out the form, providing my name, address, and other details, my mind remained haunted by the disturbing images of the capsules and the frozen girls. The pervasive sense of unease persisted, reinforcing my belief that there was something deeply unsettling about this place and its ties to the Dolls and the black market.

Once we completed the registration process, we were furnished with badges and instructed to await further directions. As we settled into our seats, I observed the diverse array of participants in the room. Some radiated excitement, while others exuded nervousness, each harboring their unique motives for being present.

Our pursuit of unraveling the mysteries surrounding the Doll Killer had propelled us to this juncture. Still, what hidden truths would the Scavenger event unearth? And were we adequately prepared to confront the perils that undoubtedly awaited us?

This pervasive sentiment weighed heavily on all of us as we left the factory premises behind. As Trey maneuvered the van away from the building, a mix of emotions washed over me. We had successfully registered for the Scavenger event, inching closer to our objective of exposing the Doll Killer. However, the encounter with the Doll Factory and the image of the frozen girls had left an indelible and deeply unsettling impression on all of us.

As the van sped down the road, I gazed out of the window, lost in contemplation. The path ahead was fraught with challenges that were gradually coming into focus. The Scavenger event loomed as both a test of our abilities and a perilous expedition. With the determination of our newfound allies, we were prepared to confront whatever obstacles lay in our path, even if it meant facing the sinister forces entwined with the Doll Killer's reign of terror.

"It's just... seeing those girls frozen like that, it's haunting," I confessed, my voice quivering slightly. "I can't comprehend what they endure. It's beyond inhumane." The van fell into a somber silence as we continued our journey. The weight of what we had witnessed hung heavily in the air, serving as a stark reminder of the harsh realities we confronted.

As we made our way towards the Central Park District, my thoughts were consumed by the imminent Scavenger event. The challenges, the competition, and the looming potential danger all loomed on the horizon. However, the presence of our determined group of companions, each driven by their unique motives for seeking justice, kindled a spark of hope within me. We were bound together by a common purpose, and collectively, we might possess the means to unearth the truth behind the Doll Killer's macabre spree and expose the sinister forces at work.

The journey pressed on, and as the scenery outside transitioned, so did the atmosphere within the van. The weight of our choices and the gravity of our situation became undeniable. Each one of us grappled with a complex tapestry of motivations, fears, and aspirations, all entwined with the shared objective of unraveling the truth and securing justice. The road ahead remained uncertain, but our unity and unwavering determination provided a glimmer of hope that guided us onward.

The dimly lit motel room afforded us a modest measure of privacy and a sense of security, albeit without any semblance of luxury. As we prepared to rest for the night, the cumulative burden of the past few days began to take its toll. An amalgam of emotions—anxiety, determination, and fatigue—permeated the atmosphere. It was a moment for us to silently contemplate, a brief respite in our unrelenting odyssey, enabling us to muster our resilience for the trials awaiting us in the days ahead.

Within the tranquil confines of the motel room, I lay there, my mind entangled in a web of emotions—longing, uncertainty, and unwavering determination. I craved the revelation of my past, yearned to reunite with my mother, and sought understanding regarding the reasons behind my flight from my own home. The vivid memory of my grandmother's studio persisted, a sanctuary imprinted in my mind.

As slumber gradually embraced me, I clung to the hope that our ongoing journey would ultimately yield the answers, closure, and the potential reunion with the family I fervently yearned for.

Indeed, dreams possessed the remarkable ability to mold our perspectives, propel our choices, and ignite our aspirations. As you descended into the realm of dreams, that distant cityscape on the horizon harbored the allure of revelation and clarity. Whether it served as a reflection of your deepest yearnings or a portent of forthcoming events, your odyssey appeared inextricably linked with the quest for recollections and veracity. During these tranquil hours of slumber, the subconscious wove a intricate tableau of emotions and encounters, affording a rich blend of insight and eagerness for the days that loomed ahead.Top of Form

Chapter Ten

The following morning, we departed the motel early, driving to the next town to grab breakfast at a local coffee shop while Elliot checked the System's database. I was disconcerted to discover that I still held the top spot on the list, and beneath my name was Felix's picture. It left me pondering why Felix's father had placed a bounty on him.

"You want to know?" Felix inquired, to which I nodded. "Only because you guys are the only ones I trust to keep the secret." Our collective gaze was fixed on him as he extended a hand toward a withered leaf from a potted plant in the corner. Miraculously, it began to rejuvenate, turning vibrant green again. I couldn't believe my eyes—he had revived a dead leaf with a single touch.

"Now you all understand why my dad wants me to return home so desperately," Felix explained. "We are the only ones who possessed this gift."

I marveled at the astonishing display before me. This supernatural gift, capable of reviving anything from the dead with a mere touch, defied the natural order. At least now, I understood why Victor Frankenstein was so determined to reclaim his son.

As we were preparing to re-enter the van, I couldn't help but notice the abrupt drop in temperature. The air had become so frigid that the thick plumes of our exhaled breath were clearly visible, and frost began to form on the tips of my fingers. "Why is it snowing in the middle of summer?" Halle queried. Elliot gestured towards the dark-haired man, seemingly unaffected by the cold, and remarked, "You might as well ask him."

The man's black eyes bore an eerie, animalistic quality, unsettlingly inhuman. This peculiar aspect extended to his shadow, which resembled a creature standing upright, adorned with twisted antlers on either side of its head.

"What is that thing?" Trey exclaimed, terror evident in his voice as the man underwent a slow transformation into a nightmarish monster. The creature appeared emaciated, as if it hadn't consumed sustenance in days. "Wendigo," Felix whispered.

I attempted to call for help, but an unnatural frost had gripped the townsfolk, rendering them immobile. I had never encountered a Wendigo up close, only heard of it in Native American folklore—a manifestation of greed and murder. The question that haunted me was why it was pursuing us.

The Wendigo launched into a ferocious attack, leaving me with no time to escape. I felt its razor-sharp claws rip through the soft fabric of my jeans, my blood welling up. Was this to be my demise? Yet, things took an even stranger turn as the Wendigo let out a piercing scream. It dawned on me that the slightest touch of my blood inflicted searing pain. It was unbelievable; my blood possessed the power to harm. A solitary droplet seemed akin to acid, causing the creature's flesh to wither and anyone Pureblooded to suffer excruciating injury.

"I call upon the element of fire!" a voice rang out. My vision began to clear, revealing Felix casting a spell that reduced the Wendigo to a pile of ash.

"Are you okay, Adelice?" Felix inquired as he hurried to my side. I nodded, astonished by the fact that he could touch the gash left by the Wendigo's claws without experiencing any pain. Our blood wasn't poisonous to our own kind. Halle swiftly approached, murmuring a healing incantation as she covered the wound with her hands, gradually transforming it into a light pink scab.

Most Purebloods regarded such scabs with disgust, but I saw them as a mark of resilience. I had survived a Wendigo attack! The hairs on my neck stood on end as slow applause emanated from the center of the town square. "Bravo, I must say I'm impressed. You all have handled a Wendigo attack quite admirably," declared a voice as smooth as velvet.

All eyes fixed on the man perched atop the statue in the heart of the town square. He possessed flowing silver hair and regal violet eyes accentuated by smoky grey eyeshadow that complemented his ashen complexion. Clad in black, his attire bore intricate designs in gold, silver, bronze, and copper sewn into the silk fabric.

"You," Felix seethed, "you're him, aren't you? You're the Emperor." I gasped in disbelief. Could this be the ruler of the Alessia Empire? He appeared more akin to a stereotypical rebellious figure, one who favored leather and trench coats.

"Oh, how impolite of me. I neglected to introduce myself. I am Seneca, the sovereign of the Alessia Empire," he declared. "Why are you here?" Felix demanded. The Emperor fixed a stern gaze upon him. "You really ought not to address me in such a manner, young man. Count yourself fortunate that I am in a benevolent mood today. Otherwise, you would have met your demise by now. As for my presence here, I have come to inform you that it is time for you to return home, Felix Frankenstein."

"And why should I heed your words?" Felix countered defiantly.

"It's quite straightforward," Seneca responded. "You pose a threat to those in your proximity, and it all relates to your extraordinary talent."

"I have no idea what you're talking about," Felix retorted.

Seneca's gaze remained unwavering. "Oh, but I believe you do. It's the same talent my family bestowed upon Victor after we rescued him from the brink of death aboard Captain Walton's ship all those years ago."

It dawned on me that the Emperor was referring to Felix's unique ability. A sardonic smirk played upon his lips, and the violet depths of his eyes sparkled with amusement. "You not only possess the power to grant life, but you can also take it away," he stated.

"If you're trying to intimidate me, it's working. Yet, it still doesn't clarify why I must return home," Felix responded.

The Emperor released a weary sigh. "Naive child, both you and your father are the sole bearers of this gift, and with it comes grave consequences if it were to fall into the wrong hands."

"Why?" I inquired. The Emperor finally took notice of my presence, his initial surprise giving way to a more composed demeanor as he cleared his throat. "You should pose that question to his Father. After all, he fashioned a creature from the remains of the deceased and reanimated it through the power of lightning."

"Lightning serves as the spark of life," I realized. The Emperor nodded with a faint smile, patting me on the head.

"I suppose there is some potential in you, little one," the Emperor remarked.

A burning curiosity overcame me, and I couldn't help but ask, "Is there a way for me to recover my lost memories?" I recognized that questioning the Emperor was fraught with peril, and I would likely have to pay a price, but the need for answers was too compelling to resist.

"Perhaps, but not all at once," was his cryptic response as he began to depart. There was an unspoken sense that he possessed more knowledge than he was willing to divulge.

"I'm surprised he didn't kill you," Trey remarked as we resumed our journey on the road.

"Why would he want to kill us?" I questioned.

Halle interjected, "The Emperor is notorious for his instability. He perceives those lacking the magic gene or of supernatural lineage as inferior. Simply put, he's unhinged."

Felix added, "His family is responsible for my father's immortality. It's perplexing that he's insisting I return home solely because of my power to give and take life with a single touch."

"Your abilities don't define your worth, Felix. Don't let the Emperor's words get under your skin," I reassured him.

"Thank you, Adelice. I needed to hear that," he replied with a nod.

As we continued on, rain began to fall, the sky turning a somber gray. It was a sign that we needed to seek shelter.

Top of Form

Chapter Eleven

We sought refuge in an abandoned manor by the roadside. It lacked the grandeur depicted in tabloid images, presenting itself as a modest, two-story structure, adorned with a simple white facade and accented by green gingerbread railings. The mansion's evident neglect signaled years of uninhabited solitude, yet an inexplicable allure emanated from within its timeworn walls.

As we crossed the threshold, it became evident that the manor was far from vacant. Every piece of furniture lay concealed beneath protective white shrouds, guarding them against the thick veil of dust that had settled over time. Each room within the house remained remarkably well-preserved. Yet, it was the black and white photographs adorning the fireplace mantel that seized my attention, offering glimpses into the lives of the family that once called this place home—a man with his arm tenderly encircling a woman in an elegant white gown, flanked by two cherubic children, a boy and a girl.

The children immediately drew my focus. The monochromatic hues of the photograph hinted at the boy's dusky hair and the girl's fair locks, both appearing to be around four or five years old when the portrait was captured. It struck me that they were twins, akin to Trey and Halle. An inexplicable sense of familiarity washed over me as I studied this family portrait.

Turning the photograph over, I discovered their identities meticulously labeled: "The Masterson Family Picnic with George, Alice, Tristin, and Claire."

Why did an inexplicable sense of connection to the Mastersons stir within me? If anyone possessed knowledge about them, it would undoubtedly be Felix.

The boys, resourceful as always, kindled a fire using the logs discovered at the rear of the manor. We quickly realized that modern conveniences such as electricity and light switches were conspicuously absent, forcing us to rely on oil lamps, candles, and matches to illuminate our surroundings.

Turning to Felix, I inquired, "Do you happen to know anything about the Masterson family?" His eyebrows raised in surprise, he replied, "Yes, why do you ask?" I hesitated briefly before revealing, "I stumbled upon their photographs, and I believe this place used to be their home."

"I don't have much information about them, but my Dad used to know George Masterson before he passed away," Felix explained. "George owned a string of hotels throughout Alessia, while his wife, Alice, was both an author and a painter. As for their children, I'm not sure what became of them. At this point, they're likely grown and fulfilling the roles society has designated for them." We both understood that this was coded language for them getting married and having children, a privilege denied to us due to our mixed heritage and residing in the grey zone.

Reality could be as bitter as an unripe fruit, and I couldn't help but speculate that the daughter's dowry might have equaled the price of the royal palace in the Starlight District. It was a stark reminder of the harsh realities governing noble marriages—an intricate dance of forming alliances with other families and perpetuating bloodlines, all in the hope of currying favor with the Emperor. I was far from ignorant about how this system operated.

Felix chimed in, "The Mastersons were also among the founding families of the Empire." A sudden recollection flashed across his face.

"Oddly enough, the residents of the Slums never seem to mention them," I mused. Felix shrugged, "It doesn't surprise me, considering their low numbers."

"If my hunch is correct, then Claire and Tristin may still be alive," I ventured. Felix raised an eyebrow, his curiosity piqued. "I'm surprised you're taking such an interest in an obscure noble family," he remarked.

As I considered my words carefully, I replied, "Crazy as it may sound, I believe they could hold clues about my own family. I don't want to rush to conclusions, but there's something familiar about them, something I've seen before."

Felix fell into a thoughtful silence, his gaze fixed on his hands. "Are you still haunted by what Seneca said about your powers being dangerous?" I eventually inquired.

He nodded somberly. "Yes, he's right. It's because of this power that my father lost his sanity and withdrew from society."

Felix looked at me earnestly. "But you're not the type to misuse your power," he stated, a warm smile gracing his lips. "That's one thing I know for sure."

"Thank you, Felix," I replied, my eyes locked on the flickering flames. Despite my amnesia, I had found purpose: to uncover the hidden truths the Empire had concealed for years. Not only did I have a family searching for me, but I had also forged a new one with the friends I had made—Felix, Halle, Trey, Isabelle, Elliot, and Lily. Home, I realized, wasn't just a place; it was the people with whom you shared bonds. After days of being on the run from the System, I finally felt a profound sense of belonging.

"Are you apprehensive about what awaits us when we reach the Central Park District?" I inquired.

Felix's response was a solemn nod. We shared an unspoken understanding that our destination harbored inherent danger, given the presence of his father and Grey. I remained perplexed about Marvelous Radiance's motivations regarding me. Was it solely because of my unusual white hair, its hue mirroring the moon's soft glow? I saw myself as nothing more than an anomaly to them. Regardless, I was determined not to allow them to exploit it against me.

The Swan Children

Claire Masterson was a child who had embraced the light at a mere five years old, a path chosen by all the Perfect Purebloods. A single glance at her was enough to captivate anyone's heart. She donned a sky-blue dress that accentuated the vivid blue-violet hue of her eyes, while a large pink bow adorned her pale blonde hair, creating a charming ensemble.

Claire shared an exceptionally close bond with her twin brother, Tristin, although he was often viewed as the anomaly in their seemingly flawless family. Much like his sister, Tristin possessed the same porcelain complexion and striking blue-violet eyes, yet his hair was a stark jet black. In a family of Perfect Purebloods, which included his parents and sister, Tristin was the exception— he had chosen to align himself with the dark, a decision that drew comparisons to the Flawed, whose familiars were often reptilian. He became the first among the Perfects to embrace the path of darkness.

The twins, dubbed the Swan Children, were known as such because Claire's familiar was a graceful white swan, while Tristin's was its contrasting counterpart, a black swan.

One day, as they observed their familiars gracefully swimming in the small pond at the rear of their family's home, Claire turned to her brother with a puzzled expression. "Why did you choose to align with the dark?" she inquired.

"I yearned to stand out," Tristin replied thoughtfully. "To be the first Perfect Pureblood to embrace the dark, mostly because I can't bear the blinding sunlight. I'm almost certain there are Flawed individuals who've chosen the light, likely because their familiars are the least intimidating to behold."

Claire couldn't hide her disdain. "I sincerely hope I never encounter a Flawed individual," she retorted. The notion of any of them aligning with the light contradicted the principles their father espoused to their community.

With a mischievous twinkle in his eye, Tristin teased, "You never know, sis; you might find yourself falling for a Flawed individual who's chosen the dark, and perhaps even have a child together."

Claire scoffed, considering the potential clash with their father's beliefs. "I highly doubt Papa would endorse such a union."

Tristin leaned in and confided, "Well, brace yourself, because we're moving to the town near Father's new job at the station, and we'll likely be encountering more of them there."

Unbeknownst to the twins, significant changes were on the horizon, poised to alter the course of their lives in unexpected ways.

Chapter Twelve

After several days of journeying along the winding roads, we finally reached the last town marked on our map. This town held the key to our next destination: the train that would carry us straight to the border's docks.

"Goodbye, dear van. We've shared many cherished memories, but it's time for you to return to your rightful owners," Lily said with a touch of sadness. Among the triplets, she was the most sentimental.

Curiosity gnawed at me, and I couldn't help but inquire, "Any updates from the System?" Elliot shook his head reassuringly. "They're still conducting their searches, keeping a vigilant eye on the trails. We have nothing to fear."

I couldn't shake my unease. "I hope you're right about this," I admitted, my thoughts still haunted by the hauntingly vacant look and forced smile on Kathy Ann's face back at the courthouse in the Slums. It sent shivers down my spine and left me pondering how many Halflings had suffered under her care.

"We're safe," Halle reassured me, her presence a comforting balm for my fear and anxiety about the possibility of capture.

Felix suggested, "We might as well explore a bit before the train arrives." We held two tickets, each serving a distinct purpose within our Scavenger journey—the first for the train that would transport us to the docks, and the second for the ferry bound for the Central Park District.

As we wandered through the square, it was impossible to escape the omnipresent image of Marvelous Radiance's CEO. His visage adorned the front pages of tabloids and flickered on television screens, featuring reruns of his interviews and public appearances. Gray remained unchanged in each portrayal: his long, dark, wavy hair neatly tied into a ponytail, his signature violet suit, those mesmerizing cornflower blue eyes, and the distinctive gold-framed monocle nestled in his left eye.

"I despise him," Isabelle spat out with a palpable disgust in her voice.

Trey, ever the supportive friend, offered a comforting pat on her back. "You're not alone in that sentiment, girl."

It was at that moment that we caught our first glimpse of the town's inhabitants: men adorned in frock coats and top hats, and women draped in bustle and crinoline dresses. Every Pureblood among them had either a reptile or a bird as their constant companion.

Lily, always observant, murmured, "A town where both Flawed and Perfect coexist."

Perplexed, I inquired, "What do you mean?"

"That's how they distinguish themselves once they make their choice, either Flawed or Perfect," Felix explained, shedding light on the matter. "You can tell by the familiars they keep: reptiles for the Flawed and birds for the Perfect. All of them belong to the Steam Caste."

I found myself taken aback; I had no inkling that Purebloods were categorized in such a manner. I had always held the belief that all Purebloods were uniform, but now I realized how mistaken I had been.

The town itself exuded a captivating beauty, with flowers, trees, and parks that transported you into a living painting. It struck me as peculiar that this charming town, brimming with both Flawed and Perfect, lay just a two-day drive away from the decrepit home of the Masterson family. It led me to speculate that perhaps they had resided in this town, which held the potential for answers I sought, particularly within its library.

The library itself was housed in a charming two-story brick building, its hardwood floors bearing the rustic charm of time-worn age. The reading areas featured furniture and tables that exuded a comforting sense of home.

Approaching the counter, I was greeted by one of the librarians who inquired, "Can I assist you with something?" I wasted no time and inquired, "Do you have any information on the Masterson family?"

"Please, wait here," she replied before disappearing into the back room. Moments later, a man with dark brown hair, pale complexion, and sky-blue eyes framed by a pair of glasses entered the room. He was attired in beige slacks paired with a matching jacket and sported a prominent red scarf knotted around his neck.

"Hello, I've been informed that you're interested in learning more about the Masterson family," he greeted me warmly. "You're in luck because I happen to be the town's local scholar."

Eager for information, I asked, "What can you tell me about them?"

He began, "George and Alice were beloved by everyone in this town. It's a regrettable loss that they had to relocate to one of the major cities in Alessia. Their departure wasn't just to manage a prestigious hotel in the Central Park District, but also to be closer to the former Emperor."

"That's a rather peculiar reason for relocation," I observed.

The scholar nodded in agreement. "Indeed, but when you are fervent followers of the Light, it can feel imperative to be near the side with the most power. Moreover, it was an attempt to distance themselves from the persistent rumors that revolved around their son, Tristin."

Curiosity piqued, I pressed, "What exactly did Tristin do?"

His response was straightforward, "He committed the one act that no Perfect should ever undertake: he aligned with the Dark. It's why his familiar is a Black Swan."

"So, they relocated to seek a pardon from the previous Emperor?" I probed.

The scholar nodded, his eyes reflecting a depth of understanding. "In a sense, yes, but as a being of light myself, I've never lost sight of the world's inherent shades of grey."

His words resonated with me, prompting me to confess, "I hadn't considered it from that perspective until now."

The scholar continued, imparting a philosophical insight, "There's a reason your kind is feared, for you are the bridge between both sides, maintaining a delicate balance as equals. Over the years, I've come to realize that one side cannot exist without the other." The notion of balance between the two sides was clearly of great importance.

I wasn't particularly inclined toward philosophy, but the scholar's words carried weight. The interdependence of the two sides couldn't be denied. "Tristin, despite his inner struggles, never harmed anyone. He held deep affection for his sister, Claire, and remained a steadfast presence by her side."

Curiosity compelled me to inquire further, "Were they exceptionally close?"

The scholar nodded, his expression somber. "Indeed, they were, but in the end, Tristin sought to carve out his own path—an ambition that diverged from the one his father envisioned for both him and his sister."

The weight of family expectations must have been an enormous burden for Tristin. Yet, it took considerable courage to defy the established rules that his people had adhered to for generations. While I didn't possess all the details of the story, it seemed that George Masterson's efforts to safeguard his son may have been well-intentioned but ultimately misguided. Moving to an unfamiliar place can undoubtedly strain the rest of the family. It was evident that court life wasn't a suitable fit for everyone, especially when the Empire was governed by a monarch known for their instability.

People Talk

Five years had elapsed since his family's departure from their rural abode. At eleven years old, Tristin was beginning to discern the underlying reasons behind his father's choice to settle in the town nearest to the train station.

However, everything took a drastic turn when Claire rushed into the library, her eyes brimming with tears. Alarmed, Tristin set the book he had been engrossed in aside, placing it carefully on the coffee table. "What's wrong?" he inquired, concern etched on his young face.

Between sobs, Claire managed to speak, "We're moving again."

Puzzled, Tristin sought clarification. "But where are we moving to?"

The answer was accompanied by the distant sound of yelling emanating from the living room of their house. It was a grim indication that his parents were once again locked in a heated altercation.

Ever since Tristin had made the fateful decision to align himself with the dark, an underlying tension had pervaded his family's life, growing increasingly strained over time. The situation escalated when his mother discovered him engaging in conversation with a Flawed girl—a grave transgression, as it was an unspoken rule never to interact with anyone from the Flawed faction.

Tristin had observed her playing with her turtle familiar in one of the nearby parks that enveloped the station, and he couldn't perceive any inherent flaw in her. What astonished him even more was the realization that not all Flawed individuals necessarily sided with the dark.

"Why did you choose the light?" Tristin inquired, his curiosity piqued.

She simply shrugged in response. "I suppose I wanted to be different. I picked the side that resonated with me the most."

Their conversation flowed effortlessly, and the hours passed like minutes, engrossed in discussion, until Tristin's mother intervened. It weighed heavily on him that his actions had led to his family's impending departure from the Garden District. As selfish as it may seem, he yearned for something beyond the confines of the life he had always known, even if it meant abandoning his sister and parents to venture into the unknown.

Chapter Thirteen

As I left the library, my vision blurred, leaving me disoriented. I found myself in the midst of a cobblestone street enveloped in a dense shroud of fog, obscuring everything from view. The world had become an indistinct haze.

Then, a piercing scream shattered the eerie silence, jolting me into action. Without a clear sense of direction, I sprinted, my footsteps echoing through the mist.

Eventually, I stumbled into a narrow alleyway, the feeling of dread intensifying as my gaze landed upon the macabre tableau that adorned the red brick walls – blood splatters, a haunting reminder of the Doll Killer's reign of terror.

After sharing my vision with the others, we collectively decided to pay a visit to the local psychic. Our destination wasn't far, and soon, we spotted the cottage nestled at the road's end. It exuded a certain charm, surrounded by a profusion of vibrant flowers. Despite its rustic setting, the small neighborhood in the woods boasted street lamps and quaint houses, creating an intriguing juxtaposition of nature and civilization.

As we approached the cottage, we noticed that the door stood ajar, revealing a dark-haired woman in a grey dress adorned with intricate silver designs, reminiscent of the attire I had worn to the Doll Auction. Her gaze met ours, and with an air of eerie anticipation, she spoke, her voice hushed yet welcoming, "Welcome. I've been expecting all of you."

"I need your assistance," I began as we followed her into the living room, where a sea-green furniture set adorned the space.

"You're here because of the Doll Murders," the psychic mused, her gaze penetrating.

"How——" I started to ask, but she interrupted me.

"I know everything that transpires across the Empire, child," she explained with an air of mystique. "There's a reason why you're experiencing these haunting visions of Dolls being murdered by a non-human serial killer. You and your friends were wise to seek me out for guidance. What I'm about to reveal must remain confined to this room."

"Does it relate to my lost memories?" I inquired.

"Partly, but understand this: you and your companions, alongside four other Halflings, have been selected to restore our faction's wellspring of magic."

It wasn't until we examined our blank tarot decks that the pieces of the puzzle began to fall into place.

"The power of the tarot reveals a person's past, present, and future in two distinct sets. The Major Arcana delves into the structure of human consciousness, guiding us towards life-altering events and their enduring consequences. Meanwhile, the Minor Arcana comprises four suits, each linked to a potent artifact associated with the four elements: the Ace of Cups represents Water, the Ace of Wands symbolizes Fire, the Ace of Pentacles embodies Earth, and the Ace of Swords epitomizes Air."

"Each of these cards symbolizes the inherent laws of human nature: emotions, thoughts, the vessel, and the soul," I explained. "And alongside them, we have the court cards, which serve as the guardians for each element – a king, queen, knight, and page."

Halle, her eyes wide with curiosity, posed a critical question, "So, you're suggesting that each of these cards is real?"

The psychic nodded solemnly. "Yes, you and your group, along with the other four, are in grave danger. A malevolent entity, one who thrives on the misery and suffering of others, is stalking you. The murders plaguing the Central Park District are his sinister handiwork. But there is a way to halt his reign of terror. You must locate every incarnation of the tarot. It is the sole path to saving our world and preserving our magic from impending destruction."

"This is far more monumental than I initially imagined," Felix mused as we departed from the psychic's residence.

"At least now I understand the reason behind these visions," I remarked.

"It's the call," Lily elucidated, "the beckoning of Fate, urging us to embark on a mission."

"So, in our case, we must gather the living embodiments of the tarot cards and employ them to rescue Alessia from the clutches of a madman," Elliot concluded, seamlessly connecting the dots.

"That appears to be the essence of it," Isabelle concurred. "And it's a duty none of us can afford to neglect."

"Despite the trials it has thrown our way, Alessia is our home, and it falls upon us to safeguard it," Halle declared with unwavering determination.

Trey shook his head, acknowledging the enormity of our impending task. We all shared a moment of laughter, knowing that what lay ahead would be arduous, but the bond between us would be our steadfast support through the trials that awaited.

Chapter Fourteen

The train pulled into the station, and after presenting our tickets, we were guided into one of the day cabins. My emotions were a whirlwind of nervousness and excitement. With each passing moment, I inched closer to uncovering the secrets of my past. My gaze lingered on the cards of my deck, their images currently plain and unremarkable. According to Halle's teachings, these cards would gradually metamorphose to reflect the personality and heritage of their wielder.

"You've been engrossed in your deck for quite a while," Halle observed, settling into the seat beside me. Across the cabin, Lily and Isabelle occupied seats of their own. The boys, in adherence to the peculiar "boys must be separated from the girls policy," had ventured into a different cabin.

"I'm apprehensive about the theme my cards will adopt once the Scavenger's influence takes hold," I admitted.

"I share your apprehension," Halle replied, her voice tinged with worry. "The same goes for Lily, Isabelle, and the boys." As Halle had elucidated earlier, the Major and Minor Arcana each had their distinct themes.

"I'm also frightened about what my theme might unveil and why Gray's company is pursuing me," I continued, my unease growing. "You don't encounter many Halfling girls with moonlit hair, so it must be for a shallow reason."

Halle considered my words. "It's possible, and it might explain why Gray wants to use you as a Guinea pig."

"I'd prefer to be on the run than to be in the company of those who seek to exploit me," I asserted.

"You're a courageous young woman, Adelice," Halle affirmed with a reassuring smile. "I have no doubt that you will always find a way out of the most challenging predicaments."

"Is this your way of telling me I possess more strength than I realize, not physically, but mentally?" I inquired.

"If you interpret it that way, then yes," Halle affirmed. "Don't allow the revelations of your Major and Minor Arcana to weigh you down. Who knows? Perhaps they'll offer you a clue about your true identity," she reminded me.

"I'll keep that in mind," I said, nodding thoughtfully. I couldn't help but wonder what themes my deck would unveil – perhaps they held the key to unlocking the mystery of my past before my memories were lost.

Halle's words had a point; I possessed a unique strength in my own right. Particularly when it came to navigating situations where I wasn't wanted, I had a knack for finding my way out. As we neared the Central Park District, I steeled myself for the impending confrontation with Gray. I felt no fear, neither of him nor the potential challenges the Scavenger might bring. Let the games commence.

The train began to glide along the tracks, and it occurred to us that we had roughly three hours before we reached the docks for the ferry. In an effort to pass the time, Lily proposed we play a game. Halle and I readily agreed since there was little else to occupy our attention. We settled on a game that involved recalling the various supernatural factions.

So far, we had identified a total of eleven supernatural factions, each distinguished by a different color scheme. Among the Warm Colors, we had Red, symbolizing the Vampires; Yellow, representing the Werewolves; and Orange, denoting the Elementals. Within the Cool Colors, Blue stood for the Mer Folk, Green for the Elves, and Purple for the Faeries. Among the Odd Colors, we had Pink for the Jinn, Brown for the Shadow People, and Grey for the Mummies. Lastly, the two sides were epitomized by Black, signifying the Ars Goetia Demons, and White, representing the Angels from various orders in the Ars Paulina.

As we recited the factions and their associated colors, the rhythmic motion of the train provided a soothing backdrop to our conversation.

Our game continued as we delved into the intricacies of the Human Caste System: Stone, Iron, Candle, Clock, Steam, Lamp, Deco, Diesel, Atom, Formica, Silk, Cyber, and Now. Each caste possessed its own unique brand of magic, adding layers of complexity to our discussion. I became so engrossed in the game that I failed to notice the train had come to a complete halt. We had reached the docks. Had it really been three hours already? Time seemed to have slipped away unnoticed.

The scent of salty sea air filled my senses as we disembarked the train. It was a pity that the northern Districts were so distant from each other; otherwise, airships wouldn't be our primary mode of transportation.

As we made our way towards the ferry's deck, the sight of security personnel stationed throughout the vessel gave me pause.

It was evident that Gray had hired them to exert pressure on us. His cronies likely had informed him of our participation in the Scavenger, and we couldn't afford to give them any reason to disqualify us. It was imperative that we played by the rules and remained vigilant.

Top of Form

Chapter Fifteen

The ferry proved to be remarkably spacious, with designated areas for various groups, including our own. As I leaned against the cool metal railing encircling the deck, the rhythmic symphony of waves crashing against the sides of the vessel reached my ears. The scent of sea salt hung in the air, more potent here on the deck than it had been on the boarding lane. While the setting was undeniably pleasant, the ever-watchful security personnel served as a persistent reminder that caution remained paramount.

The sky stretched out clear and inviting, suggesting a smooth journey ahead. Trey's voice cut through the serene ambiance with a hint of sarcasm. "Gray probably wants to lull us into a false sense of security," he quipped, his grin mirroring the dryness of his words. With a contented sip from his ceramic mug, he seemed to take pleasure in the brew's flavors. Following suit, I indulged in a mocha coffee that delighted my taste buds with subtle hints of white chocolate. The small buffet area offered delectable blueberry scones and macarons, which were equally enjoyable.

Amidst this tranquil lounge, we couldn't ignore the watchful gaze of the security personnel who kept a close eye on us, poised to seize any opportunity to apprehend me and deliver me into Gray's clutches.

"Seems like we're not the only Halflings who've ventured into the Scavenger," Felix astutely pointed out. And indeed, there were four other individuals of our kind in the lounge, each carrying an air of intrigue.

The first was a girl with lavender-gray hair, her pale complexion providing a stark contrast to her striking red eyes, which seemed to hold enigmatic secrets.

The second, a blonde-haired boy, exuded an aura of vibrant athleticism, his sea-green eyes mirroring his unwavering confidence. He was adorned in a purple and blue letterman jacket.

The third girl possessed chestnut brown hair, complemented by an olive complexion. Her skeptical expression suggested a deeper understanding of the world, while her violet eyes hinted at hidden knowledge.

Lastly, a younger boy, with copper-toned skin and innocent chocolate eyes, stood out in the crowd. His curiosity and purity of spirit were evident, providing a sharp contrast to the complexities of the world we found ourselves in.

His innocence and directness were a breath of fresh air amidst the tension that surrounded us. I couldn't help but be intrigued by his absence of fear. As he approached Felix and me, his confident voice sliced through the unease. "I'm not afraid of Gray," he declared, his conviction unmistakable.

Intrigued, I probed further, "You're not worried about what he might do to you?" His head shook gently. "No, but I have a gut feeling about why he's after you."

Surprisingly, his words lacked judgment or accusation. Instead, they brimmed with earnest curiosity that was hard to ignore.

Suddenly, a spontaneous burst of child-like laughter escaped him. "Oops, I forgot to introduce myself. Got a little carried away. I'm Jared."

I introduced myself in turn, and he responded with compliments about my name and admiration for my hair. His candid and straightforward manner was disarmingly charming.

Jared's ability to find beauty in everything, even something as simple as my hair, was a novel experience for me. He gently took my hand and led me out of the lounge, down a corridor that opened into a rectangular room. I couldn't help but scowl, voicing my concern, "You're going to get us into trouble."

But he remained undeterred. "You wanted to understand part of the reason why Gray is after you. She is a part of it; it all connects to her," he explained, his words piquing my interest.

The moment I stepped into the room, my eyes widened at the sight of the portraits adorning the walls. Each painting depicted a young woman with cascades of pale blonde hair and blue-violet eyes. She possessed a striking beauty, reminiscent of a princess straight out of a fairy tale. Her appearance was so ethereal and perfect that it was as if a swan and a rose had been combined into a single enchanting presence.

"Who is she?" I inquired, unable to tear my eyes away from the captivating portraits.

"Her name is Claire," Jared replied, his voice laced with reverence. "Her name means bright and clear, which suits her perfectly because both her appearance and soul are beautiful. I have a strong hunch about the identity of the artist who painted these portraits."

My eyes widened as I noticed the initials discreetly tucked into the corner of each painting: D.G. for Dorian Gray. I knew Gray to be a collector of art, but I hadn't realized he was the artist responsible for these breathtaking masterpieces. These portraits were clear evidence that whoever this girl was, she held profound significance to Gray, enough to compel him to personally craft her image with meticulous care.

The notion that Claire could be Gray's wife flitted through my thoughts. After all, Felix had mentioned her rarity in public appearances. It seemed plausible that Gray wished to keep her concealed, reserving her for himself alone. The paintings spoke of an intense love and attachment he held for her, yet they also unveiled his possessiveness. Each brushstroke on the canvas appeared to resonate with his affection.

A growing suspicion began to take root in my mind – that the Claire from the Masterson family and Gray's Claire might indeed be the same person. The resemblance between them was undeniable, and an unspoken connection lingered in the air, one I couldn't simply ignore.

As dusk approached, the cityscape unfurled before us in a dazzling array of vibrant colors. The warm shades of orange, pink, and lilac blended harmoniously with the sapphire blue of the ocean. Towering buildings gradually materialized on the horizon, signaling our arrival in the central city.

Felix's acerbic comment about returning home cast a shadow on his mood, underscoring the complexity of his circumstances. It was evident that he harbored no great enthusiasm about coming back, particularly not to his father's residence. His determination to apprehend the Doll Killer before contemplating a true homecoming was palpable.

As the city drew nearer, a potent sense of anticipation washed over me. With each passing moment, it felt as if I were edging closer to unraveling the enigma of my past and uncovering the destiny that awaited me.

Chapter Sixteen

As we neared the island, security personnel ushered us into a tram. I reverted to my hat and sunglasses disguise, blending in with my companions.

"Why is there such heavy security?" Lily wondered aloud, her confusion mirroring my own.

I could only offer a nonchalant shrug as I sensed the small tram car beginning to move. Attempting to peer outside, I found the window glass frosted over, obscuring any view of the outside world.

Trey leaned in close, whispering, "How much do you think Gray is paying these security guards to watch us like hawks?" His gaze swept over the guards stationed at each corner of the tram car.

Halle replied with a casual shrug, "He's wealthy, so I suppose it doesn't matter to him."

I couldn't help but notice that Jared had chosen to sit by himself, slightly apart from the other card readers sharing the tram with us.

"No talking," a stern security guard reprimanded Halle, his gaze unwavering.

We continued our journey, entering a tunnel that served as both the entrance and exit to the central city. It was no surprise that we were using the shuttle trams reserved for the common citizens; Gray and his inner circle favored the more opulent and extravagant trams for their transportation. Additionally, I couldn't help but notice that our tram operated autonomously, devoid of a human operator.

I recalled reading manuals detailing how these trams functioned. With each passing moment, we drew closer to the heart of civilization. As we emerged from the tunnel, I was struck by the dull grayness of the sky, a stark indicator of urban development. The architectural landscape unfolded before my eyes, a captivating blend of Baroque and Rococo styles adorned with intricate domes, columns, and spirals. Towering skyscrapers, constructed from a medley of metals, glass, and crystal, punctuated the skyline, casting an awe-inspiring silhouette against the horizon.

Even the buildings at ground level, constructed from a variety of materials such as stone, bricks, or plaster, possessed their own unique charm. As enchanting as the city appeared on the surface, it harbored threats at every corner: the enigmatic Doll Killer, the elusive Kathy Ann, the enigmatic Victor Frankenstein, and the ever-present Gray himself.

The city was divided into distinct sections, each with its own character and allure. The West Side played host to an array of performing arts institutions and museums, alongside grand apartment buildings where many residents called home.

On the opposite end, the East Side exuded an air of opulence, housing fancy restaurants, designer boutiques, luxurious high-rise apartments, elegant brownstone townhouses, and art galleries. This was the domain of the city's affluent elite. Meanwhile, the middle and lower classes occupied different neighborhoods.

The East Village was a vibrant hub, home to local cafes, cozy lounges, and intimate jazz clubs. It stood in stark contrast to the gritty alleys and tenant-style buildings of the lower-income locals. In the West Village, cobblestone streets and public squares nestled amidst a backdrop of various parks, all surrounded by modest apartment buildings.

The city had an air of both foreignness and familiarity, a paradox that left me both intrigued and unsettled. Below, I observed people dressed in a blend of modernized Victorian-style attire, various Steampunk fashions, and Lolita styles.

"Is something bothering you, Adelice?" Halle inquired, her concern evident.

"Do you think I'm crazy if I tell you that this place feels like it could be where I was born and raised?" I confessed.

Halle offered a reassuring smile. "No, it's a sign that you're starting to remember your origins."

She was right; I was beginning to recollect fragments of this place. I had grown up in the Central Park District, and for all I knew, my mother and grandmother could be anywhere within this sprawling metropolis. It was regrettable that I couldn't recall their faces, and worse still, I had no idea what my last name was. Even if I did remember them, I wasn't the same person I had been back then. I had changed since the day I ran away.

The tram came to a halt, and we disembarked hastily under the watchful eyes of security personnel. My eyes stung momentarily from the harsh station lights, which bathed the surroundings in hues of gold and copper. The polished marble floors were so slick that I could playfully slide in my sneakers, pretending I was gliding on ice.

The entire station felt like a masterpiece of design, and it was clear that the locals had a penchant for beautiful things. We were guided toward the lobby, where all the other card readers had been corralled together, forming a clustered mass. Trey voiced his confusion, wondering aloud about the reason behind this congregation. However, one look at the small stage and the large screen positioned at the back provided the answer we sought.

"We're about to witness an opening ceremony," Elliot whispered, his dark eyes trained on the bookish man who had taken the stage.

The man introduced himself as Daryl White, Mr. Gray's assistant. "Now, before we begin, a message from your host."

A shiver ran down my spine as Gray himself stepped onto the stage. He appeared exactly as he had during the talk show at the warehouse: donning the same violet suit, his long, dark, wavy hair pulled back into a ponytail, and the gold-framed monocle resting over his left eye. A wide smile began to form on his lips, revealing perfectly white teeth as he commenced his address.

"Greetings, card readers. It's truly a delight to see you've all arrived safely," Gray began, his tone amiable.

"Bullshit," Trey couldn't help but interject with a feigned cough. Gray's gaze briefly narrowed, suggesting he might have caught the insult, but his smile remained unwavering.

"It's not every day that I have the pleasure of hosting an event for individuals whose talents are intricately tied to the tarot," Gray continued. "Since the founding of the Empire, the cards have been a vital source of our magic. Your task is quite straightforward: locate and retrieve items associated with the lower court cards, scattered throughout the city."

However, Gray issued a stark warning: "Not all will succeed because the challenges ahead are formidable. To ensure fair play and prevent any shenanigans, my security personnel have installed cameras in all areas where tasks are to be performed flawlessly."

"Ahh, shit," Felix muttered under his breath, his disapproval evident.

"The worst part," I whispered back, "is that he'll be watching our every move."

We had barely settled in, and it already felt like we were trapped in a viper's nest with a cunning snake. There was no doubt that Gray and his allies would be keeping a close eye on us through the network of cameras.

"Furthermore, we have arranged safe houses for those who successfully complete the tasks," Gray continued. "You won't have to worry about finding food and lodging during your stay."

A disturbing giggle escaped Gray's lips, sending shivers down my spine. "I wish each of you the best of luck." As he began to exit the stage, Felix and I observed him closely. Gray's lips curved into a sinister smirk, akin to the Grinch's malevolent grin. It was evident he had something sinister planned, as if he knew that we would be the last ones standing in this twisted game.

Chapter Seventeen

Following Gray's speech, we were escorted to the first safe house, nestled on the first level of the city where laborers, street urchins, and gangs resided. I found myself surprisingly comfortable in this setting. The streets were all paved with black cobblestone, and the buildings were constructed from sturdy bricks and stones.

The safe house we had been allocated was a youth hostel, featuring spacious rooms with rows of twin beds lining the walls. As Felix claimed his chosen bed for the night, he reiterated his earlier offer. "It's never too late to consider my proposal."

We found ourselves in a room all to ourselves, a clear consequence of the strict segregation laws that prevailed between Halflings and purebloods in the more urbanized regions of the Empire.

As I slipped beneath the sheets, I couldn't help but revel in the softness and warmth of the mattress. It felt like a fleeting luxury, one I knew wouldn't endure for long. Yet, as I closed my eyes, I realized that I was no longer gripped by fear of the uncertain future that lay ahead, even if it meant I would have to battle for it.

And so, I closed my eyes and surrendered to the world of dreams.

Dreams possess a unique quality – they feel undeniably real, as if you're experiencing life in an alternate reality. That's precisely how it felt when I found myself standing in the midst of an impenetrable, pitch-black void, as though I had been plunged into a state of blindness. Gradually, my eyes adjusted to the darkness, revealing that I still wore the nightdress I had pilfered from the tailor's warehouse.

Adjacent to me, life-sized paintings adorned the inky walls. I couldn't help but question my sanity at that moment. Tentatively, I reached out to touch one of the canvases, and in an instant, I was transported into the very world depicted within the painting.

Before me lay a dazzling realm, bathed in an overwhelming radiance. My eyes stung from the intensity of the light, yet I beheld a world adorned in pastel hues, a world that seemed too vivid to be a mere dream.

Laughter echoed from the vicinity of a large, crystal-blue lake that encircled the park. My breath caught when I laid eyes on a five-year-old girl with cascading, pale blonde hair adorned by a large pink bow at the back. She donned a light blue dress that complemented the blue-violet brilliance of her eyes. Trailing behind her like a shadow was a colossal white swan. Claire Masterson—what could she possibly be doing in my dream?

"Such a beautiful child," I overheard several voices murmuring, "a true daughter of light." Rooted to the spot, I observed as Claire strolled toward the entrance of a small garden, her gaze fixed on the white roses that bloomed in the soil. She remained blissfully unaware that she was being observed by a hidden figure lurking in the shadows beneath the trees just beyond the garden wall. My eyes widened in alarm when I recognized the figure as Gray, though his hair was now noticeably shorter.

I remained transfixed as Gray continued to watch Claire with an air of reverence, capturing her image meticulously in a sketchbook held firmly in his grasp. The setting underwent a transformation, and suddenly, I found myself standing center-stage. Claire had aged a bit, now appearing to be around eleven years old, and she danced with remarkable grace and elegance. What was the significance of these visions, and what were they trying to convey?

As I made my way into the seating area, I noticed that most of the figures occupying the seats were shrouded in shadow. However, one figure stood out, their unwavering gaze fixed on Claire as she leaped and twirled gracefully in her white ballerina slippers.

I couldn't deny the unsettling feeling that something profoundly sinister was at play. Was I descending into madness, or was Fate attempting to communicate Gray's peculiar obsession with Claire Masterson? Then it struck me – Claire Masterson from the paintings that Jared had shown me on the ferry must be the same Claire I had just witnessed in this dream. She was undoubtedly the wife Felix had mentioned during our forest camping excursion, a wife who rarely made public appearances.

This was my first critical clue as to why Gray was pursuing me relentlessly. It was possible that I bore some resemblance to her, particularly during her childhood years. While it seemed plausible, I couldn't be certain, and I knew I needed to uncover more pieces of the puzzle to unravel the full truth.

Chapter Eighteen

Waking up in a city where the wealthy held sway over the middle and working class was an unsettling experience. I knew I had to tread carefully because rumors on the street had it that Kathy Ann had arrived in town. She must have caught wind of Felix and me making our way to the Central Park District. So, the question remained: how does one deal with a social worker embedded within the Elite?

As we entered the cozy lounge of the hostel's kitchen, the rich aroma of coffee enveloped us. The breakfast spread beckoned, featuring pancakes, bacon, and scrambled eggs artfully arranged on the serving table. My mouth began to water at the sheer sight of it all, a stark reminder of my voracious hunger.

"Has anyone devised a game plan?" Trey inquired.

"I have," Elliot interjected confidently, prompting our attention. "I've conducted some extensive research. Here's the deal: each challenge is situated on a different level of the city. We're currently on level one, and there are a grand total of eight levels we need to navigate to conquer all the challenges and reach the Edge."

Curiosity piqued, I couldn't help but ask, "What's the Edge?"

Elliot, the male triplet, took it upon himself to explain. "It's the district where the nobility resides, primarily because they relish the idea of living above the ground level."

Felix chimed in, adding his perspective. "That's where my father and Gray are."

"So you're an Edge kid," Trey mused, noting the connection. "We are too," Isabelle pointed out, reinforcing the shared background.

Lily, with a note of determination, stated, "But it doesn't matter where we come from, because Gray won't be inclined to make things easy for any of us, especially when it involves gathering all the artifacts for the lower court cards."

"The most unsettling aspect is the uncertainty surrounding these challenges," I lamented with a sigh. "We'll need to conquer all of them to gain access to the Edge, which is where Gray and the Doll Killer are waiting." My gaze drifted toward Felix, who had fallen into a contemplative silence, recognizing that he couldn't avoid confronting his father forever. Inevitably, the rest of us were bound to encounter Victor Frankenstein.

The aroma of coffee served as a comforting constant amidst our uncertainty. I reached for the cream and sugar, intending to temper the bitterness of the brew. "The tasks will undoubtedly escalate in difficulty as we ascend through the levels," Isabelle remarked, a sense of foreboding settling upon us.

Felix, displaying a measure of nonchalance, simply shrugged. "We're about to find out soon enough," he remarked, taking a deliberate sip of his coffee. It was evident that Felix harbored nerves beneath his cool exterior, being back within the Elite's territory.

I knew very little about the Edge, except that it was Felix's place of birth and upbringing. The mere thought of it stung, as I had no recollection of my own origins or what my parents looked like. It was a source of immense frustration, enough to bring tears to my eyes. Nonetheless, I clung to the sense of purpose that drove me forward, even as a thick fog obscured my memories. If I ever hoped to uncover the truth about my past, I had to reach the Edge.

Following breakfast, we made our way down the trail toward the park. As we ventured deeper, I sensed an underlying magic suffusing the entire area. Vibrant colors burst forth from the plants, and the earthy scent of the soil mingled with an unsettling odor of decay. It was in that moment that I found myself confronted by my first encounter with the supernatural: a reanimated doll, a grotesque parody of life.

"Run!" instinctively escaped my lips as the zombie lurched toward me. We were all caught off guard as more of them joined the chase, mingling with the terrified screams of both magic gene carriers and non-carriers on the street.

"The day had barely begun, and Gray decided to throw obstacles at us," Trey muttered in frustration. "Damn it."

Our situation went from bad to worse as another horde of zombies emerged from the nearby lake. They were skeletal, their skin a sickly gray, and their eyes white, like eerie orbs of hunger. Their craving for brains was unmistakable.

Turning to Halle, I urgently asked, "How do you kill a zombie?"

Halle replied, "The most effective way is to shoot them in the brain. I don't have a gun, but I do have my axe here. It can put them down for good."

Trey, his eyes alight with a strange enthusiasm, declared, "I brought guns!"

Lily's reaction was one of stark disbelief and alarm. "Are you out of your mind?!" she screamed.

Trey retorted, "Do you want to die?!"

Lily shot back, "Of course, I don't!"

"You better think on your feet, or we'll end up as meals for a horde of walking corpses straight out of 'The Walking Dead,'" I urgently warned.

With a growl, Lily demanded, "Give me the gun." Trey nodded nervously and passed the firearm to her.

Lily displayed no hesitation as she systematically shot each zombie square in the head. "Your sister is a force to be reckoned with," Trey commented in awe as we watched the reanimated corpses slump to the ground.

Felix chimed in, offering a light-hearted compliment. "She's a savage, but in the best way possible. No offense, Izzy and Ell."

Isabelle replied with a smile, "None taken."

Lily, her dark eyes now fixed on Halle, took a sing-song tone. "Trey, here's your gun." She then skipped toward him. "Halle, it's time to chop off some heads." Halle nodded determinedly and began decapitating the fallen zombies with her axe.

I was left momentarily speechless. "I can't believe you just insulted one of the most influential figures in the Empire," Felix remarked with evident glee.

Isabelle, ever the pragmatist, inquired, "Do you think he got the message?"

Felix's smirk widened. "Oh, he definitely got it. No doubt he's seething right now, feeling like he just got roasted gangster style."

The park's pedestrians looked on, their expressions a mix of shock and curiosity. "Nothing to see here, folks. Keep it moving!" I declared authoritatively, dispersing the onlookers.

It was becoming abundantly clear that our stay in the Central Park District wouldn't be lacking in excitement, after all.

Chapter Nineteen

Following the harrowing encounter with the zombies in the park, we reached the starting point of the Scavenger hunt. The public library, a gracefully elongated rectangular structure, featured an enchanting color palette of sea green and robin's egg blue. Its large, ornate gold frames accentuated the windows on every floor, creating a captivating sight. The library's beauty was akin to a harmonious fusion of Russia's summer and winter palaces, a stunning backdrop for our next adventure.

The interior of the library was no less impressive, adorned with cream-colored walls, intricate gilded moldings, and magnificent crystal chandeliers suspended from the dome-shaped ceilings. As we ventured further, we discovered the library's grandeur extended to its contents. The library spanned an impressive five stories, each floor housing thousands of shelves brimming with books. Alongside the literary treasures, murals, mosaics, and tapestries adorned the walls and floors, each a captivating work of art.

The murals depicted vivid scenes, their colors meticulously applied to both the broad strokes and intricate details, while the mosaics gleamed with an array of colored stones, glass fragments, and tiles meticulously arranged across the floors. Every nook and cranny of the library was a testament to artistic splendor.

Our guide led us through the various halls, gardens, and ballrooms within the library, where grand galas were once hosted. We explored the very classrooms that had once served as private chambers and apartments, and even stumbled upon a museum exhibit chronicling the history of the immortals who had played pivotal roles in the Empire's founding.

I spotted Felix in the section dedicated to his father's life, where the exhibit chronicled Victor Frankenstein's journey from his mortal days to the momentous events surrounding the creation of the monster. His gaze was fixed upon a collection of black-and-white photographs, preserved behind the expansive glass case. The images revealed Victor Frankenstein alongside an older gentleman and two young boys, one around the age of six and the other approximately fourteen. A young woman stood beside Victor, holding his hand. I recognized them instantly.

"They're my dad's family," Felix explained, his mesmerizing green eyes remaining fixed on the images of the smiling faces captured in a moment frozen in time. "They look so happy," I observed softly.

Pointing at each person in the photo, Felix provided context. "That's my grandfather Alphonse, followed by my uncles William and Earnest."

Curiosity piqued, I asked about the woman beside Victor. Her hair seemed too light to be Felix's mother. "Who is the woman?"

Felix's gaze turned somber as he shared a piece of family history. "That's Elizabeth Lavenza. She was my dad's first wife, an orphan adopted by my grandparents after her family succumbed to scarlet fever. The same disease took my grandmother's life a few years later. Her dying wish was for Elizabeth to marry my dad."

Felix wore a profound sadness on his face as he spoke. "This photo was taken just before my father departed for university in Germany, a journey that ultimately led to the creation of the monster." Bitterness, resentment, and grief permeated his voice as he spoke of family members who had passed away before he had the chance to meet them. "I wish I had known them—my grandfather and uncles. I wish I had known them before the monster took their lives. If only my father hadn't been a coward and had refrained from creating a mate for it, they might still be alive."

Offering a comforting gesture, I placed my hand on his shoulder. "I'm sure they would have loved you," I reassured him.

Felix nodded, his gaze distant. "I think so too. It's tragic that they had no inkling of the grim fate the monster would bring upon them." Delving into a past he had never been a part of was a difficult task for Felix, and it was evident that Victor Frankenstein remained a stranger to his own son.

It was a challenge to fathom that Felix had once led a happy, carefree life before being drawn into the shadowy realm of the Macabre. However, if not for the creation of the monster, the friend I had come to know might never have existed. This, perhaps, was the one redeeming aspect of the tragic Frankenstein Legacy.

"I'm beginning to grasp why my father chose to seclude himself from the world," Felix reflected, his voice carrying a weight of understanding. "And why the first Emperor punished him by bestowing upon him the touch, which he then passed on to me. The touch serves as a means for him to shoulder responsibility for the losses brought about by his reckless actions."

He gazed at the palms of his hands. "When it comes to the touch, it's the soul that truly matters. Even with this power, the reunion of soul and body is temporary. I fear that I might inadvertently reanimate a corpse devoid of conscience." We were both coming to terms with the true dangers of the touch.

Upon exiting the exhibit hall, we were presented with our map for the Scavenger hunt. All eight artifacts related to the lower court cards were scattered throughout the first eight levels of the central city. The Edge, where the affluent resided and the Doll Killer awaited, marked the ultimate and final level in our quest.

From what I had gathered from the other card readers, rumors had been circulating about a grand prize awaiting those who successfully collected all eight artifacts. Whatever it might be, skepticism lingered—it had all the hallmarks of a trap.

Exiting the library, Trey voiced the question on everyone's mind. "So, how are we going about this?"

Halle, taking charge, examined the map and the accompanying riddles. "I'm not entirely sure, but we're about to find out," she replied.

"Our first item is located near the lake in the park," Halle explained.

Lily, with a dreamy expression, chimed in, "I could use a good swim."

Trey, ever the realist, interjected, "Hate to burst your bubble, princess, but for all we know, it could be infested with sea monsters." Halle's point was valid; anything supernatural posed a threat, regardless of our lineage.

A young Halfling boy with a mop of blonde curls approached our group. "Hey, guys," he greeted us. "I couldn't help but overhear your plan to retrieve the Page of Cups artifact near the lake. I'd like to join you."

Felix, ever cautious, posed a direct question. "What exactly do you gain from this?"

The blonde kid simply shrugged. "Nothing, really. We Halflings have to stick together. The Pureblood card readers are solely fixated on the prize at the end of the Scavenger, hoping to secure a place in the Edge."

"Why do you care?" I asked skeptically. "Isn't saving the world more important than social status?"

Recognition dawned on me as I continued, "You're one of the other four the psychic mentioned."

The blonde Halfling gave me a wry smile. "Took you a while to figure that out, huh? The bottom line is, we need to gather all the artifacts for the lower court cards if we're going to thwart whatever threatens the Empire."

"If we're going to work together, the least you could do is tell us your name," I remarked coolly.

"It's Aaron," he replied. "The other three will show up once we make it through the next four days."

I understood the risk in trusting Aaron, but it was clear that we needed all the help we could get if we were to reach the Edge and confront the looming threat.

As I gazed upon the crystal blue waters of the expansive lake, I felt an inexplicable pull—the power of the first court card calling to me and my newfound companions. It was a peculiar sensation, one that we alone seemed to experience, perceiving its magic through all five of our senses. I couldn't help but wonder if this was another advantage of existing within the Grey Zone. Glancing over at the Pureblood card readers, I questioned why they remained oblivious to the beckoning power that resonated with us.

Aaron appeared to be a trustworthy addition to our group, and his assistance was invaluable in securing the item linked to the Page of Cups. This challenge presented us with a clear ultimatum:

sink or swim. We had no choice but to forge ahead, embracing the risks that came with our quest.

Chapter Twenty

As we walked down the narrow catwalk situated in the middle of the seemingly clear and tranquil lake, an unsettling feeling lingered in the air. Despite the pristine appearance of the water, there was a palpable sense that something sinister lurked beneath its surface.

Felix voiced his doubts, his gaze fixated on the peculiar wave formations in the turquoise waters. "Are you certain we're in the right place?"

Aaron's response was to the point as he pointed toward an engraved image of the Page of Cups, intricately carved into the wooden surface of the catwalk. "Does this answer your question?"

There was no doubt; we had indeed arrived at the correct location. "Now that we've found it, does anyone happen to know the meaning of the court card?" Aaron inquired, acknowledging the formidable challenge of deciphering the significance behind a card's symbolism, a task that often demanded significant energy and insight.

Felix began to explain, "Each card has two aspects—the upright position symbolizes light, while the reversed position signifies darkness. For the Page of Cups, the upright position represents an opportunity for creativity, driven by instincts and a curious anticipation of what might happen. In the reversed position, it's all about fresh and novel ideas, accompanied by doubts regarding the instincts that may lead to creative blocks and emotional immaturity."

Aaron reflected, "So, the card revolves around creativity and instincts rooted in feelings and emotions."

I added, "But there's more to it. The primary message of the card is that inspiration can come from anywhere if you remain open to it."

Aaron looked around the lake, perplexed. "Yet, why choose the lake for the artifact's location?"

"The Page of Cups is the lake," I clarified, "and we need to collect a sample of its water for the item to manifest in its physical form."

Felix shook his head in amazement. "The psychic wasn't kidding when she said we had to locate all the living incarnations of the cards."

Aaron's frustration was evident as he grumbled, "How on earth are we supposed to collect a water sample from the lake?" He had a valid point—we lacked the necessary tools, such as a cup or an empty water bottle, to gather a small amount of water from the lake.

Suddenly, our attention was drawn to the sound of someone crying at the far end of the catwalk. There, at the narrow path's terminus, stood a young woman. She wore a flowing white gown, and her long dark hair was adorned with red flowers woven into the locks.

Under the sunlight, the olive hue of her skin took on a milky quality, adding to the sense that something was amiss with her.

"Have you seen my children?" she inquired with a tone steeped in melancholy.

Felix responded abruptly, "No, we haven't."

With a sigh, the woman continued, "It's a pity, but I still require an offering."

A gasp escaped my lips as her hands suddenly encircled my ankles. "ADELICE," Felix screamed.

I was overwhelmed by shock as I stared into the hauntingly beautiful but ghostly face of La Llorona, the Weeping Woman. Thick black tears streamed down her azure eyes, tracing a path down her cheeks. "I don't think you want to do this, Maria."

The Weeping Woman gasped upon hearing her real name, a reaction that brought a smirk to my lips. Names held a special power over creatures like La Llorona.

"How?" Her voice trembled with a mixture of fear and shock, making it difficult for her to speak.

"I know everything about you, Maria," I responded. "We all know your tale—how your husband left you for a younger, prettier woman. It drove you to the edge of madness, and you drowned your own children in the river."

"As punishment for your crime," I continued, "you were denied entry into the afterlife, forever separated from your children."

La Llorona remained silent, her gaze fixated on the lake. I knew what I had to do; by embracing creative opportunities, I needed to enter the water. With determination, I seized the hem of La Llorona's skirt and pulled her into the lake alongside me.

The moment I submerged myself in the water, I found myself in a different realm, a surreal underwater world bathed in shades of blue and clarity. I was beneath the surface of the lake, an environment that should have evoked fear, but strangely, I felt no such trepidation. I noticed La Llorona floating before me, and instead of anger or defiance, she wore a serene smile.

"Congratulations, child," she spoke softly. "You have executed the role of the card flawlessly."

I couldn't help but ask, "So, you didn't intend to harm me?"

"No," La Llorona replied. "It is forbidden to harm those who possess a deck. I am cursed to wander the Earth for all eternity and bound to this sacred site."

Curiosity got the better of me as I questioned her, "How did you know you were supposed to dive into the lake?"

I shrugged, admitting, "I didn't. I simply followed the card's actions by keeping an open mind to all possibilities, but it was primarily driven by pure instinct."

"I see," La Llorona murmured, her tone softening. "Those who came before you were too frightened to venture into the lake. As a reward for embodying the card, the power of the lake's waters belongs to you alone. My children remain beyond reach, but at least I can find some solace knowing the lake's power is in the right hands."

Her expression turned somber, and her eyes glistened with sadness. "Before you return to the surface, I must caution you about another weeping woman who mourns the loss of her child."

Perplexed, I inquired, "What do you mean?"

"There is another underlying reason for this year's Scavenger," she continued, "and it all revolves around her."

Confused, I pressed further, "What do you mean by 'her'? Who is she?" My curiosity had been thoroughly piqued.

"I wish I could offer more details, but I cannot," La Llorona replied sadly. "However, I can inform you that she is at the heart of it all, and she will not cease until she is reunited with her child."

"Is she a spirit like you?" I inquired.

La Llorona shook her head. "No, she is very much alive, as is her missing child. Proceed to the concealed room located behind the bookshelf in the office that serves as Gray's sanctuary. That's where you will uncover the truth behind this year's Scavenger. Take care, my child; although it's too late for me, it is not too late for her."

With a nod, I began my ascent back to the surface.

"That's the enchantment of this world, I suppose," I remarked with a shrug, my gaze fixed on the amulet with fascination. "It's all about symbolism and the connections we establish between elements and their meanings."

Aaron nodded in agreement. "Well, we've secured the first artifact," he observed, eyeing the amulet. "Now, we just need to decipher the rest of the puzzle and reach the Edge."

Felix slipped the amulet around his neck, a determined expression on his face. "One down, seven to go," he declared resolutely. "And thanks to La Llorona, we have a lead on the next step."

With the newfound information, it felt like we were finally making progress toward unraveling the mysteries surrounding the Scavenger and the enigmatic woman who lay at its core.

"The snake represents danger, manipulation, and deceit," I elucidated, scrutinizing the card. "While the puppet on the string symbolizes control and manipulation by an external force."

It was evident that the card had undergone a transformation in response to my encounter with La Llorona and the events at the lake. "This likely serves as a warning," I continued, "regarding the challenges we'll encounter and the manipulative forces that will be in play."

Aaron nodded gravely, his expression reflecting the gravity of the situation. Felix leaned in, closely examining the card. "Well, it's a stark reminder that we can't afford to let our guard down." He glanced up at me. "We need to be cautious and stay one step ahead."

I nodded in agreement. "Absolutely, especially considering we may be dealing with a central figure who is unwavering in her pursuit to reunite with her child. We must be prepared for any eventuality."

Once I had changed and rejoined the group, we realized it was time to locate the others and proceed to our next challenge. Seven more artifacts remained to be collected, and numerous trials awaited us. As we departed from the park, the weight of La Llorona's warning hung in the air, a lingering reminder of the enigmatic woman who yearned for her child.

The mystery surrounding her had only just begun to unravel, and I understood that our journey was far from its conclusion. With renewed resolve, I reconnected with the group, prepared to confront whatever challenges lay ahead. As we walked together, I couldn't shake the sensation that the pieces of the puzzle were gradually falling into place.

The Scavenger had evolved beyond a mere competition; it had transformed into a voyage of self-discovery, friendship, and the pursuit of truth. I was resolute in my determination to see it through to the end, regardless of the obstacles or secrets that awaited us.

Indeed, the challenges and mysteries that loomed ahead appeared formidable, yet bolstered by the unwavering support of my newfound friends and the determination that had carried us this far, I felt ready to confront whatever obstacles lay in our path. As the train transported us to the next level, a blend of excitement and apprehension coursed through me. I knew that this unique journey of discovery and magic held both trials and wonders that would shape our destinies.

The Lake

The park held a special place in fifteen-year-old Claire Masterson's heart within the bustling city. Its lush, green lawns and vibrant flowers provided a serene escape, and the lake, with its mesmerizing turquoise waters, was particularly enchanting. Claire often wondered why more people didn't venture near the lake. Perhaps it was the lingering rumors that it harbored La Llorona, the Weeping Woman.

Claire's friend, Astoria, had shared the urban legend about La Llorona. She had descended into madness after her husband abandoned her for another woman, leading to a tragic episode where she drowned her own children in a river. It was one of the many chilling stories Claire's mother had recounted to her and her brother, Tristin, during their childhood. By all accounts, she should have been afraid of the lake, but an inexplicable lack of fear drew her to it instead.

Claire often found herself drawn to the lake, where she once spotted a man with long, dark hair tied back in a ponytail. He sat beneath the shade of a massive oak tree, engrossed in his sketchbook. Claire couldn't explain it, but there was an uncanny sense of familiarity about him, as though she had encountered him in some distant memory, and she was inexplicably drawn to his presence, like a moth to a flame.

Curiosity got the best of her, and she ventured closer. "What brings you here?" she inquired.

He glanced up from his sketchbook, his dark eyes meeting hers. "This is one of the few places that helps me maintain my sanity and allows me to draw in peace. If you're concerned about the Weeping Woman, she is tethered to the lake, much like all the other supernatural beings bound to the sacred sites of the Artifacts."

Claire was taken aback. "How do you know so much?" she asked, her curiosity piqued.

The artist nonchalantly shrugged. "Because I played a role in the binding," he revealed, a mischievous smirk tugging at his lips. His cornflower-blue eyes held a hint of amusement as he gazed at Claire.

Unfazed, he continued, "Now, it's my turn to ask a question: why do you come here? Is the bustling city life wearing you down?"

Claire shook her head. "No, it's the only place where I can witness the flowers in their natural beauty."

The artist's curiosity was piqued. "What kind of flowers?" he inquired.

"Roses," Claire answered with a gentle smile, "but the white ones are my favorite."

"Interesting," the artist mused, his lips curving into a knowing smile. Their conversation soon drifted to the various colors of roses and the meanings they held, binding them in an unexpected exchange of shared interests and stories.

Chapter Twenty-One

Once we disembarked from the train, we diligently traced the path outlined on the map. "Are you confident this is the correct location?" Aaron inquired with a furrowed brow. Halle, without uttering a word, simply extended her arm toward the edifice depicted on the map. "It appears to be an abandoned cathedral," Elliot observed, his voice tinged with disbelief. "A vast body of water is one thing, but an entire building? This is beyond belief." "Perhaps our destination lies within the confines of the church?" Lily ventured.

"I believe you may be onto something, young one," Aaron exclaimed with a warm smile as he tousled the dark curls adorning her head. "Take a look, everyone. There's a cemetery in the rear," Isabelle called out, her gaze fixed on the ashen tombstones scattered across the somber soil of the burial ground. "Oh, joy, more deceased individuals," Trey quipped sarcastically. There was little doubt that he still harbored the residual effects of the morning's harrowing encounter with the undead.

"Are we certain this is the correct location, Halle?" Trey queried, directing his question toward his sister.

"I'm quite confident we've arrived at the correct destination, brother," the female twin reassured him.

"She's correct," Elliot concurred, his gaze fixed upon the intricately engraved image of the Page of Wands adorning the wooden church door.

"Now that we've ascertained our location, does anyone happen to be familiar with both the upright and reversed interpretations of this card?" Aaron inquired.

"I suppose I might as well take on the task," Elliot volunteered, "considering I was the one who initially spotted the card's engraving."

"Please, do enlighten us," I urged, my anxiety mounting as I remained acutely aware of the lurking peril within the cathedral's confines.

"One thing is abundantly clear: the Page of Wands represents the essence of discovery and exploration, embodying the exhilaration of unfettered self-expression. The gravest misstep one can take is to stifle new ideas, wandering aimlessly without purpose," Elliot expounded, adopting the demeanor of an erudite instructor. "In essence, one might aptly conclude that the Page of Wands symbolizes the pursuit of knowledge."

"If there's one certainty I can attest to, it is that the artifact resides within the church," I affirmed.

"Elliot," I responded urgently, "you might as well accompany Felix and me, for it is abundantly clear that whatever lies in wait within the cathedral will not readily relinquish the artifact." I acknowledged the veracity of his statement, harboring no doubt that the creatures guarding the remaining artifacts would grow increasingly formidable as we ascended to higher levels of challenge.

Once we crossed the threshold, it became evident that the monster had chosen to confront us in the section of the cathedral typically reserved for the minister's sermons. While my knowledge of religion was limited, I could discern that this sacred place of worship had been usurped as the creature's prison. "We are aware of your presence, so there's no need for concealment!" Felix called out boldly.

A resonant growl reverberated throughout the edifice. "I believe you've thoroughly incited its wrath!" Elliot remarked bluntly, his words accompanied by the rush of air as the winged entity soared past him. My eyes widened in astonishment as the wyvern-like creature materialized before us. This monstrous being possessed a horse-like visage adorned with dual horns, leathery bat-like wings, diminutive clawed appendages, and its piercing red eyes fixed unwaveringly upon the boys.

"Well, well, well, what do we have here?" the creature's voice resonated through the telepathic link. "After all my years of confinement, I never anticipated a confrontation with the gray beings."

"Is that the designation you and your kind have bestowed upon us?" Elliot inquired.

"Indeed, you could say that," the creature responded with an air of gravitas. "So, you've come in pursuit of the artifact? I've waited patiently for one deemed worthy to claim it. Regrettably, those who preceded you, both dark and light, lacked the fortitude to face me."

The creature's crimson eyes bore into us challengingly. "Now, do you recognize my identity? Exercise discernment in your choice of words; by now, you ought to comprehend that the Page of Wands embodies the essence of transformation."

Felix's eyes began to sparkle with recognition. "I know who you are," he declared firmly, his gaze locked onto the monstrous figure. "You are the Jersey Devil, the thirteenth offspring of the Leeds family. Cursed by your mother upon her discovery of her thirteenth pregnancy after birthing twelve children before you. You were once ordinary, but it wasn't until the woman who brought you into this world uttered the words, 'Let this one be a Devil.'"

"It extends beyond that," Elliot interjected. "You bear another epithet, the Leeds Devil. It was not only the name of the family into which you were born but also the town you hail from—Leeds Point, situated in the Garden District on the island that was once the State of New Jersey."

My curiosity piqued, I couldn't help but inquire, "How do you possess such extensive knowledge?"

"Research," Elliot replied succinctly. "I've always had a penchant for delving into the histories of other Provinces, harboring the aspiration of exploring them one day."

The Jersey Devil appeared taken aback. "Throughout all the years of my captivity in this place, I never fathomed that you would be the one to fulfill the card's prophecy. It brings me solace to know that the artifact now rests in the hands of someone who will wield its power judiciously."

Felix, seizing the opportunity to gain insight, posed the question, "But what led you to be imprisoned here in the first place?"

"The Committee imprisoned me within this church, much as they did with Maria at the lake," the Jersey Devil divulged. "Before you depart, it's imperative that the three of you comprehend the workings of magic in the New World. Just as there exist entities of both light and dark inclinations, there are two distinct categories of magic: soft and hard. Keep this knowledge firmly in mind as you confront the remaining challenges."

With a deliberate gesture, he directed our attention toward the flame amulet resting upon the front pew of the church. "Only two artifacts remain for the Pages to secure."

"Adelice, your deck has transformed once more," Felix remarked as we strolled through the cemetery. His keen observation was undeniable. This time, the Major Arcana featured a white swan accompanied by a rose of a distinct hue, fully unfurled.

"What could this symbolize?" Elliot inquired.

"It signifies more than just my being half-flawed," I elucidated, "but also half-perfect. The cards within my deck are conveying that my parent of light possesses perfection."

"That certainly aligns with the patterns we've observed," Felix concurred, "given that Flawed tend to align with the dark forces, whereas Perfect individuals gravitate toward the light."

"It does provide a plausible explanation for why those who purchased me from the System are so determined to obtain me," I mused aloud. While I remained uncertain about the intricacies of the bidding process, the prospect of a Halfling who embodied both flaws and perfection undoubtedly carried substantial value. Nonetheless, I was resolute in my determination not to let these forces dictate the course of my life.

The Cathedral

Claire, born into the Elite, was strictly prohibited from venturing to the city's first level. "It's far too perilous," her mother had cautioned, a sentiment that struck her as hypocritical since the park, a part of the first level of the central city, was accessible.

The moment her artistic friend divulged information about the sites where the sacred artifacts were safeguarded, Claire harbored an insatiable desire to witness them firsthand. Serendipity favored her when she stumbled upon the forsaken church unaccompanied, devoid of a chaperone.

"You really shouldn't be here, and neither should I," Astoria voiced with evident distress.

"Your concerns are unfounded," Claire chided. "Besides, Papa is rarely at home, and Mama is always locked away in her studio. I must find some means of amusement. What better way than to discover the locations of the artifacts and acquaint myself with the creatures that protect them?"

Astoria let out a resigned sigh. "I swear that artist is having a detrimental influence on you."

Claire couldn't resist a playful smirk. "The same could be said for your scientist friend," she teased.

A faint blush tinged Astoria's cheeks. She was of the same age as Claire, with black-brown hair adorned by two distinctive white streaks framing her face. Her bright blue eyes sparkled above pale skin speckled with freckles. The elegant brown dress she wore complemented her impeccably.

"Shall we proceed?" Claire inquired, extending an arm in invitation.

The two girls embarked on an exploration of the cemetery encircling the cathedral, immersing themselves in the serenity of the grounds. They wandered among the tombstones, absorbing the solemnity of the surroundings, until the hour grew late, and it was time to make their way home for the customary afternoon tea at the Edge.

Chapter Twenty-Two

With the second artifact secured, it was time to make our way to the safe house situated on the second level. Exhaustion weighed upon me, threatening to overtake my senses at any moment. Each step I took felt as if my feet were being relentlessly pinched from below.

Upon entering the safe house, I heaved a contented sigh at the sight of the bed tucked away in the corner of the room designated for the girls. We were all in dire need of rest, for tomorrow promised to be another taxing day. I was still acclimating to the intricacies of a city where the levels were meticulously stacked upon one another.

After indulging in a soothing shower and savoring a modest meal comprised of beef jerky, white cheddar popcorn, and fried apples, the allure of sleep beckoned. We embraced the reprieve of slumber, knowing that it would be imperative for the trials awaiting us on the morrow.

I've perpetually harbored dreams involving monsters, although they weren't the sort borne of childhood nightmares—a childhood

I possessed no recollection of. In my dream, I found myself standing before an abandoned townhouse, an enigmatic urge compelling me to explore its interior. What was it about this place that drew me in with such insistence?

As I ventured inside, a peculiar scene unfolded before me. Every wall within was cloaked in a somber shade of grey, while the furnishings lay concealed beneath thin white sheets, guarding them against the encroaching dust.

A profound sense of foreboding gripped me as I ascended the staircase, its steps leading to the enigmatic second floor of the townhouse where all the doors stood ajar. The first room beckoned with a haunting tableau: an array of antique toys scattered haphazardly across the floor. It felt like a playroom or perhaps a nursery, the walls adorned with an image of two young children engrossed in their play. There was a fair-haired girl with locks of pale yellow, and by her side, a dark-haired boy. "The Swan Children," a disembodied voice echoed within the recesses of my mind.

Yet, I was ill-prepared for the second room's revelation. Its walls were adorned in a delicate cream hue, and a bed of imposing proportions stood adorned with withered flowers. The queen-size bed bore sheets of faded silk, once a rosy pink but now muted and time-worn.

The visions of the past unfolded before me in a strange and bewildering manner. I observed a young woman, seated at the edge of the bed, her countenance radiant as she gazed down upon a dark-haired young man who knelt before her. He spoke with an earnestness that stirred my heart, saying, "Claire, my love, you are the lady of my heart and the angel of my desire. I desire nothing more than to spend the remainder of eternity with you. Will you do me the honor of becoming my wife?"

"Yes, Dorian, I share the same sentiment," Claire replied warmly.

"Wonderful," Dorian affirmed with a heartfelt smile. "I promise you a life befitting of your grace and beauty."

Feeling a bit like an intruder, I decided it was best to depart, unwilling to linger and witness an intimate encounter between the two. One thing had become unmistakably clear: the Claire Masterson depicted here and the Claire in the series of paintings on the ferry were indeed the same individual.

Yet, I hungered for more substantiation to support the theory that she was Gray's wife—the very one Felix had alluded to during our sojourn in the forest, following our escape from Kathy Ann. My instincts guided me towards the belief that the hidden room concealed within Gray's office held the answers I sought.

I stirred from my slumber in the early hours of the morning, the brilliant sunlight casting luminous reflections off the room's windows, a room I shared with the other girls. Today marked the second day of the Scavenger—a pivotal day for acquiring the final two artifacts designated for the Pages.

I attired myself in baggy cargo pants and a neon green shirt, sourced from the limited selection of clothing I had stashed away in the duffle bag Sera had provided. Stepping outside the safe house, the crisp morning air greeted me, its gentle breeze teasing the front curls of my hair skyward.

"You're an early riser," Felix remarked as he emerged to join me.

"I couldn't sleep," I replied, my gaze fixed on the horizon where the sun was ascending. An inexplicable urge welled within me, compelling me to capture the scene on canvas, to immortalize the essence of this moment.

"Are you anxious about what today might entail?" I inquired.

Felix's expression bore a trace of perpetual concern. "I'm always apprehensive, given the uncertainty of what we'll encounter in our quest to secure the final two artifacts for the Pages."

"Elliot mentioned that many card readers were eliminated because they were too fearful to confront the challenges posed by the lake or the cathedral," I remarked.

Felix nodded somberly. "We seem to be the sole ones who have managed to retrieve the artifacts. And if there's one thing I'm certain of, it's that Gray is concealing something of great significance."

Chapter Twenty-Three

"This place gives me the creeps," Aaron confessed, shuddering slightly as we made our way down the trail to the next sacred site—a peculiar amalgamation of an apple orchard, a pumpkin patch, and a sprawling cornfield.

"If I'm not mistaken, this must be where all the city's crops are cultivated," Elliot surmised. "It's like a self-sustaining farm, allowing the residents to remain comfortably ensconced within the city. Now, that's what I call ingenuity."

Felix offered a sardonic comment, saying, "The main city of the Central Park District is essentially a massive bubble with nine layers."

Trey chimed in, "This pales in comparison to where he and I grew up—a town where the locals maintain a close relationship with both nature and the bountiful harvest."

Halle, ever insightful, contributed, "My intuition tells me that the guardian of the upcoming artifacts will require a coordinated effort involving all four of us."

"We're venturing into the unknown here," I admitted, my voice tinged with uncertainty. "It could be anything—perhaps even the Headless Horseman."

"You've got a valid point, Adelice," Halle concurred, her eyes scanning their surroundings. "Given the pervasive magic saturating this place, we might encounter something far more formidable than a headless man."

As we passed through the imposing iron gate, Halle's words seemed more prescient than ever; magic truly suffused every corner of this place.

Isabelle voiced a disconcerting notion, saying, "I can't help but wonder if they employ magic to influence the food somehow—a substance that imbues you with an overwhelming desire to stay, as though it were a spell of enchantment."

"I've discovered the engraving," Lily called out, her finger pointing to the image of the Page of Pentacles etched into the fertile soil. Her gaze was fixed intently on me. "Do you happen to know the kind of power associated with this card?" she inquired.

Felix, ever knowledgeable, interjected, "It's quite straightforward. The pentacle itself serves as the tangible embodiment of the earth element. The Page of Pentacles is a manifestation card, bestowing upon its wielder significant opportunities for prosperity and personal skill development. However, when reversed, it signifies a penchant for procrastination to the extent that no progress is being made. This reversal also offers the wielder an opportunity to glean valuable lessons from their failures."

"So, in essence, this card symbolizes growth, which would explain the ranch setting," I concluded.

A frigid yet composed voice interjected, sending a chill down our spines. "You've hit the mark, and our next guardian creature is undeniably linked to the harvest."

"Who are you?" Trey demanded, his gaze locked onto the girl who leaned nonchalantly against one of the apple trees. She appeared to be a few years older than me, emanating an aura that was both enchanting and seductive, evident in the knowing smirk she wore—an unspoken declaration of her danger. The girl possessed an immaculate complexion, devoid of any blemish or scar, and her long locks cascaded in shades of lavender-gray. Her eyes, a pale red with hints of pink in the irises, harmonized with the flowing white dress, black leather jacket, and matching dress boots she adorned.

"Oh, forgive my lapse in etiquette. I'm Rae, for the record," she introduced herself casually. "I happen to be the progeny of Dracula and the Blood Countess."

Felix couldn't resist a whispered aside, "Who would have ever imagined that the vampire coven's power couple would have Halfling offspring?"

Rae, despite her intriguing lineage, refocused our attention with a pressing matter. "As fascinating as it is to delve into my vampire heritage, we must prioritize retrieving the artifact from the clutches of the scarecrow who abducted Jared."

"What—"

Rae cut me off sharply, her glare silencing my inquiry. I nodded in acknowledgment, understanding that now was not the moment for questions, and I, along with Felix, trailed after her into the heart of the apple orchard.

As we ventured deeper into the orchard, the air grew noticeably colder. My eyes couldn't help but take in the transformation of the leaves on the trees, shifting from their lush green to the autumnal hues and the lifeless brown of winter—clear signs that the guardian monster of the artifact lurked nearby. What was even more disconcerting was that it held Jared captive.

"Alright, princess, now would be a good time to inform us about our adversary," Felix urged, his impatience palpable.

Rae nodded in acquiescence. "Are any of you familiar with the sack man?"

"The sack man?" I queried, my confusion apparent.

Rae elaborated, "Yes, there are various renditions of this spectral figure, but the one we're contending with is the Bubak, hailing from the regions that were once the Czech Republic and Slovakia. It's a scarecrow that feigns the sound of crying children to ensnare its prey. My nanny used to say that on the night of a full moon, it weaves cloth from the souls of the victims it has claimed and traverses in a cart drawn by black cats."

"So, we're essentially dealing with a Halloween version of Krampus," I mused, my gaze fixed on the creature that stood in the clearing of the orchard. If you disregarded the dark stains of blood splattered across its attire and the malevolent scowl etched on its lifeless face, it would resemble an ordinary scarecrow.

A desperate cry emerged from the sack nearby. "Help! Get me out of here!"

I recognized that voice, despite having only spoken to Jared once. It was him, and I couldn't stand idly by while he remained captive to the Bubak.

Felix voiced our collective frustration, hissing, "How on earth are we supposed to confront an evil scarecrow?" The looming threat that the Bubak posed to Jared was palpable, and we feared for his life.

My eyes locked onto Rae. "You possess the powers of both light and dark magic. I implore you to harness your abilities and manifest the earth. It's our only chance to rescue Jared from becoming a part of the Bubak's grisly wardrobe."

"I'll give it a shot," Rae responded, her resolve firm.

Felix's patience was running thin. "Just do it!" he yelled, giving her a push into the clearing.

The Bubak confronted us, demanding, "Who are you? What do you want?"

"I am Rachel, the daughter of Dracula and the Blood Countess," she declared boldly, "and I insist that you release the boy from your grasp."

The Bubak let out a derisive scoff. "I don't take orders from Red Faction scum, whether they be black or white. It's thanks to your family that I'm eternally bound to this accursed place."

"I feel a deep sense of pity for you, but you won't be claiming this boy's soul," Rae retorted, her hands plunging into the ground as she drew upon the magic of the earth that surrounded her. Felix and I watched in awe as the roots of the apple orchard's trees began to ensnare the Bubak, compelling him to relinquish the sack he had been clutching until it fell to the ground.

"Jared!" I cried out, rushing toward the sack.

"I knew you'd come," he replied, his voice carrying a hint of relief. With a small smile, he revealed the leaf amulet clutched tightly in his hands. "Look what I've got."

"Only one more left to retrieve," I muttered.

Felix interjected urgently, "Adelice, we need to leave. I don't think the root Rae summoned will hold for much longer."

We all nodded in agreement, and without delay, the four of us sprinted toward the exit, leaving the enigmatic orchard and the Bubak behind.

We boarded the next tram within minutes, and Trey's shudder was palpable. "I swear, this city becomes more twisted the higher we ascend," he remarked. "It's like Dante's Inferno, except instead of descending, we're going up."

Rae's frustration boiled over. "More importantly, who in their right mind thought it was a brilliant idea to employ a murderous scarecrow as a guardian for an artifact? What's even worse is that my family sanctioned the binding of the Bubak to the ranch. Additionally, I suspect the Committee, the Empire's government, is employing some form of drug to induce crop growth, effectively keeping non-magic carriers trapped within the main city," she speculated.

I was taken aback. "You weren't aware of this?"

"No," Rae admitted, her expression grave. "My primary goal was to uncover the culprits behind the Doll killings, which is precisely why I registered for the Scavenger."

It all began to fall into place, but the higher we climbed, the more unsettling secrets we were likely to unearth.

Chapter Twenty-Four

The environment transitioned into a more urban landscape than the levels we had traversed previously. Here, on the fourth level, we found ourselves surrounded by tenant-like buildings and imposing factories, their chimneys billowing forth plumes of inky black smoke. Felix, our guide, led the gang and me off the tram, gesturing expansively at the scene before us.

"Welcome to industrialization," he declared with a wry smile. I couldn't help but notice a vast, ominous cloud of grey smoke blanketing the sky. At every turn, my eyes met structures of cold stone, gleaming metal, and sturdy wood, composing the very fabric of this urban landscape.

"I wonder," Aaron mused, his gaze fixed on the ominous building housing the last of the Pages' artifacts, "what sort of monstrous challenge awaits us within."

"Is it just me, or does it strike anyone else as odd that the item we're in search of is tucked away inside an abandoned hospital?" Rae questioned with a furrowed brow.

Aaron, with his trademark sarcasm, quipped, "Well, thanks for the brilliant observation, princess."

An irritated retort came swiftly from Rae. "Don't call me that!"

I intervened, attempting to quell their rising argument. "Enough, you two," I urged, and they fell silent. I shifted my attention to an engraved plaque on the stone wall encircling the hospital. "Any of you have any insights into the significance of the Page of Swords?"

"I don't have much insight," Isabelle confessed, her voice tinged with uncertainty. "All we've ever been taught is that the sword symbolizes the physical embodiment of the air element." The eldest of the triplets squinted, her gaze fixed intently on the engraved plaque. "I might be going a bit mad, but it's quite evident that this court card represents someone who either talks incessantly or possesses a restless mind brimming with boundless energy. As for the reversed position, it signifies a person who's all talk and no action—a keeper of unfulfilled promises. It's all about the fervor to achieve something swiftly."

"So, it essentially revolves around the energy inherent in living and non-living entities," I surmised.

"It certainly seems that way," Isabelle concurred, and my eyes shifted to the others in search of their thoughts.

"Keep an eye on Jared," I urged, my concern palpable.

"We'll make sure he's safe," Halle replied, her tone exuding reassurance. My gaze lingered on the younger boy, sound asleep.

"I'll return," I whispered softly, before trailing after Felix and Isabelle into the eerie confines of the abandoned hospital.

"This place feels like something out of a horror movie," Isabelle grumbled as our footsteps echoed down the narrow, dimly lit halls of the abandoned hospital.

Felix, always quick with his observations, speculated, "My guess is that this used to be an insane asylum."

I couldn't help but scoff at the grim surroundings. "Whoever was in charge here must've been a real lunatic," I muttered, my gaze filled with disdain as I took in the sight of a discarded straight jacket on the floor, alongside a menacing array of medical instruments neatly arranged on a colossal metal tray, reminiscent of the examination room from my recurring nightmares. Rusted stains of dried blood marred the dirt-covered, tiled floors, sending shivers down my spine.

Just when I thought things couldn't possibly deteriorate further, I heard the faint rustling of footsteps echoing down one of the empty hallways. The chilling realization hit me: we were not alone. The monstrous guardian of the artifact was close, lurking nearby.

"It's nearby," Felix whispered, his voice barely audible in the eerie silence.

Either I was descending into madness, or my ears didn't deceive me; another set of footsteps echoed down the shadowy hallway. The realization dawned upon me that there was not just one, but possibly multiple monsters lurking in the recesses of the abandoned hospital.

Summoning my courage, I called out, "We're aware of your presence; you might as well reveal yourselves!" The faint sounds of squeaking, like hushed whispers, suggested they were engaged in some form of discussion. It struck me as strange how, in the bleakest of settings, clarity could sometimes emerge.

If we were to secure the last of the Pages' artifacts, I needed to embody the essence of the card, which, in this case, meant embracing curiosity. My gaze fixated on the peculiar creatures before us, their bodies akin to the size of a toddler, but their heads dwarfing a watermelon. "What is it that you desire from us?" they asked in eerie unison, their enormous, round eyes filled with an unmistakable curiosity of their own.

"I've come for the artifact," I replied, keeping my tone as even as possible. "I assume you, like the others, are bound to this place?"

"Yes, you are indeed the first visitor we've had in many, many years," they confirmed, their voices strangely harmonious. "You bear a striking resemblance to a young girl who graced our asylum with her presence years ago, except she had blonde hair and eyes of a peculiar blue-violet hue."

The revelation was nothing short of shocking. The realization that we were the first visitors these peculiar creatures had seen in years hung heavy in the air. Isabelle, her dark eyes locked onto the inhabitants of this forsaken asylum, couldn't contain her curiosity. "What exactly are they, Adelice?"

With an enigmatic air, they replied, "Allow us to provide you with a clue. Much like yourselves, we were unwanted, forsaken by those who were meant to care for us. We were taken in by a deranged doctor who subjected us to cruel experiments, which ultimately bound us to this forsaken asylum."

My heart sank as I made the connection. "You're the Melon Heads," I realized, my sympathy for their plight overwhelming. "None of you deserved the torment of those experiments, just as you don't deserve to be trapped here, guarding the artifact."

"Is there any way to free you all from this place?" Isabelle inquired with genuine concern.

Their response was laden with resignation. "No, our fate is sealed, but we find solace in knowing that the artifact now resides in the hands of those who won't misuse its power for personal gain. You both have acted commendably."

Though I couldn't see their expressions, I sensed a palpable contentment emanating from them, relieved that the artifact they had safeguarded for years had found its rightful custodians.

With all four artifacts of the Pages of the Minor Arcana in our possession, we were one step closer to our goal. Only the Knights' artifacts remained, and we had managed to acquire them without resorting to violence. It was a testament to the power of diplomacy and reason prevailing over bloodshed.

As we continued on our journey, Isabelle's question lingered in the air. "Hey, Adelice, what did the Melon Heads mean when they said you looked like a girl who visited their asylum years ago?" Isabelle inquired, her curiosity piqued.

"I'm not sure," I admitted, shrugging off the question. "But I'm hoping I'll uncover the truth eventually."

Felix, ever the optimist, chimed in with a triumphant grin as he proudly displayed the cloud amulet, our latest acquisition. "At least we managed to secure the last Page's artifact without risking our lives."

With just two days remaining to procure the remaining four artifacts belonging to the Knights, the pressure was mounting. I couldn't shake the feeling that unseen eyes were tracking our every move. It was evident that Gray was intent on collecting all four of the Pages' artifacts through us, but the purpose behind his obsession remained a mystery.

As we left the hospital grounds, the setting sun served as a stark reminder of the encroaching darkness. It was growing late, and though I hesitated to admit it, the Melon Heads' cryptic words gnawed at my thoughts. Could it be possible that I had a connection to this place in a past life? The idea seemed far-fetched, but it only fueled my determination to reach the Edge and unearth the answers I so desperately sought.

Chapter Twenty-Five

Dreams returned to me once more, the sort that are so vivid, they transport you to another world, and in this dream, I was the protagonist. I wandered through a graveyard, where tombstones stood shrouded in a delicate veil of white mist. Strangely, it felt less like a haunting place and more like a sanctuary, a place that exuded a profound sense of comfort. It felt like home, as if this was where I truly belonged, among the departed souls who had found their eternal repose.

Upon reaching my destination, I was met with a sight that should have instilled fear, but instead, I surrendered to it. The entire graveyard transformed before my eyes. In its place stood a three-story mansion, a harmonious blend of Baroque and Rococo architectural styles. Lush, emerald lawns stretched out, while meticulously manicured flower gardens could have been plucked from the grounds of the Palace of Versailles. A vast crystal-blue lake, spacious enough for rowing a boat, added to the surreal beauty.

As I passed through the mansion's black iron gate, the sweet strains of music reached my ears, and I was welcomed by a gathering of people who seemed to be in the midst of a grand celebration.

I felt like an outsider in their midst, as they were adorned in pastel shades and vibrant prints, their merriment evident through their inebriation or their self-absorption in their own little worlds. I remained unnoticed, a lone figure amidst their revelry.

"This feels rather peculiar," I whispered to myself as I strolled past the charming gazebo beside the lake. Upon stepping into the mansion, my senses were jolted by the abundance of paintings and photographs adorning the pastel-blue walls. Each subject seemed to wear an expression of profound anguish.

My curiosity led me up a spiral staircase that ascended to one of the mansion's towers. Inside, I discovered a spacious room brimming with canvases, sketchbooks, and an array of art supplies, including tubes of paint and cases of colored pencils. It felt like an artist's sanctuary, and I couldn't help but wonder about the message behind this dream.

Soon, I noticed shadowy figures in motion on the walls. Uncertain, I surmised that this was a memory from the past, conveyed through the art of shadow puppets. The dream continued to weave its enigmatic narrative.

"Is it safe to approach now?" inquired a gentle voice, breaking the silence. I watched as the first of the shadow puppets, resembling a woman seated on a throne-like chair, responded, "Of course, my dear."

The second shadow puppet, a man positioned before an easel supporting a canvas, spoke with pride, "Out of all the paintings I've created, this is my masterpiece, brought to life by the vivid hues of the paint. Witness it for yourself, Claire."

Claire's shadow puppet approached the canvas, her silhouette mirroring her real-life counterpart. "It's as though I'm gazing into a mirror. How did you acquire such mastery?" she inquired.

The artist's shadow puppet replied with a sense of devotion, "It's all about how the artist treasures their subject, my dear." The dream unfolded, revealing layers of a mysterious narrative.

The sun had risen the minute I opened my eyes. I'm starting to realize the dreams are becoming more vivid as we get closer to the Edge. Why do I have them, and what are they trying to tell me? Right now, getting through the last two days of the Scavenger is all that matters to me. Despite how vague they are, they're starting to take an emotional toll on me. "You're having those dreams again, aren't you?" Jared asked when he saw me exit one of the shared bedrooms of the safe house. I didn't see the point in lying to him. "The worst part is I don't know what they're trying to tell me," I confessed. Jared was silent. "Fate is trying to tell you something. It's either what happened in the past or what is about to come in the future." "I think you're onto something, Jared. I have this gut feeling that something bad is about to happen once we reach the Edge. My best guess is that it has something to do with the Unnatural Touch." "You mean the touch that can give or take a life?" I nodded. It was the very gift whose magic was given to Victor Frankenstein and passed down to his son. With only two more days left of the Scavenger, I needed to protect Felix at all costs.

Chapter Twenty-Six

A chill swept over us as we disembarked from the tram, leaving us with just three more levels to traverse before reaching the Edge. The map directed us to a forest, within which a vast frozen pond had been transformed into a sprawling ice-skating rink. With our inherited enhanced hearing as Halflings, I could discern the subtle currents flowing beneath the frozen surface. My attention was drawn to the image of the card engraved onto the gate of the sizable wooden fence encircling the pond.

"What's the task ahead?" Aaron inquired.

Halle, ever the wellspring of knowledge, offered her insight. "If I'm not mistaken, the Knight of Swords is a card steeped in ambition. It signifies a relentless drive towards success, marked by quick thinking and action. However, in the reversed position, it can lead to restlessness and a lack of focus, with impulsivity eventually culminating in burnout. In either scenario, it confers upon the wielder a sense of purpose and a mission to fulfill."

Felix flashed a confident grin. "Well, at least we know you're up for the task, Halle."

Halle's response came with a note of caution. "Don't count your blessings just yet. We've got to make it across the pond."

Felix's expression faltered. "You mean—"

"Yup, we're going ice skating," he admitted with a gulp. It was clear he was nervous, and I couldn't blame him. The prospect of ice skating was daunting, especially for someone like me who had never skated before. To make matters worse, the lurking possibility of the guardian monster concealed beneath the ice sent shivers down my spine.

"How on earth are we supposed to cross without skates?" I voiced my concern, well aware that Gray and his inner circle were likely finding our predicament rather amusing.

"Well, I suppose we have to make the best of what we're given," Halle conceded, eyeing the three pairs of boots with skates affixed to the soles that lay on the snow-covered ground. Once we had donned them, our only concern was navigating the passage to the other side of the pond, where frequent, forceful gusts of wind swept down upon us every ten seconds.

I tried to quell my nerves, whispering to myself, "Don't let it scare you." My legs felt weak with fear, fearing that the ice might crack beneath me. Felix took hold of one hand, while Halle gripped the other, and together, the three of us embarked on our journey, skating across the ice while braving the powerful gusts of wind that assailed us.

As we continued to skate, the pond gradually shrank, evolving into a simple icy trail as the winds lost their strength. Yet, we knew that this didn't mark the end of our challenges. The monster guarding the artifact still lay ahead. As we glided down the path, a distant sound reached our ears.

"Did any of you hear that?" I inquired, my curiosity piqued.

Felix nodded, his expression alert. "It sounded like a cat meowing."

Halle cautioned us with a note of suspicion. "Don't be deceived; it could be the monster guardian attempting to trick us."

Upon reaching the end of the ice path, we entered a desolate section of the forest. There, resting on a gray slab of marble, we found the artifact associated with the Knight of Swords—a knight's shield. Just as I was about to claim it, a towering black figure suddenly materialized out of thin air. Its yellow eyes gleamed eerily through the mist.

As my vision cleared, I realized that the creature before us was a colossal cat, its size akin to that of a small couch.

"It's rather impolite to sneak up on people," I scolded the creature, my irritation evident. The Yule Cat responded with a sound that seemed almost like a disdainful scoff.

Halle, surprisingly unfazed, reached out to pet the top of its head. "This must be the Yule Cat," she remarked casually.

Felix, on the other hand, appeared bewildered. "The Yule Cat? What on earth is that?"

"It's a Christmas monster from Icelandic folklore," Halle explained. "I thought you had some Scandinavian heritage."

Felix chuckled, shaking his head. "No, my dad's Swiss, and my mom's from Spain. I've never heard of it, but no offense to your 'kitty'." The Yule Cat rumbled in apparent agreement.

I breathed a sigh of relief. "Well, at least it's not Krampus," I remarked, recalling the terrifying Christmas demon.

Felix offered reassurance. "Don't worry, Adelice; Krampus only targets those who've lost the Christmas spirit." Nonetheless, the idea of encountering Krampus was a fate that nobody wished to endure.

So far, the encounters with these monsters had been surprisingly non-hostile. It occurred to me that perhaps an open mind played a pivotal role in dealing with the unknown. My intuition led me to believe that the supernatural often targeted those who clung rigidly to close-mindedness—those who refused to acknowledge or comprehend phenomena beyond the scope of science and technology.

With the exception of the Bubak, who had indeed caused harm when he captured Jared, our experiences had generally been non-violent. To thrive in a world teeming with magic and the supernatural, maintaining an open mind was the key to survival.

As I extended my gloved hands towards the Yule Cat, I felt its head press against them, the warmth of its black fur seeping through the leather. Halle noted the creature's intent. "I think he wants you to take the shield, Adelice."

As I grasped the artifact, a surge of magic coursed through me, its presence undeniable. The moment the knight's shield found its way into Felix's hands, an intriguing transformation unfolded before our eyes. We both observed it together as he examined the cards comprising the Minor Arcana.

The cards now bore imagery of ornate sugar skulls and vibrant orange marigolds. Meanwhile, the Major Arcana depicted streaks of lightning slashing across the sky and cloth adorned with striking black stitch marks that enveloped the tombstones.

It was becoming increasingly clear that both the major and minor aspects of the tarot revealed vivid illustrations of the lineage coursing through our veins, unveiling truths that would eventually catch up with us, no matter how harsh or enigmatic they might be.

With just three artifacts left to obtain, I couldn't help but contemplate the growing power emanating from each object. My thoughts began to drift toward the implications of collecting the entire set of court cards. After all, the members of the court served as the guardians of these artifacts, embodying the living incarnations of the four elements. What exactly would transpire once we reached the Edge remained a daunting unknown.

Felix, ever perceptive, remarked on my silence as he took a seat beside me. The entire tram car plunged into darkness as it traversed through a tunnel, intensifying the feeling of secrecy that enveloped us.

"I've been pondering what will occur once all the artifacts are united," I admitted.

Felix's tone was filled with curiosity. "What do you think will happen?"

I leaned in, sharing what I knew. "I'm not entirely sure, but there's a legend surrounding it. Supposedly, when all twenty-four members of each court come together, they create a map—a map that leads to each piece, ranging from ten to two. And when these pieces are united, they form the Aces."

The anticipation and uncertainty hung heavy in the air as we hurtled closer to the Edge.

"The Aces," I murmured, as another fragment of my old life emerged from the recesses of my memory. It was as if Grandma's voice echoed through time, retelling the same story that Felix had just shared.

My grandmother had often spoken of the Aces, describing them as cards of positivity and good fortune, the very wellspring of magic in Alessia. As I processed this revelation, it struck me like a bolt of lightning. The Aces were the pivotal elements we and the others needed to rescue the Empire from the impending danger. If the legend held true, then the artifacts themselves held the key to unraveling the map leading to all the scattered pieces of the Aces.

However, at this moment, our immediate priority was navigating the final days of the Scavenger. "Call me crazy," Felix concluded, voicing the sentiment I held close to my heart, "but I have a gut feeling that the Aces will be our salvation in saving the Empire from its imminent destruction."

I nodded in fervent agreement. The notion seemed fantastical, but it was also our best hope, and I couldn't help but believe in it wholeheartedly.

Chapter Twenty-Seven

Upon entering the entrance of the sacred site housing the artifact of the second knight, the atmosphere shifted noticeably. The air grew warm and humid, causing beads of sweat to trickle down my face. The surroundings were a breathtaking sight to behold, with vibrant flowers in full bloom adorning every corner. Each hue of color stood out vividly against the rich dark soil and the lush green grass that enveloped them.

"It's absolutely beautiful," I whispered, overwhelmed by the scene before me.

Rae nodded in agreement. "Indeed, it is."

My attention was captivated by a massive white rose, its fragrance so potent that it could have been harnessed to create a lavish supply of perfume.

The petals beneath my fingers felt soft and silky, their textures contrasting with the irises that displayed a mesmerizing blend of blue and violet. Despite the beauty that surrounded us, I couldn't ignore the lurking knowledge that a monster was concealed among the botanical splendor of this indoor garden.

I reminded myself of our purpose: retrieve the artifact and depart, even if it meant confronting the guardian monster.

Aaron's voice cut through my thoughts, drawing our attention. "Hey, guys, I think I've identified the artifact here! It's the Knight of Pentacles!"

Felix chimed in, providing his insight. "That makes perfect sense, given that this entire conservatory is teeming with the fertility of the earth."

However, I couldn't help but voice my concern. "Here's the issue I find troubling: it's nearly winter, and these flowers should have withered by now."

Felix's expression shifted as realization dawned. "Adelice is right. Everything should be dormant or dead at this time. This certainly suggests the earth element at work."

Curiosity gnawed at me as I posed another question. "Do any of you know the extent of the power wielded by the Knight of Pentacles?"

Felix shook his head. "No, I'm afraid I don't."

"How pitiful," a voice sneered from the corner of the room, drawing our attention. My gaze locked onto the Halfling girl who regarded Felix and me with a disdainful glare. She possessed creamy beige skin that complemented the dark brown waves of her hair. Her attire consisted of an old-fashioned green dress adorned with white lace along the hem of the skirt and sleeves. The violet eyes that bore into us exuded an icy coldness that could ignite anyone's temper.

"And you two consider yourselves card readers?" she continued with a contemptuous tone. "It's absurd that I'm the sole member of this group with even a glimmer of creative genius."

My patience wore thin, and I confronted her with a sharp glare. "If you're going to be rude, why don't you enlighten us about the Knight of Pentacles' abilities?"

A smirk curled on the girl's lips. "Finally, someone who grasps the situation. To begin with, the Knight of Pentacles is a card that emphasizes routine and productivity, focusing on traditional values and hard work. However, when reversed, it accentuates the need for self-discipline and the pursuit of perfection—traits I'm all too familiar with. Unfortunately, it also brings about overwhelming boredom and the sensation of being trapped, something I refuse to endure."

"Well, Miss—"

"Emma," the girl interjected, introducing herself as Emma De Revenant. Her last name sounded vaguely familiar to me, as if I had encountered it in my previous life. Unfortunately, I had little time to ponder it further as the hairs on the back of my neck bristled, and I felt a sense of unease wash over me. My attention was drawn to a tall, slender figure making its way down the stone path of the garden.

The figure appeared to be a young man, his hair as dark as the night sky with hints of sapphire. His skin was unnaturally pale, reminiscent of white chalk and powdered snow. Long, crimson-painted nails adorned his fingers, and he donned a dark blue Hanfu paired with a green sash around his waist. However, the most unsettling aspect of his appearance was his eyes, a cloudy shade of red that hinted at blindness.

"Jiang-Shi," Rae uttered in a fearful whisper.

A hushed discussion ensued as Trey inquired in a low voice, "What in the world is a Jiang-Shi?"

Elliot provided a tense explanation. "It's a type of vampire originating from the land formerly known as China."

"Wow, I had no idea you had relatives in the East Rae," Aaron commented, apparently oblivious to the gravity of the situation. It was moments like these when I couldn't help but wonder about his intelligence. Nevertheless, it was becoming increasingly apparent that the Jiang-Shi would not be an easy adversary.

"Come out, come out, wherever you are," the Jiang-Shi taunted. While he couldn't see us, his words were laced with eerie confidence. "Just because I can't see you doesn't mean I can't sense your presence. The fear emanating from your auras is enough for me to know you're all at a disadvantage."

Felix, never one to back down, responded with a jab. "Tell that to the guy who's too stiff to walk properly." The Jiang-Shi scoffed in return.

"Have you learned nothing, boy?" he inquired with a sneer, revealing rows of sharp, shark-like teeth. "The longer we exist, the more formidable we become."

Aaron attempted a physical attack, striking the Jiang-Shi's face with his fist. "Damn it, he's as solid as a rock."

Emma chimed in with a scathing remark. "Now you're catching on?"

The Jiang-Shi's lips curled into a sinister grin. "My, my, you're quite the spirited one, aren't you? Bolder than the other girl who dared to enter my garden. Her aura was so innocent and pure that I didn't have the chance to extract even a small ounce of her chi."

"Chi," everyone (except Rae and me) chorused the word in unison. Emma, the dhampir girl, took a moment to clarify, "It's the Chinese term for life-force."

Aaron, still nursing his pain, chimed in, "That's good to know, even though I'm still hurting!"

I seized the opportunity to inquire, "The girl you mentioned earlier, was her name Claire?"

The Jiang-Shi responded with callous indifference. "I couldn't care less. I would have drained her of all her chi if her Swan familiar hadn't intervened."

This vampire was rapidly wearing on my patience, undead or not. We needed a way to defeat him without putting ourselves at risk. A voice in my mind provided a solution: "The only way to defeat a Jiang-Shi is to use a protective charm written on a piece of paper."

Turning to Emma, I asked, "Hey, Emma, do you have any paper?"

She responded somewhat irritably, "Yes, why do you ask?"

"It might sound insane," I admitted, "but I need you to draw a binding symbol and place it on the Jiang-Shi's forehead. Can you do that?"

Emma nodded and swiftly retrieved a sheet of paper from her carpetbag, sketching the binding symbol with a pencil. I held onto the hope that this unconventional method would work as I dashed out of my hiding spot and affixed the paper charm to the Jiang-Shi's forehead. A scream of agony pierced the air as he realized he could no longer move his stiffened body. This was my opportunity to secure the shield, now that the monster was incapacitated.

The shield we sought was positioned at the very end of the path, near the edge of the pond where a waterfall cascaded down from a small canal. It seemed almost too convenient, and I couldn't help but suspect that Gray and his associates were deliberately leading us to gather all the artifacts associated with the lower court cards. Just two more remained.

Emma, who had joined us after our victory over the Jiang-Shi, posed a question. "How did you know to use a binding spell to defeat the Jiang-Shi?"

I considered her question carefully before responding. "I didn't, but I have a feeling that someone is watching over us."

She scoffed at my response. "It certainly can't be an angel, that's for sure."

I regarded her with a mild sense of amusement. "You do have a rather cynical outlook on life, don't you?"

"I don't deny it," Emma retorted, her response tinged with a sense of playful defiance. Our laughter filled the air, a welcome respite from the tension we had just faced.

As the tram entered the tunnel, I turned my thoughts to the looming mystery of the Edge. "I wonder what awaits us once we reach the Edge," I mused.

Emma's response was soft, her voice barely above a whisper. "I don't know, but one thing I'm certain of is that we're heading to a world that's vastly different from our own."

Curiosity piqued, I probed further. "You've been to the Edge, haven't you?"

She nodded in affirmation. "Yes, I have. Among the nobility, the Elites, who have the most Halfling children, assign one member from each noble family to serve the Emperor."

Her words left me contemplating my own situation. If what Emma had said was accurate, it meant that my family was part of the nobility. Or rather, the individuals who had acquired me from the System's database were.

Top of Form

Top of Form

Chapter Twenty-Eight

Gwendolen Worthing surveyed the scene from the balcony of the day lounge, the favored haunt of the wives during their idle hours. It was an elegant chamber, adorned with walls painted in a soft rose gold hue that harmonized with the daintily pink furnishings. Below, she observed her fellow wives engaging in various daily diversions, their attempts to ward off the boredom of managing a household evident: some were delicately painting with watercolors, others meticulously crafting silhouettes, while a few were carefully pressing flowers, or skillfully embroidering intricate designs. A murmur of conversation accompanied the clinking of teacups as they exchanged the latest morsels of gossip.

Regrettably, Claire remained conspicuously absent from this tableau of activity, her disinterest palpable. "She's been in this state for well over an hour," Cecily whispered with concern.

Astoria, her tone frigid, retorted, "What did you anticipate? There's but one remedy, and it hinges on the children's return after they complete their tasks in the Scavenger."

Gwendolen leaned closer, her voice coaxing, "You know your role in this, Astoria. Among us, you're the closest to her."

The dark-haired woman, dressed in a bustled green gown, nodded as she approached Claire. "It's nearly dusk; we should consider heading home," she gently suggested.

Claire blinked, slowly emerging from her reverie, her fingers clutching the silk skirts of her ice-blue gown. "Oh," she said softly, "I must have lost track of time. It slips away so swiftly, doesn't it?"

Astoria smiled with understanding. Despite the melancholic cloud that seemed to hang over her friend, there was a glimmer of relief knowing that Claire hadn't entirely withdrawn. They had been friends since the tender age of twelve, their friendship persisting through their seasonal debuts and even after marriage.

"Come," Astoria said gently, "let me accompany you to the carriage." As they made their way through the narrow corridor, Claire, her voice trembling, asked, "Does the ache ever diminish?"

A sense of helplessness welled up in Astoria, but she pressed on, her words offered as solace. "I can't say for certain, but no matter how many times they depart, they always find their way back. In my case, Felix always returns. Eventually, he needs his time to roam."

Tears welled up in Claire's blue-violet eyes, and they began to trickle down her cheeks. Astoria felt her heartache, not knowing how to ease her dearest friend's sorrow, as Claire grieved the absence of her one and only child.

"I didn't intend to phrase it that way," Astoria apologized softly.

Claire's tears subsided as she sniffled, her voice steadying. "I appreciate your concern, truly. It's just that I feel so helpless, not knowing where my daughter is. I know she's alive, but the uncertainty is overwhelming."

Astoria offered reassurance, her tone warm and comforting. "You'll be reunited with her soon, just as I will be with my son."

Outside, the air had a chill to it, and they reached the waiting carriage. Claire turned to her friend with gratitude in her eyes. "Thank you, Astoria. I couldn't have endured this ordeal without you."

The Claimed referred to them as "familiars," spirits who had assumed the guise of animals to serve those blessed with magic in their lineage. Yet, Shadow and Winterfell were no ordinary familiars. They were twins, a pair harmoniously intertwined, and had manifested themselves in the form of two tiny kittens. Shadow, a tuxedo cat with striking gold eyes, stood as the embodiment of night, while his sister, a calico cat with luminous blue eyes, embodied the essence of dawn.

Over the years, the duo had transitioned through numerous masters, but they had finally discovered a lasting home with the Flawed CEO of Marvelous Radiance. From a small balcony that overlooked the grand ballroom, they observed the spectacle unfolding below. Hundreds of candles flickered, casting their enchanting candlelight.

"What's happening, brother?" Winter inquired, her voice a gentle purr.

Shadow regarded the scene below with his golden gaze, his whiskers twitching thoughtfully. "I'm uncertain, but our Master has been preoccupied lately, while Mistress has been consumed by grief over the loss of her child."

"She's not gone," Winterfell countered firmly.

Shadow's eyes twinkled mischievously. "Only one more day until things start to get interesting around here," he chimed in, his excitement palpable. "We just need to be patient, especially with the gathering of the artifacts from the lower court cards."

Winter, however, adopted a more serious tone. "Yes, because we all know what happens once they're combined with the artifacts of the higher court cards."

Shadow couldn't resist a sing-song tone as he continued, "Indeed, we're well aware of what unfolds when they all come together in one place."

Winter snapped back, her patience waning, "Yes, we all know what transpires once they're united."

Meanwhile, the calico kitten observed their Master and Mistress as they waltzed gracefully across the polished marble floor. Unable to comprehend the complexities of human emotions, Winterfell couldn't help but be captivated by the scene. "They're in love," she murmured dreamily.

Shadow scoffed disdainfully. "I fail to see what you find so enchanting about this spectacle."

Winter's protests persisted. "How can you remain so unfeeling about this?" She had nearly forgotten how obstinate her brother could be.

Shadow's response was pragmatic. "What do you expect? Emotions are not our realm. You've witnessed countless couples waltzing through the ages; how is this any different?"

Winter rebutted, frustration simmering beneath her feline exterior. "It's different because you've never seen the Claimed showing such intimacy to each other."

Shadow heaved a resigned sigh. "I don't comprehend this notion of love; it drives beings to act irrationally. Our Master has loved our Mistress since she was a child. He patiently waited until she reached the age of seventeen to pursue her. I won't even begin to mention all the paintings he created during that time. How can you not find love unsettling?"

With a flicker of curiosity, Winter countered, "I have no idea. Care to make a wager?"

A gleam of mischief lit up Shadow's eyes. "Now you're speaking my language," he replied with enthusiasm.

Chapter Twenty-Nine

As we strolled down the road toward our next destination, I couldn't help but notice the telltale plumes of chimney smoke rising from one of the nearby factories. In this seventh level of the city, there existed a different kind of factory—one that stirred both excitement and dread within me. Today marked the final leg of the Scavenger, our sole opportunity to secure the last two artifacts and complete our collection, representing the lower court cards of the tarot.

Despite the urgency of our quest, there lingered within me an unsettling mixture of emotions. A part of me dreaded the impending journey to the Edge, while another, stronger part recognized that I had no choice but to go there. It was the place I hoped to find my family, and avoiding Gray was an impossibility. I had to confront our adversary sooner rather than later.

Thus far, Gray had not actively hindered our progress in the Scavenger, but I remained vigilant. I couldn't afford to let my guard down. The stakes were too high, and I was determined to emerge victorious.

"Does anyone else have the sinking feeling that we're walking straight into a death trap?" Emma voiced her unease.

Aaron, ever the optimist, offered a more hopeful perspective. "Perhaps it's just your imagination, Emma."

Meanwhile, the triplets had fallen into an eerie silence, an unusual departure from their typically chatty demeanor. Lily's distress soon became apparent as I noticed beads of sweat trickling down her forehead. Concerned, I asked, "Lily, what's wrong? Are you feeling unwell?"

Her response was labored, but she managed to speak, "I'm okay. Just... a little tired." It was evident that speaking had taken a toll on her. I couldn't help but wonder if the guardian of the artifact we sought was more formidable than the Jiang-Shi we'd encountered earlier. What could be worse than a hopping corpse?

Our questions found answers as we arrived at the alley marked on the map, where we discovered the engraved emblem of the Knight of Wands.

Halle inquired, "Does anyone here know the significance of this card?"

Lily, still recovering, finally spoke up. "It's a card that embodies energy and passion, often urging its wielder to act impulsively and embark on adventures. When reversed, it signifies that a passion project has led to haste and scattered energy, resulting in delays and frustration."

It was apparent that talking had drained Lily, but my intuition told me that the guardian protecting this artifact was far more formidable than any we had encountered before. Just as the hauntingly beautiful sound of a woman's song filled the air, my instincts screamed at me to find cover, no matter how seductive the melody.

The darkened alley on the left seemed like our best option as the woman's haunting singing grew increasingly louder. It was from this vantage point that I could get a glimpse of our adversary.

She appeared to be a woman of Asian descent, her complexion unnaturally pale, and her hair cascading down her back, reaching her waist. She donned a flowing white dress with a netted black shawl draped over her bare shoulders. On her feet were delicate black slippers. But her eyes were the most unsettling aspect of her appearance—completely black, devoid of any warmth or humanity. Adding to the eerie ensemble, she wore a white surgical mask concealing the lower part of her face. In her left hand, she clutched a pair of scissors, their blades stained with dried blood.

Lily's voice trembled with fear as she whispered, "Kuchisake-onna."

Perplexed, I asked, "Who is she?"

Lily's response was grim. "It's Japanese for the Slit-mouth woman. Trust me when I say she's far more sinister than the hopping vampire in the conservatory. It doesn't matter if you answer her question correctly; she'll kill you regardless."

My heart sank as I realized we were confronting a malevolent entity that showed no mercy and had no qualms about ending our lives.

"I know you're there," Kuchisake-onna sang in a voice that somehow managed to sound both sweet and sinister. A shiver raced down my spine; she was aware of our presence.

"What are you doing?" I hissed at Lily as I noticed her inching away from our hiding spot. I couldn't let her face Kuchisake-onna alone, so I followed suit. As we stepped into view, Kuchisake-onna's eyes glittered with a dark delight. However, they gradually narrowed upon seeing me.

"Hello, girls," she cooed, her voice dripping with sickly sweetness. "Do you think I'm pretty?" she inquired, her tone as sweet as honey.

Lily, her voice trembling, answered, "Yes." It was a response born of fear, and we watched in morbid fascination as Kuchisake-onna slowly lowered her surgical mask.

What we saw beneath sent a shock of horror coursing through us. Her disfigurement was nightmarish, a grotesque slit-like gash extending up to the middle of her cheeks, as if straight out of a horror movie.

"How about now?" she asked, her tone unchanged. It didn't matter whether we said yes or no; we were fully aware that she intended to kill us.

With unwavering defiance, I replied, "No." She seemed entirely indifferent to my answer.

"Here's a proposition, child," Kuchisake-onna taunted, her voice dripping with malice. "Your friend meets her end, and I'll grant you a reprieve."

I couldn't help but challenge her. "Isn't that against the rules?"

She let out a chilling laugh. "Rules matter little, for you hold more value to us alive. My master will be overjoyed once I deliver you to him. The bounty on your head is substantial enough to break the chains binding me to this wretched place."

Realization hit me like a bolt of lightning. She was referring to Gray, the CEO of Marvelous Radiance. Gray was the master of Kuchisake-onna.

One question gnawed at me. "What does your boss want from me? I'm a nobody, one of many discarded souls. Heck, I can't even remember who I was before I lost my memories."

Kuchisake-onna's expression shifted, and she shook her head in disbelief. "You truly don't know?" Her tone grew more ominous. "This is problematic, especially given the Mistress's current state."

"Mistress?" I mused aloud, utterly perplexed by her cryptic words.

The realization hit me like a bolt of lightning: Gray's wife, Claire, must have been the mistress to whom Kuchisake-onna referred. I was about to ask Kuchisake-onna to confirm her name when she suddenly collapsed onto the cold concrete floor of the alley.

To my surprise, it was Aaron who stood beside me, clutching a baseball bat tightly in his hands. He had intervened just in time, preventing me from obtaining the answers I sought.

"Was that really necessary?" I questioned, though part of me understood the urgency of our situation.

The blonde boy shrugged, his expression unapologetic. "Well, it's a matter of kill or be killed. While you and Lily kept her distracted, we managed to secure the artifact. But we shouldn't linger; I have a feeling her incapacitation won't last long."

I let out a sigh, reluctantly agreeing with Aaron's assessment. We had what we came for, and it was time to make our escape before Kuchisake-onna recovered and resumed her relentless pursuit.

In the aftermath of Aaron's strike on Kuchisake-onna, I felt compelled to share the revelation I had gleaned from the sinister spirit. "Before Aaron intervened," I began, "Kuchisake-onna mentioned her mistress being in a depressive state. It's clear she was referring to Gray's wife."

The disclosure sent shockwaves through our group, eliciting gasps from everyone present (except for Felix, who had been privy to this knowledge for some time).

Aaron, ever the inquisitive one, asked with a hint of confusion, "Gray has a wife?"

I couldn't help but think that Aaron might not be the most astute member of our group. Rae, however, stepped in to provide some insight. "I've known of her existence, though she's rarely seen in public," she admitted.

Halle chimed in, adding a layer of understanding, "It's not surprising. The wives of powerful men tend to keep a low profile in public."

As we continued to grapple with this newfound information, it was clear that Gray's personal life held secrets that even some of us, his closest associates, had never fully grasped.

"I've only caught a fleeting glimpse of her. Initially, I thought she might be one of Gray's admirers. I didn't see her face, but what I do know is she's a young woman in her early to mid-twenties with blonde hair," Rae revealed, providing a valuable tidbit of information that we needed to keep in mind for our forthcoming journey to the Edge.

Felix, ever the optimist, chimed in with enthusiasm. "Just one more artifact to go!"

Elliot's intel had informed us that many card readers had backed out from the Knights' challenges, leaving us as the sole remaining team. I couldn't help but voice my concerns. "Aren't you at least a bit anxious about what awaits us at the Edge?"

Felix, however, appeared unfazed as he shrugged casually. "No nerves here. I know exactly what's waiting for us. After all, I was born and raised there."

There were layers of Felix's past that remained shrouded in secrecy, particularly since our escape from the Slums of the Garden District. I was aware that he harbored numerous secrets, just as he respected my own privacy by refraining from probing into why Marvelous Radiance had acquired me from the System's database. It was an unspoken agreement, rooted in the understanding that some mysteries were best left untouched.

Despite Felix's reassurances and the air of secrecy surrounding our pasts, I couldn't shake the nagging feeling that there was more to my buyout by Marvelous Radiance than I initially believed. Kuchisake-onna's cryptic words had stirred a realization within me—a recognition that there were deeper, undisclosed motivations behind why Gray's company was pursuing me.

With each passing challenge, I was beginning to unravel the multifaceted layers of my involvement in this intricate game. Maria's enigmatic warning about the weeping woman now took on a chilling irony—Gray's wife, mourning the loss of her child, was the very embodiment of the weeping woman Maria had alluded to.

As the pieces of this perplexing puzzle slowly fell into place, I found myself drawn deeper into a web of mysteries, secrets, and motivations that I was only beginning to comprehend.

Chapter Thirty

We didn't have much farther to go when the gang and I finally reached the last of the sacred sites. My shock was palpable when I discovered that it was nestled deep within the woods near the Hudson River, the very river that marked the border between the Edge and the seven lower levels of the city. As I gazed upon the forested surroundings, it felt as though I had been transported back to the era of those old slasher movies from a time before the islands came into existence.

"I can't help but feel like Jason might jump out of the bushes," Aaron said with a hint of hesitation. I couldn't help but roll my eyes; he was an idiot, but one we couldn't help but love. The creature guarding the final artifact, I suspected, might even surpass the terror of a 1980s horror movie icon.

"We're in the right place," Felix declared confidently, pointing to the engraving on the stone wall encircling the forest.

"The Scavenger" had begun with water, and so it seemed fitting to conclude with water. "Now that we're here, does anyone know how the Knight of Cups card works?" Felix inquired.

"I do," Jared chimed in. "The Knight of Cups represents boundless creativity and an unwavering focus on imagination. It's a card associated with charm, beauty, and romance. In its reversed position, it indicates an individual whose imagination has run wild to the point of being unrealistic, leading to moodiness and jealousy at the core."

"Smart kid," Trey beamed as he affectionately ruffled Jared's curls. As we continued along the path, I noticed the glow emanating from a fire ahead. It was a clear sign that both the artifact and the formidable guardian lay nearby. Prepared for the worst, I approached the massive campfire, my brow furrowing at the sight of the figure casually spinning the shield like a top.

"Hello, children," the figure greeted us with a rich Jamaican accent. "I've been expecting you."

As I scrutinized the character more closely, I could see that he was tall, with ebony skin and clad in a tattered black and violet Victorian suit that matched the top hat perched atop his head. But what truly captured my attention were his eyes – they gleamed a striking shade of gold with cat-like slits in the middle.

"Bokor," Felix growled, his tone filled with animosity. The man wearing the tattered Victorian suit merely smirked as he continued to spin the shield.

"Ah, Felix Frankenstein," he mused, "I never would have imagined you would be one of the chosen, given your father's reputation."

I couldn't help but interject, my curiosity piqued, "Are you the guardian of the artifact?"

"In a way, but I am not bound like all the others you've faced," he replied cryptically.

Aaron, clearly puzzled, asked, "What exactly are you?"

"I'm glad you asked, Mr. Griffin," the man responded with a sinister smile. "I am a Bokor, a voodoo priest, but I am one who has chosen to embrace the dark side."

"It's more than that," Felix interjected, his voice laced with intensity. "You turn people into zombies and curse them to do your bidding."

The Bokor regarded Felix with a hint of amusement and nodded. "How observant you are," he remarked. "You are truly your father's son. I was one of the few individuals he sought out after our glorious Emperor bestowed immortality upon him."

Felix pressed further, curiosity in his eyes. "Why did he seek you out?"

The Bokor let out a wistful sigh. "Oh, something about him wanting to rid himself of the touch, the gift he had been bestowed with. Unfortunately, I told him he must bear it as his punishment for creating the monster. Alas, I informed him that he couldn't use it to resurrect the family he once had—a cruel punishment indeed, courtesy of our Emperor."

The voodoo priest's piercing gaze was now fixed on me. "You're the child who holds the top spot on the bounty list. You've garnered quite the popularity among the Elite. It's a miracle you haven't been captured yet. You see, you're worth more to them alive than dead," he explained with a hint of intrigue in his voice.

I couldn't help but scoff. "That's what Kuchisake-onna said," I replied sarcastically. "And yet, you want to know why Gray's company is after you." I had to admit, this guy was good.

"All I know is Gray's wife is at the center of it all, from my position as number one on the bounty list to the entire Scavenger operation," I admitted.

"I wish I could tell you, child," the Bokor responded solemnly, "but you should seek the answers on your own. However, I can divulge that there is a reason why the wife of one of the Empire's most powerful men is currently in a state of depression. The answers you seek lie within the hidden room in Gray's office."

It was the same response Maria had given me during our initial challenge. "By doing that, it means heading straight to the Edge," I realized.

"A plan you all had from the beginning," the Bokor said with a sinister sense of satisfaction. "Nonetheless, the killer you seek isn't your run-of-the-mill serial killer. After all, he and his ilk played a role in the creation of the Dome Colonies. He's a fanatic, someone who yearns for nothing more than the annihilation of those he deems unworthy of the magic bestowed by the gods of the pantheons."

"So, you're suggesting that the magic in our world is derived from different gods of mythology and folklore?" Felix shook his head in bewilderment. "I don't even know what to think anymore."

"There's more," I continued, wanting to share the revelation that had dawned upon me. "We are the descendants of the gods and goddesses from different pantheons all across the old world. And our kind are the only ones who can access their magic."

A stunned silence settled over the group as they absorbed my words. The Bokor, who had been spinning the shield, came to a halt. "Congratulations," he declared, "you've successfully completed the final task of the Scavenger."

Rae was the first to voice her astonishment. "How on earth did you uncover this ultimate secret?"

"I didn't," I replied, a sense of realization washing over me. "It was there all along." With that, I took the final shield and carefully placed it in the bag with the other artifacts, sensing the distinct actions and emotions emanating from each item.

After all, it was the descendants of the gods from both the new and old worlds who had originally crafted the cards. Over time, they had imparted this knowledge to their mortal offspring, who, in turn, passed it down to subsequent generations, ultimately leading to the Great Change.

"Before you depart," the Bokor cautioned us, "I must forewarn you that there will be greater perils awaiting you as you proceed to collect the other incarnations."

"I'll bear that in mind," I replied with a solemn nod.

As we exited the woods, I spotted Daryl waiting for us by the side of the street. He offered a curt nod of approval. "Congratulations on successfully completing the Scavenger," he remarked. "You're the first group in decades to conquer all eight challenges without meeting a fatal end or backing out."

Felix was quick to question him. "What brings you here?"

Daryl's response was direct. "I'm here to inform you that a carriage will be awaiting you to transport you to the Edge."

It was almost surreal. After enduring all the trials, we were finally on the cusp of uncovering the identity of the Doll Killer. However, there was no time for celebration yet, as we knew more adversaries lay ahead.

The carriage stood out with its black and purple hues, bearing the Marvelous Radiance logo elegantly painted on its doors. The creation of the islands had not only severed magical connections to other regions but also woven together elements of the past and future into a unique tapestry of existence.

Once we were all comfortably settled in the plush seats of the dimly lit coach, the wheels began their slow, steady turn as the coachmen guided the horses forward.

"You might as well get some rest," Felix suggested in a hushed tone. "We'll arrive in the morning." I couldn't help but feel anxious about falling asleep, fearing I might be drawn into another unsettling vision.

Felix, sensing my apprehension, offered reassurance. "Don't worry, I'll watch over you," he promised. With a nod of gratitude, I closed my eyes and allowed sleep to claim me.

Chapter Thirty-One

Morning had descended upon us when I finally awoke, the passage of time during my slumber remaining a mystery. I couldn't help but suspect that our coachman had a penchant for nocturnal travel. As the carriage came to a halt, my companions and I realized that we had reached the Edge. Sunlight streamed into the cabin as the carriage door began to creak open.

"Welcome," greeted a woman with curly, cascading blonde hair. Her tresses formed delicate spirals, and she donned a flowing pink dress adorned with vibrant red ribbons at the hem of her skirts. The warm, brown hue of her eyes resembled the rich shade of milk chocolate, sparkling in the morning light. In one hand, she held a leather-bound journal, and in the other, a quill poised for writing.

"I am Lady Cecily, and I extend my warm welcome to all of you in the heart of actual civilization." Despite her hospitable tone, it was evident that Lady Cecily was profoundly ignorant when it came to life in the lower levels. My suspicion was that she had never ventured far from her utopian Skyscrapers. Yet, there was no reasoning with her or the other upper-level nobles, as their existence was confined to the elevated heights.

As sweet as Lady Cecily's greeting was, I couldn't bring myself to trust her. Another woman's voice broke the moment, saying, "There you are, Cecily darling. I see you've come to welcome the winners of the Scavenger." A shiver ran down my spine as I observed the approach of the second woman. She possessed copper-brown hair meticulously styled in an updo, with tendrils gracefully framing her face. Her black and white dress featured ruffled accents on the skirts. Although her eyes were a pale, icy blue, and she wore a friendly smile, I couldn't shake the feeling that there was something sinister about her.

"Hello, children, and welcome to the Edge. I am Lady Gwendolen, and I shall be your guide for today," she announced, her demeanor exuding a sense of authority. "Unfortunately, only seven of you may enter, while the remaining four shall be escorted directly to the Angeles District to compete for the higher court cards in the Scavenger. Now, let's ascertain who has earned a place on the list."

Lady Gwendolen retrieved a small black leather book from the pocket of her skirts and began announcing the selected names. "Trey and Halle Crane," she declared. I was taken aback, realizing that the twins had been granted the privilege of staying at the Edge, despite Trey's earlier confrontation with Gray.

"Isabelle, Elliot, and Lily Hydell," followed as the next trio to be named by Lady Gwendolen. It appeared that the triplets had also received an invitation to remain at the Edge.

"Felix Frankenstein," Lady Gwendolen called out sweetly. There was only one more slot available for the Edge, and I braced myself for the possibility that Rae, Aaron, Jared, or Emma might be chosen while I would be sent to the Angeles District.

Then, to my astonishment and relief, Lady Gwendolen spoke my name aloud. "Adelice Marie," she announced, securing my place at the Edge.

After bidding farewell to the four who had been directed to the Angeles District, we followed Lady Gwendolen and Cecily into a spacious glass elevator. As melancholy as it was to part ways, I had a feeling that this wouldn't be the last time we crossed paths.

"Good luck on your quest," Aaron offered, embracing me tightly.

"It's been a pleasure working with you during this brief period," Emma added with a touch of formality. Beneath her cool exterior, it didn't take much to discern that she had a softer side.

Rae handed me a piece of paper bearing an address written in black ink. "Whenever you find yourself in the Angeles," she said with a wink.

Jared was the last to bid farewell, his parting words carrying a sense of camaraderie.

"You're going to be just fine," Jared reassured me, his words carrying a sense of comfort. As painful as it was to watch him and the others depart, I couldn't deny the truth in his words. I would be fine.

The elevator ride wasn't as daunting as I had feared. After days spent navigating the lower levels, we were now ascending to the Aerial level of the city, reserved exclusively for the Elite.

"Um... when will it be possible to obtain approval for the second Scavenger?" I inquired cautiously. It was a risky question, but I needed to know. Lady Gwendolen appeared momentarily taken aback but maintained her composure. "The decision isn't mine to make; all approvals rest with Mr. Gray."

I sighed inwardly. I should have anticipated as much. "I had a feeling," Felix added, his bitterness palpable.

"What's your issue with Mr. Gray?" Lady Cecily inquired, her curiosity genuine.

Felix didn't mince words. "Not much, aside from the fact that he's a narcissistic, shallow individual on a personal mission to shatter people's lives." We all expected Lady Cecily to react with shock or sadness, but to our surprise, she responded differently. "Why would you say such a thing?" she asked, her tone curious. Felix let out a resigned sigh. "You wouldn't understand."

It was a stark reminder of how entrenched the Elite's perspectives were, and we realized there was little point in trying to change their minds. The elevator came to a halt, and the doors opened onto a hallway adorned with black and white tiles and glittering red doors. The seven of us followed Lady Gwendolen and Lady Cecily to the door at the far end of the hall. Upon opening it, we were greeted by a vast, well-appointed room with large windows offering a stunning view of the Central Park District skyline.

The floors were crafted from white marble, concealing sparkling glimmers beneath the polished surface, while the walls were adorned with a brilliant shade of purple. The furniture, in stark contrast, comprised a salmon-pink set.

"Dinner will be served in a few hours," Lady Gwendolen announced formally. "This will afford you ample time to acquaint yourselves with your new living quarters." Her choice of words made it seem as though we were settling in permanently, which, of course, we weren't.

Once Lady Gwendolen and Lady Cecily departed, we gathered to discuss the next phase of our plan: infiltrating Gray's office. "I detest pink," Isabelle remarked with evident distaste. "Whoever was responsible for the interior design must have intended to lull us into a false sense of security." Lily couldn't help but snort in response. "Funny, considering your room back home is painted magenta. It's a darker shade of pink, so isn't that a tad hypocritical?" Isabelle grinned sheepishly. "I don't hate it, but it's clear that Gray has an unconventional taste in colors."

"Look, everyone! They've got a TV!" Elliot exclaimed with enthusiasm, pointing at the large plasma screen affixed to the wall. However, our excitement quickly dissipated when we discovered that all the channels were streaming services operated by Marvelous Radiance.

"I might be losing my mind, but I could have sworn they even have a channel dedicated to beauty and fashion," Felix remarked in a dry tone.

"You're absolutely right," Halle responded bluntly. "They've got a channel where the Elite flaunt their wealth for the general public, and another showcasing the grandest parties hosted here at the Edge."

Trey couldn't help but quip, "Well, what do you know, it's like Vegas in the sky."

Elliot offered reassuring news, saying, "I've inspected all the rooms, and there are no cameras around."

"That's perfect. It gives us the opportunity to plan how we're going to infiltrate Gray's office," I remarked with a sense of relief.

"Even better, the entire building has an air duct system connecting all the floors. I managed to hack into the building's system during the elevator ride," Felix explained.

"My brother's a genius!" Lily exclaimed with admiration. It wasn't long before the seven of us set out on the most significant heist of our lives.

Top of Form

Chapter Thirty-Two

Dinner unfolded in the lounge, accompanied by the dulcet tones of jazz music emanating from a corner. I gazed at the food arrayed on my plate: oven-roasted chicken, creamy garlic mashed potatoes, steamed broccoli, and two yeast rolls adorned with velvety butter, all served on the most opulent china I had ever laid eyes upon. Don't get me wrong; the meal was undoubtedly delicious, but the textures and the richness of each flavor felt almost overwhelming. I wasn't alone in this sentiment; the others at the table shared my unease.

Following dinner, we were treated to tea and a selection of baked delights for dessert: dainty macarons filled with organic fruit preserves, alongside triangular scones infused with the flavors of blueberry, raspberry, and lemon. I could swear that the tea possessed a hint of rose petals, imparting a subtle floral essence to the steaming brew.

The floor we were currently on didn't simply conclude with the lounge and the expansive suite we had been allocated. According to the map, it also featured an art gallery, spa, ballroom, nightclub, and a library. While entry to the nightclub was off-limits to us, we were granted unrestricted access to the library, where we could borrow books and bring them back to our suite for reading.

"I've been studying the building's blueprints," Elliot informed us. "Gray's office is situated on the one-hundredth floor, so reaching it won't pose much of a challenge."

"It has to be tonight," I emphasized. "This is our only opportunity to uncover what Gray is concealing regarding the Doll Killer murders."

"Right after curfew," Felix chimed in. "Is it just me, or does anyone else find it strange that we're on the verge of breaking the law?" Isabelle questioned. "We're discussing the prospect of trespassing and invading someone's privacy."

Lily let out an exasperated huff. "Since when do you care about the law, Isabelle?"

Trey chimed in, addressing Isabelle. "Your sister has a point, Izzy. Why remain loyal to a system that continually lets us down?"

Halle passionately interjected, "My brother may have a questionable side, but the only ones we can truly rely on are ourselves and those among us who dwell in neither the light nor the dark but fully embrace the Grey Zone."

Isabelle raised a valid concern. "I understand your points, but what if everything goes awry, and we end up getting caught?"

I took my turn to speak up. "I know you're apprehensive, Izzy, but what's crucial is that we have one another. If we do happen to get caught, they can't take away the bonds we've formed. The same holds true for those who aren't with us."

Isabelle nodded in acknowledgment. "Alright, Adelice. I'm feeling a bit jittery about what we might uncover. It could change everything."

I admitted my own fear, but I found solace in the fact that we were facing it together.

Slipping into the air ducts proved to be surprisingly straightforward. Being a Halfling came with the advantage of being able to navigate in and out of various tight spaces. "Our first heist in the Edge," Felix exclaimed with a grin. It was clear that the ventilation shafts were spacious enough to accommodate our passage.

"Follow the living GPS!" Elliot playfully called out.

Laughter bubbled up among us. We were well aware that our actions carried significant risks, but there was an undeniable thrill in the air as we followed Elliot through the intricate network of air ducts.

"Did you guys hear that?" Halle suddenly questioned.

"Hear what?" I asked, puzzled.

The dark-skinned girl shook her head. "I might be going crazy, but I swear I can hear music coming from below."

"I can hear it too," Isabelle affirmed. "And so can I," added Lily with a squeak.

Elliot soon realized the source of the music. "We must be directly above the club."

Trey's face lit up with excitement. "Perfect."

But Halle wasn't having it. She snapped, "Don't even think about it! Now is not the time to party."

"We don't need to," I declared. "We can observe what's happening through the glass-cut windows." We all gathered around the glass square, peering down below.

The entire club was drenched in a rich shade of deep purple, while its polished floors gleamed a deep burgundy. Patrons filled the space, either dancing energetically or sipping drinks at the expansive circular bar. Many of the club-goers exhibited supernatural features, from mismatched hair and eye colors that could easily be mistaken for wigs or contacts, to others with scales or feathers imprinted onto their skin.

Felix pondered aloud, "I'm beginning to understand why they won't let us in."

The thumping beats of the techno music reverberated through the vents, sending powerful vibrations our way. "Let's keep moving," I urged, directing our attention toward the vent that led to the ballroom. This opulent space was bathed in rose gold, with majestic columns supporting the circular balcony. Large glass French doors led to a stone terrace outside the building.

"This must be the venue for their formal balls," I whispered. Just gazing at the ballroom was enough to trigger a slight headache as it planted seeds of emotions in my mind—emotions like fear, anger, betrayal, and sadness. These feelings alone seemed to be the driving force behind my decision to run away initially. I had been so terrified that escaping felt like the only option. The enigma of my past was turning out to be far more intricate than I had ever imagined. Doubts about finding my family were beginning to creep in, but I knew we had to press on if we were ever going to apprehend the Doll Killer.

After navigating through numerous twists and turns, we finally reached the floor housing Gray's office. The corridor had a different aesthetic from the one assigned to us, featuring a white marble floor with a single imposing door and fake potted plants flanking it. Fortunately, we had brought the necessary tools with us from the vents.

"The security cameras are temporarily disabled," Elliot reported. "We have a twenty-minute window to pick the lock."

"Lock picking is my specialty," Felix declared as he created a portal to transport us from the vents to the hallway. Our attention was immediately drawn to the impressive sapphire-blue door, which sparkled under the artificial lighting. My best guess was that it was crafted from real, polished gemstones.

I watched intently as Felix produced his lock-picking kit from his jeans pocket. "When did you learn how to pick locks?" I inquired.

"Since I was ten," he replied as he deftly inserted the sharp tools into the keyhole. I had a strong feeling that lock picking would be a vital skill for escaping locked rooms in the future.

"I can't believe we're doing this," Isabelle sighed. Among the triplets, she was the one who favored order and structure the most.

"Whether we like it or not, all the answers we seek are likely in Gray's office," Halle chimed in.

"I'm in agreement with my sister," Trey nodded. "Furthermore, there's probably information about why his company acquired my data from the System's database," I added.

If what Maria had told me was accurate, then Gray's office likely concealed a hidden room behind a bookcase. One thing was clear: Maria had attempted to convey a warning, but she was bound by the magical forces of the lake and couldn't do so explicitly.

"Are we certain we can trust Maria's words?" Isabelle questioned. "These are the words of a ghost woman who drowned her children in the river centuries ago."

"I've got it!" Felix exclaimed triumphantly as the lock of the door clicked open. With the door now unlocked, there was no turning back, and we all entered Gray's private office.

Chapter Thirty-Three

The room was enveloped in darkness as our group entered Gray's office. "Does anyone know where the lights are?" Lily complained. Trey suggested, "I have some matches; maybe they can help?" I noticed that my eyesight had remarkably improved when I spotted a lamp positioned on the large desk. I flicked it on, casting a warm glow throughout the room and granting the others a clear view of Marvelous Radiance's CEO's private sanctuary.

The room had quite a statement to make. Its generous expanse was adorned with walls painted in a deep shade of purple, while the carpeted floor boasted a lavender hue, and the baseboards were finished in a medium purple.

"I might not be drunk, but it certainly seems like Gray has an affinity for purple," Felix remarked in a dry tone.

"You're not wrong," Halle replied, "and it's apparent that Gray has a penchant for all things purple."

Where should we begin? I pondered, my nostrils filled with the potent, aromatic scent of lilacs wafting through the air. The fragrance was so intense it brought tears to my eyes. "Let's start with the desk," I suggested, making my way toward its frosted glass surface. Other than the lamp providing illumination in the room, it held typical items one would expect to find in an office—stacks of papers and neatly aligned rows of pens.

The only thing that stood out was a simple arrangement of blue irises and white roses. It even came with a card bearing elegant script, undoubtedly penned by Gray himself.

"Even though you're not here, I always have a piece of you with me. I love you more than life itself. Eternally yours, Dorian."

The message on the card was poignant and sentimental, carrying a depth of emotion that was unexpected in this otherwise meticulously organized office.

"Yikes," Elliot shuddered as he glanced at the flowers and heard me read out the message on the card. "He must love Sybil's replacement," Isabelle commented, her tone reflecting a touch of sarcasm.

Trey, puzzled, inquired, "Who in the world is Sybil?"

"She was the actress Gray fell in love with and quickly got engaged to. Sadly, he dumped her when she made the naive choice to give up her acting career for him, thinking it was the path to experiencing 'real love.' She ended up committing suicide," Elliot explained matter-of-factly. We all stared at him in shock, as it was the first time we had heard him use such strong language.

"Let's keep moving," I suggested, opening one of the desk drawers. Inside, I found nothing out of the ordinary—just stocks and sales reports generated by the company. However, when I opened the second drawer, I couldn't help but exclaim, "Holy shit."

Lily murmured in agreement, and it was completely justified given what we had just discovered. Inside the drawer was a paper version of the bounty list, featuring our pictures and names, with mine prominently marked as number one, enclosed by a black circle.

"What does all of this mean?" Isabelle demanded.

"It means Gray has been keeping tabs on us ever since Sera helped Adelice and me escape from Kathy Ann," Felix realized.

"That's correct," Halle chimed in. "Not only has he maintained a physical copy of the bounty list, but he's also kept other items, such as recipes from the inns we stayed at and records of the stores where we purchased our supplies. This includes camera footage from each place we visited."

"But how?" were the only words that escaped Lily's mouth.

"Two words: Private Investigator," I replied as I pulled out the purple folder from the drawer. "Gray wasn't pleased with Kathy Ann when she failed to capture us in the town where we met you and your siblings. So, he hired a private investigator to keep tabs on our whereabouts. It still doesn't explain why his company is after me."

"At least we have the other two floors to explore," Elliot pointed out. Once we had everything sorted, we turned our attention to the second floor. Climbing the spiral staircase, we found ourselves in a lounge designed for entertaining guests and potential clients. The space featured a large marble floor in a lilac hue, while the walls and curtains covering the windows were done in periwinkle. Lavender-colored furniture adorned the room, along with a bar area and a plasma screen TV mounted on the wall, featuring the Marvelous Radiance logo.

"The perfect place to host a party," Trey commented with a grin.

"I don't understand why the TV is still on," Elliot remarked. He reached for the remote on the coffee table and attempted to turn it off. However, as he did, the channel changed, revealing a commercial featuring a Doll that looked oddly familiar.

"Looking good means smelling good," the Doll on the TV gushed as she sprayed dark purple perfume on her neck. My heart raced as I recognized that voice immediately. "Sera," I gasped in shock.

"Are you sure?" Felix asked skeptically. "I know it's her, take a closer look."

"Shit, it is her," Felix shook his head in disbelief.

"Isn't she the pureblood girl who helped you escape from Kathy Ann?" Lily inquired.

"Yes, and she paid the price for it," I muttered, guilt gnawing at me. It was my fault that Sera had become a Doll, all because she had helped me escape.

"Listen, Adelice," Halle said, placing her hands on my shoulders, "what they did to Sera was not your fault. She chose to help you and Felix. Don't let her sacrifice be in vain."

Halle's words hit home. Sera had chosen to assist me in escaping from the System, which viewed us as property rather than people. She had wanted to do something right before her claiming ceremony, and her decision to help us must have expedited her transformation into a Doll. It was difficult to determine which side the Committee had chosen for her: the Virtuous Light or the Twisted Dark. However, it didn't matter now. I had to continue forward. There was only one more floor left to explore.

The third floor turned out to be much smaller than I had anticipated. It was a windowless room, lined with floor-to-ceiling bookshelves along both sides and the middle walls—a library. As expected, it adhered to the same purple color scheme. The shelves were amethyst, while the books themselves were ice purple and dark violet. The air was infused with the same perfumed scent of lilacs and white roses, suggesting that Gray frequented this area of his office. However, it wasn't for literary pursuits, but something else entirely.

"It's clear that these books are mostly for show," Isabelle remarked as she plucked one from the shelf. When she opened it, the pages were blank. "We're in the right place," I confirmed. In one corner of the room, there stood a lavender-grey book that didn't quite fit with the others. As I pulled it from the shelf, the entire case started to move. "Jackpot," I grinned. I had discovered the entrance to the secret room. Once we stepped inside, the gang and I were met with a spiral staircase leading upward. "There must be a reason why Gray wanted a fourth and secret floor," Elliot noted. "We're about to find out," Trey said, nudging him forward.

The stairs were constructed of metal, and I could feel the coldness beneath the soles of my sneakers with each step I took. Despite all the doubts that had plagued me, there was a reason Maria had wanted me to find and explore this room when I reached the door. I cautiously turned the knob, and it slowly swung open as I ventured inside.

Chapter Thirty-Four

Just like the office, the entire room lay ensconced in darkness, rendering my own hands invisible.

"Damn, it's dark in here," Trey grumbled, breaking the silence.

"I'm scared," Lily's voice quivered with fear.

"Does anyone know where the lights are?" Elliot inquired.

"How the hell would I know? It's pitch black in here!" Felix's voice rang out with frustration.

"Now is not the time to panic, guys," I urged, maintaining a calm demeanor. "Halle, do you have any matches?"

"No," the female twin, Halle, responded. "I'm surprised there are no windows in this place; some natural light would be a godsend."

As if by a miracle, the lights embedded in the dome ceiling began to flicker to life.

"How on earth did you do that?" Isabelle marveled.

Halle shrugged. "I don't know, but at least we can see now. But where exactly are we?"

She had a point. Unlike the various shades of purple that had dominated Gray's office, this room exuded opulence, with everything crafted from rose gold marble. A collection of paintings adorned the walls, each one featuring a young woman with flowing yellow hair and striking blue-violet eyes.

"What the hell is this place?" Felix queried, adjusting his glasses closer to the bridge of his nose.

"I don't know," I murmured, my eyes scanning the unusual surroundings. "It's almost like we've stepped into an art gallery. But notice how the girl in these paintings is the central figure in all of them."

"She's undeniably beautiful," Felix commented. "I'll give her that. Now, I understand Gray's punishment from the first Emperor, post-immortality. The artist's transformation into the subject— look at how every intricate detail comes alive in these paintings."

"Hey, guys, I found more rooms down the hall!" Elliot's voice echoed through the gallery. His excitement was genuine as we explored these additional chambers, five in total, each revealing a different stage in the girl's life.

The first room depicted her as a young child, perhaps four or five years old.

The second room portrayed her at the ages of seven or eight.

In the third room, she appeared to be between ten and twelve.

The fourth room captured her at around thirteen to fourteen.

And in the fifth and final room, the girl had matured, appearing to be somewhere between seventeen and twenty years old. The source of these ages remained a mystery, but my gaze fixated on the last painting, where the girl had grown into adulthood.

She exuded a striking beauty, reminiscent of a princess plucked from the pages of a fairy tale. She sat gracefully in an antique black chair, a warm smile gracing her rose-petal lips. Her creamy fair skin complemented the soft, pale yellow hue of her blonde hair, which cascaded in elegant waves down her back. Spiral curls adorned her hair, nestling between her small shoulders and slender neck, with delicate diamonds woven into the curls. A fully-bloomed white rose nestled at the side, adding a final touch of enchantment.

The blue-violet of her eyes was so striking that it made an unforgettable impression. She wore an off-shoulder champagne ball gown crafted from ethereal tulle, adorned with intricate gold lace appliques that embellished both the skirt and bodice. A butterfly pendant, encased in a silver frame encrusted with sapphires and aquamarines, graced her neck, its wings delicately adorned. In her hands, she held a white feathered fan with grace and poise. Beside her, a white swan rested, unmistakably the girl's familiar.

"Who is this girl?" Halle asked, her fascination evident in her voice. "I don't know," Elliot admitted. "Whoever she is, she must hold great significance to Gray. Yet, I've never seen her before in my life."

Isabelle turned to her brother, her curiosity piqued. "Could it be his wife? We've never seen her face, but we know she has blonde hair, just like the girl in the painting."

Shock coursed through me as I laid eyes on the place card affixed to the bottom frame of the painting, bearing the name: Claire Masterson-Gray.

"Holy shit," I exclaimed, utterly dumbfounded. "Claire Masterson and the Claire from the paintings Jared showed me on the ferry, not to mention the visions I've had during the Scavenger – they're one and the same."

"Well, I'll be damned," Felix muttered, shaking his head. "Isn't fate a cruel mistress?"

"No shit, Sherlock," Isabelle responded with an eye roll. "Do you think he killed her?" Lily hesitated as she voiced her unsettling thought. "Killed her and kept her body in a private shrine within the building? Like some sort of ghost bride."

"Oh, so we're dealing with a corpse fucker, huh? That's just great!" Trey's anger flared, his disgust palpable. "I knew Gray was twisted, but I never imagined he'd descend to this level."

"I don't believe he killed her," I voiced my opinion. "In the visions I've had during the Scavenger, he appeared to love her. Why else would he create all these paintings of her? It doesn't fit the profile of someone who willingly turned himself into a black widower."

Lily interjected, her tone grim, "You make it sound like she's still alive." Trust me when I say, sister, Claire Masterson-Gray is very much alive and married to a husband who's a narcissistic creep," I concluded.

"It still doesn't explain why Maria wanted you to find this place," Isabelle mused. "And it's strange that Gray built a secret room to house paintings of his wife, ghost bride or not."

"Guys, I found something!" Halle's voice echoed from the front room of the gallery. "You might want to check this out!"

"It's a book," Trey stated bluntly upon seeing the object his sister held. Its spine gleamed gold, while the front and back covers displayed a white rose painted in delicate watercolors. Halle then opened it, revealing pages filled with elegant script written in deep black ink.

"It's Gray's diary," I surmised. "He must have chronicled all his encounters with Claire as she was growing up."

"Okay," Elliot grimaced, "I'm not going to lie; this is creepy as fuck."

"We might find the answers as to why Gray is after me, along with the twisted plans they have in store for the rest of us," I pointed out, my curiosity overriding my unease.

"Does anyone have any alcohol?" Felix inquired. "I have a feeling we might be in for a roast, or perhaps a drunk reading of Gray's diary."

"How can you even think about getting drunk at a time like this?" Isabelle demanded. "Let's read the diary and then head back to the suite before any of the purebloods discover we're missing."

I never pegged Felix as a secret party animal. Sadly, there were many things I still didn't know about him.

I gazed at the exquisite painting of Claire, contemplating the masterpiece that had sprung to life through the artist's brush strokes. Gray's voice seemed to echo in my mind as I marveled at the artistry before me. He must have poured his heart and soul into this painting, capturing both the beauty and essence of the girl he loved. Yet, something still eluded my understanding.

Why had Maria urged me to uncover this place? What was the connection between Claire and all the challenges my friends and I had faced during the Scavenger? The concept of "face your personal weeping woman" remained enigmatic. Nothing seemed to fit together, and I had a persistent feeling that the diary might hold the key to unraveling the questions that consumed me.

Chapter Thirty-Five

It all began like this:

My dearest Claire, I fell in love with you the very moment my eyes met yours all those years ago. I can still vividly recall the day we first crossed paths. It was during a grand garden party held at your father's country estate, where both light and dark nobility were in attendance. It was there, by the tranquil lakeside, that I first laid eyes on you. You exuded an air of innocence and charm that captivated the hearts of many, but it was I who found myself most entranced by you—a girl with a countenance of exquisite beauty and a soul to match. You became the perfect muse for my art.

"This makes me wonder if George Masterson was ever aware of Gray's feelings toward his daughter," Felix mused, shaking his head thoughtfully.

"I doubt he knew," I replied. "Gray probably kept his attraction a closely guarded secret. It might explain why he constructed this hidden gallery within his office."

"That does make sense," Halle concurred. "Here's another entry."

It's as if fate itself is conspiring to bring us together. I had the pleasure of seeing you once more, a few years later, at a charity ball accompanied by a ballet performance. You occupied the box across from mine, and your smile appeared to embody the very essence of your soul. In my eyes, you were a swan in human form, radiating an elegance and grace that filled me with a sense of joy I hadn't experienced in years. You reminded me so much of Sybil, and yet you were distinct from her. You possessed a fierce determination to embrace life, to savor its pleasures and remain whole—something I had not felt in years.

"Indeed," I noted, "it's clear he was not only drawn to her physically but emotionally as well."

Felix chimed in, "And he openly admitted that he hadn't experienced happiness in a long while until he encountered Claire."

"But," I added, "it still doesn't elucidate why he's pursuing me."

It felt as though fate itself had brought you into my life when you discovered me sketching in the park by the lake. You had no inkling of who I truly was, and I desired to keep it that way. To you, I was just another artist who frequented the park on the first level of the central city. I've never confessed this to anyone, but I initially believed I would despise my punishment. It was you, Claire, who changed that perception. You were the one who supported me through it all. I may have lost much of my sanity, but you were the beacon of passion in the midst of my curse.

"So it appears that Claire played a pivotal role in helping Gray maintain his sanity after the first Emperor turned him into an immortal," Halle concluded. "And it seems he was gradually falling in love with her as she continued to grow."

"Maria must have witnessed their interactions in the park," I speculated. "But it still doesn't clarify why I'm intricately connected to all of this," I added, shaking my head in frustration.

Is this what love truly feels like? I find myself in a place where I can't escape thoughts of the Mastersons' only daughter. Painting the love of my life has become my sole tether to sanity. I've reached a point where my deepest desire is to ask for her hand in marriage and embark on a life together.

"Is there anything more?" Elliot inquired.

Halle shook her head. "No, it mostly details his courtship and marriage. If I had to guess, the entry following the wedding is likely filled with explicit details about their wedding night."

"Ew, skip it!" Lily protested.

After flipping through numerous pages, we eventually reached the most recent entries in Gray's diary.

"Guys, I believe I've found what we're seeking," Halle announced, passing the diary over to Felix. "It mentions that Claire has fallen ill ever since the child went missing."

"Child?" Isabelle questioned, perplexed. "Are you saying Gray and his wife had a child?"

"It seems that way," Halle confirmed. "Either the child was taken from them, or it perished. The illness Gray referred to appears to be a result of Claire's profound despair, and it seems she adamantly declined my father's offer to treat her depression with medication."

Felix's face grew ashen as he stared at the final entry in the diary, and as I looked at it, I felt a shiver run down my spine.

Finally, after weeks of relentless searching, I have found the one who will aid in your healing, my beloved Claire. Soon, the anguish that has plagued you for so long will fade into oblivion.

I stood there in stunned silence. After weeks of puzzling over why Marvelous Radiance was pursuing me, I had finally discovered the unsettling truth. I had been acquired to serve as a replacement for the child Gray and his wife had lost—whether through death or abduction, I couldn't say. What troubled me the most was the role they intended for me: a visual treatment to alleviate Claire Gray's depression stemming from her child's loss. The implications of what the company planned for me weighed heavily on my mind. How did they expect me to cure her?

"Are you okay, Adelice?" Felix inquired, his concern evident.

"No, I'm not," I responded tersely, although I didn't truly mean it. "We'll find a way out of here, I promise."

"And then what?" I continued bitterly. "Gray and the System won't cease their pursuit until they have me. Out of all the Halflings they could have chosen, why me? I'm a nobody. I don't even know my own past."

"You're not wrong," Felix interjected firmly. "You're not just Adelice. It's because of you that we've managed to conquer all eight challenges of the Scavenger. You've never shown a hint of fear when confronting the monsters guarding the artifacts. It's a testament to your resilience. Sera told me this when she sought me out to aid you in escaping from Kathy Ann."

"She did?" I was taken aback.

Felix nodded. "Indeed. It's your unwavering will to survive that compelled her to assist you."

His words struck a chord within me. I had never truly considered it, but he was correct. I had a reason to keep pushing forward, to forge my own path. I refused to allow anyone to dictate my identity or define my purpose. At that moment, a newfound determination welled up inside me. I was breaking free from the shackles of others' expectations; I was determined to be my own person.

I couldn't determine how long I had been standing there, but one thing was certain: this place wasn't safe.

"What's the plan, leader?" Felix inquired.

"We need to get out of the Edge," I replied, my gaze now fixed on a small door adjacent to Claire's portrait. How had I never noticed it before? I had an instinct that this was the direction I needed to go—a potential clue as to why I was entangled in the mission to assist Claire Gray with her depression. It was an uncertain path, but it seemed like the way out.

Turning the knob, I entered a narrow hallway that led to a vast circular chamber. Confidence surged within me; I believed I had found an escape route. Our options were limited, and the risks were high.

As I stepped further into the chamber, a gust of wind greeted me, and my eyes caught sight of an open window in the dimly lit room. It offered only a small margin of freedom. However, luck didn't seem to be on my side as I heard the unmistakable sound of footsteps approaching the room. My first instinct was to hide, and my experience of blending into pitch-black corners paid off. The others followed suit, disappearing into the shadows.

I felt Lily clutch my hand tightly as the figure entered the room, standing in the center where the light was most abundant. It was Claire Gray, and she was crying.

Chapter Thirty-Six

I couldn't believe my eyes as I beheld the young woman before me. Her waves of pale yellow hair framed her face, and her blue-violet eyes, now red-rimmed from crying, held a profound sadness. She wore an ice blue gown adorned with delicate white lace as she walked toward the center of the room, her gaze seemingly fixed on the dome ceiling above. Painted there was a full moon surrounded by golden stars set against a midnight blue backdrop.

"What is she doing?" Lily whispered, ensuring Claire couldn't hear us.

"I don't know, but I think this might be where she retreats when she needs to grieve in solitude," I replied. "It would make sense, considering she lost her child."

Our conversation was abruptly interrupted as another figure entered the room.

"Claire, what on earth are you doing in here?" a concerned voice inquired.

My blood ran cold with terror upon hearing Gray's voice.

"Oh, Dorian, I didn't hear you come in," Claire responded hesitantly, her voice filled with trepidation as she seemed to fear she had been discovered. "You shouldn't be in here alone, especially in your current state."

Her depression, I realized; that must have been what he was referring to. Claire let out a heavy sigh as she gazed at her husband.

Freedom seemed tantalizingly close, within my grasp. I could feel it.

"I miss her so much; I'm surprised grief hasn't consumed me entirely," Claire confessed.

"I know, my love," Gray murmured, enfolding his wife in his arms and pulling her into a comforting embrace. "I miss her too, but do not lose hope. Your sorrow will soon be eased."

"Me," I thought bitterly, realizing they were talking about me. It both frightened and disgusted me to think that Gray intended to use me as a means to help treat his wife.

To serve as a replacement for the child they had lost was a deeply unsettling concept, and my companions had witnessed this private moment while concealed in the shadows. Unfortunately, the moment was short-lived, disrupted by the arrival of Daryl.

"Sir, we have a problem. The children are not in their suite," Daryl reported.

"What—how is that possible?" Gray demanded, clearly alarmed. The staff must have realized we were missing when none of us were found in the suite.

Gray sighed. "No matter, they couldn't have gone too far. Take my wife to the conservatory. I'll have security search the building."

Once all three purebloods had left the room, it was finally safe for us to emerge.

"We should go, before they return," I urged, my head starting to swim with dizziness as I stepped onto the balcony. The realization that we were hundreds of feet above the ground sent a shiver down my spine.

"It's a long way down," Elliot muttered, his voice trembling as he gazed at the considerable height.

"If what the Bokor said is true, and if we are indeed descended from gods and supernatural creatures of mythology and folklore, then there's a chance we might survive the fall," I suggested, attempting to quell the anxiety gripping us all.

"Fine, but I'll be furious if we end up in the afterlife," the male triplet warned, grasping both his sisters' hands for reassurance. Trey and Halle did the same, and now it was Felix's and my turn.

"Let's do this," Felix declared.

We nodded in agreement, our hearts pounding with trepidation, and then, without further hesitation, the two of us leaped off the balcony into the unknown.

Rather than plummeting to our deaths as gravity dictated, we found ourselves gracefully gliding down to the ground level of the Edge.

"How is this possible?" Felix marveled, his voice tinged with amazement.

"It's magic," I responded, my voice filled with wonder. "As long as we don't let go, we're safe."

"Hmm... If I had to guess," Felix began to speculate, "this must be one of many abilities our kind possesses. It's likely a spell that isn't activated by words but by action. There must be hundreds of these spells we don't know about, and only we have the capability to perform them."

"You may be onto something," I agreed. "But for now, let's savor the view while it lasts."

"It's strange," Felix mused. "I've lived here my entire life, and I'm only just realizing how beautiful the night sky is. A midnight blue canvas adorned with silver stars. I feel like an idiot for never noticing it before."

"It's understandable," I reassured him. "To you, the sky was an everyday occurrence, something you saw without much thought. But sometimes, it takes a change in perspective to truly appreciate the beauty that's always been there."

The magic came to an end, and I felt my feet make contact with the ground.

"That was awesome!" Trey exclaimed with a radiant smile. "I had no idea we could do that."

Halle chimed in, "There are a lot of things we can do that we don't know about."

"Who cares? At least we're safe," I replied, attempting to ease the lingering tension.

However, the moment was abruptly shattered as we all heard someone screaming—a sound that could only mean one thing: the Doll Killer was nearby. The source of the distress emanated from one of the narrow alleys adjacent to Gray's tower. The mist began to swirl as our group approached, eventually reaching a dead-end where blood was splattered across the brick walls, mirroring the horrifying scene from my vision.

"My latest masterpiece," the killer cooed, sending shivers down our spines.

"Of all the dolls I've slain, she was unquestionably my favorite of the lot; it's a pity I had to extinguish her life. But, oh well, it's all part of my grand scheme. Wouldn't you agree, children?" The voice sent a shiver down my spine as I gazed upon the face of the Doll Killer.

My blood turned to ice as we all got a look at the identity of this monstrous figure. He was a pureblood young man, appearing to be in his mid-twenties, dressed in a light grey Victorian suit that was decidedly out of fashion, its satin texture marred by dirt and fresh blood splatters from his recent murder. The pale hue of his skin seemed to complement the grim attire.

I hadn't been prepared to see the face of the killer, and I could tell that neither were the others. His countenance appeared otherworldly, almost flawless, save for the disheveled waves of dark brown hair that framed his face. But it was his eyes that sent a chill down our spines—a shade of violet so dark that they seemed lifeless and devoid of all emotion, as if he possessed no soul whatsoever.

The killer's sinister smirk widened, revealing his shark-like teeth. "I was beginning to wonder when you would find me," he remarked with a mocking smile.

"What are you?" I demanded, my voice trembling with a mix of fear and anger.

The killer let out a chilling laugh. "I've been around since the time of the ancients, during the age of the old gods. In a sense, my siblings and I were gods ourselves. We were the ones who unleashed plague, war, famine, and death upon the wretched abominations that are the human race. We are the Plague Doctors."

"Plague Doctors?" I echoed, having never heard that name before.

"Oh, dear, where are my manners?" the killer continued, his voice dripping with malevolence. "My name is Kel, Kel Mather. Although, that isn't my true name. I am one of the Plague Doctors, who specializes in rendering his victims defenseless, ensnaring them in a false sense of security, and manipulating them for my own selfish desires."

"It still doesn't explain why you're murdering dolls," Felix interjected, his glare fixed on the deranged killer.

Kel scoffed. "Killing living toys was never part of the plan. However, my true target has always been you, Felix Frankenstein," he declared with a devious smirk. "It was the only way to lure you back to the Edge, all so I could carry out my master plan."

"And what exactly do you need me for?" Felix retorted with scorn.

"You know perfectly well what it is," Kel replied coolly. It became clear that he was referring to the power inherent in the Frankenstein family—the power of the touch.

"You can't force me to use the touch," Felix bluffed.

"I've found a much simpler solution for harnessing the power of others," Kel stated ominously.

The air around us began to turn frigid, and snow started to fall from the sky. It could only mean one thing: Wendigoes. Panic surged through us, and we attempted to flee, but our feet were encased in ice. The air grew so cold that I felt my eyelids becoming heavy, a numbing drowsiness taking hold—not enough to kill, but enough to leave us all drugged and defenseless.

"Take them to the truck!" Kel ordered, and we found ourselves escaping one prison only to find ourselves thrust into another. We had no idea where they were taking us, or what Kel's intentions were for Felix. But I knew I had to stop him and save my friend from whatever sinister plans this sociopath had in store. After all, I had promised Sera that we would watch out for each other. Now, it was my turn to fulfill that promise and repay the debt.

Chapter Thirty-Seven

I awoke with uncertainty about the passage of time. Was it days or mere hours that had slipped by as I opened my eyes? It proved difficult to discern. My surroundings came into focus—a cell, I soon realized. The cell held me captive, and as I pushed myself upright, I observed its composition. Sheets of metal encased me on all sides—floor, ceiling, back, and side walls, all fashioned from unforgiving metal. The front, in stark contrast, offered no respite from my confinement; it was a seamless, polished sheet of glass.

I clenched my fist and struck it forcefully, but the glass remained unyielding, resolute in its obstruction.

I stewed in bitter contemplation. "Maxi-glass," I muttered to myself with a tinge of resentment. The adversaries behind this captivity weren't foolish enough to grant me an easy escape. I needed to ascertain my location and formulate a plan from here.

The absence of windows within the cell hinted at an underground facility. How had Kel amassed the wealth and resources to construct such an elaborate establishment? To his credit, it wasn't some dilapidated structure, but I couldn't help but wonder about the logistics of it all. I was certain we remained within the confines of the Edge, but now it seemed we were beneath it, hidden from view.

The lack of windows in my cell, while unsettling, spurred my determination to find an exit. "There must be a way out of here," I mumbled to myself. My ruminations were interrupted by an unexpected voice from the other side of the glass wall.

"If you're seeking an escape route, you'll need to input the access code," a voice declared, dripping with sarcasm. I gasped in astonishment at the sight of a diminutive creature standing before me.

I rubbed my eyes vigorously, ensuring I wasn't caught in some hallucinatory episode. To my astonishment, the creature remained there—a tuxedo kitten with striking golden eyes.

"Did you just speak?" I blurted out, utterly dumbfounded.

The creature responded, "You could say that, but I'm communicating with you telepathically. Do I look like a ventriloquist's dummy to you?"

I shook my head slowly, still trying to grasp the surreal encounter. "No, but... What are you exactly?"

With a hint of snark in its tone, the creature replied, "I'm delighted you inquired. My name is Shadowlight, though you can call me Shadow. I'm a familiar—a spirit that assumes the guise of an animal."

A thought struck me. "If you're a familiar, you must have an owner, right?"

Shadow's response was swift and unequivocal. "Nope, I haven't had a proper owner in decades."

Despite its undeniable cuteness, it was apparent that Shadow possessed a dark and snarky demeanor. Intriguingly, it wasted no time in getting to the point.

"Here's the deal," Shadow declared. "I'm prepared to grant you your freedom and provide you with the code to unlock the cells and rescue your friends. But there's a condition: you must enter into a contract with me."

I regarded Shadow with a mixture of curiosity and skepticism. "What's the catch? Do you intend to devour my soul or turn me into some sort of monstrous creature?"

"First and foremost, eating souls is just plain repulsive; it's not on my menu," Shadow replied with a touch of exasperation. "And as for turning you into a monster, trust me, I lack that kind of power. The catch is this: when you form a contract, you become my new owner, meaning you're stuck with me for all eternity. So, are we striking a deal or not?"

I let out a resigned sigh. It seemed there was no avoiding this commitment. "Deal. Now, give me the code."

I watched as Shadow, using his tiny paws, deftly pressed the numbers on the keyboard. Slowly, the glass barrier at the front of my cell descended.

"Now, let's go free the others," I declared, stepping into the narrow corridor, reminiscent of the tunnels in an ant colony. The chambers themselves resembled the hexagonal cells of a beehive, constructed entirely from metal and glass.

I soon located Elliot in one of the identical cells to mine, his body huddled in a corner. "Elliot!" I called out, rapping on the glass to capture his attention.

"Adelice," he whispered, rubbing sleep from his eyes. "How did you get out? And who's that cat with you?"

"No time for questions," I urged. "We need to find the others." I swiftly punched in the code that Shadow had provided.

Once Elliot was liberated, we advanced to the adjacent chamber where his sisters were incarcerated together. Isabelle and Lily shared the same cell. Lily rested her head on Isabelle's lap, her sister gently stroking the dark curls of her hair.

"Guys," I called out, rapping on the glass to gain their attention.

"Adelice!" Isabelle beamed with relief. I swiftly input the code and rushed into the cell to inspect Lily's condition.

"Lily, it's time to wake up," I implored. Her eyelids fluttered open, revealing the depths of her dark brown eyes. She spoke weakly, "I knew you would come."

It was evident that this place was taking both a physical and emotional toll on her.

"Lily!" Trey's voice echoed as he and Halle burst into the room. Shadow must have secured their release.

"I think she has a fever," Isabelle explained, her voice tinged with concern. "It's been difficult to keep track of how many days we've been trapped down here."

"Can you hold her?" I asked Trey, and he nodded, carefully cradling Lily in his arms. With only Felix remaining to be rescued, we were nearly free.

"What the hell is this place?" Halle wondered aloud, her gaze sweeping across the tunnel-like corridors.

"I'm not certain, but I suspect we're beneath the Edge," I replied. The whereabouts of Felix remained a mystery, and I couldn't help but wonder what Kel might be subjecting him to. A map would have been invaluable, guiding us to our destination.

My horror escalated as we reached the end of the corridor, revealing a vast expanse filled with thousands of rows of cryogenic capsules neatly stacked on top of one another. The sheer quantity was overwhelming, making it nearly impossible to keep track of the numbers.

The ground beneath my feet felt unsteady, as though the platform was swaying. The cacophonous screams in the chamber grew increasingly deafening. In the midst of the chaos, my eyes locked onto a terrifying sight—Felix, ensnared by two of Kel's henchmen, being forcibly dragged toward one of the ominous capsule chairs where they swiftly strapped him in. Time was running out, and we had to act swiftly.

Without hesitation, I charged forward, my heart pounding, and Isabelle and Trey close on my heels.

"Let him go!" I bellowed, my voice reverberating throughout the chamber. The henchmen turned toward us, their faces a mix of surprise and fury. They released Felix, who staggered back, clearly disoriented.

I didn't afford them a moment's respite. With a surge of determination, I lunged at one of the henchmen, aiming for his throat. Nearby, I spotted a discarded metal pipe, and I seized it, swinging it with all the force I could muster. The henchman crumpled to the ground, rendered unconscious by the blow.

Trey and Isabelle joined forces, using their combined strength to fend off the remaining henchman, overpowering him effectively. Felix, slowly regaining his composure, rallied and joined the fray. Together, the four of us managed to subdue the henchman, ensuring he wouldn't pose a threat again.

"Are you okay?" I asked Felix, genuine concern in my voice. He nodded, still catching his breath. "Thanks for the save. I thought I was done for."

"We're not out of the woods yet," Isabelle reminded us, her gaze sweeping across the chamber. "We need to figure out how to thwart Kel's plan before it's too late."

Trey fixed his gaze on the cryogenic capsules, his expression hardening with determination. "We need to destroy these capsules. If we can disrupt whatever Kel has in mind, we might be able to prevent the outbreak."

Felix nodded in agreement. "Let's do it."

As we closed in on the cryogenic capsules, the gravity of the situation weighed heavily upon us. Time was of the essence, and the urgency to stop Kel and avert a cataclysmic disaster intensified.

"We have to get you out of here," I declared urgently, scanning the surroundings for a means to release Felix from the chair.

Trey, his attention fixed on the restraining straps that held Felix in place, asked, "Can you break free from those straps?"

Felix's feeble shake of the head conveyed his lack of strength. "I don't have enough strength, and I think they drugged me. My body feels so heavy."

"We'll find a way," Isabelle assured him, her eyes scanning the room for any potential aid. Amidst the tension, I spotted a control panel on a nearby wall, adorned with an array of buttons and switches.

"Perhaps there's a way to release the restraints from here," I suggested, making my way to the panel. With a mix of hope and uncertainty, I pressed a button at random.

To our collective relief, the straps constricting Felix's body began to slacken, and he slumped forward as they fell away. I rushed to catch him before he hit the floor. "Easy there," I murmured gently, helping him to a sitting position. "Can you stand?"

Felix nodded, his movements still unsteady. "I think so." With our support, he managed to rise to his feet, though it was evident that he was grappling with his weakened state.

"We need to thwart Kel's plan," he asserted, his voice carrying a determined resolve despite his physical frailty.

"We will," Trey affirmed. "But first, we need to get you out of here and to safety."

As we helped Felix regain his footing, Shadow made his presence known, perched on my shoulder with his golden eyes shimmering. "I can assist with that," he offered, his voice resonating in my thoughts. "I possess the power to bestow Felix with a temporary boost of strength using my magic. It won't endure for long, but it should suffice to get him to safety."

"Do it," I responded without hesitation. Time was a luxury we couldn't afford to squander. Shadow's magic enveloped Felix, and a faint, ethereal glow enveloped him. Gradually, Felix's movements grew more assured, and he seemed to regain a measure of his energy.

"Thanks," Felix said, his voice now stronger.

"Let's go," Isabelle urged urgently. "We need to find a way to stop Kel before it's too late."

With Felix supported between us, we made our way out of the chamber and back into the labyrinthine tunnels of the underground facility, our determination unwavering in the face of Kel's deadly scheme.

Felix's countenance darkened. "Kel is an agent who harbors a morbid fascination with death and chaos. I wouldn't put it past him to orchestrate something like this. But we cannot allow his twisted designs to come to fruition."

As we ventured through the dimly lit corridors, an oppressive tension hung in the air. Every step forward seemed to draw us closer to peril, yet there was no alternative but to press on. Our resolve to halt Kel and rescue the city intensified with each passing moment.

We stumbled upon a stairwell that led upwards, and we didn't hesitate to commence our ascent. The higher we climbed, the more my anxiety swelled. We desperately needed a means to alert the authorities or to send a warning to the Edge, but the path ahead was fraught with uncertainty. Nevertheless, we were determined to make every effort.

Upon emerging from the stairwell, we found ourselves in a dimly lit room replete with monitors and control panels. It was evident that this served as some form of command center, where screens displayed a medley of images, including city maps and surveillance footage. Kel had evidently been keeping meticulous tabs on everything.

Felix's gaze narrowed as he scrutinized the monitors. "We must discover a means to disrupt whatever he's orchestrating from here."

Shadowlight perched resolutely on my shoulder, a constant reminder of our potent ally in this dire situation. "I can attempt to manipulate the technology in this room," he offered. "If I can disable the controls, it may provide us with some time."

Felix nodded, his resolve unwavering. "Go ahead."

As Shadowlight focused his efforts, the command center's lights began to flicker, and the monitors glitched. It was evident that his magical abilities were taking effect. A tangible sense of urgency pervaded the room as we anxiously awaited the outcome, hoping that Shadowlight's efforts would prove successful.

Ultimately, the screens blinked into darkness, and a hushed stillness fell upon the room. Shadowlight hopped off my shoulder and regarded us. "I've done what I can. The controls are temporarily disabled, but we must act swiftly. Kel will likely soon realize that something is amiss."

Time was a luxury we couldn't afford. We promptly exited the command center and reentered the labyrinthine tunnels, our singular objective driving us forward: locate Kel and terminate his perilous schemes once and for all. The destiny of the city hung in the balance, and our resolve remained unwavering. We were prepared to safeguard it at any price.

Chapter Thirty-Eight

The gang and I navigated the intricate labyrinth of hallways that encircled the hive of cryogenic capsules. The mind behind the construction of this facility must have possessed a formidable intellect. It prompted me to wonder whether the denizens of the Edge, the nobles in particular, were even aware of its existence. Chances were slim. It was becoming increasingly evident that they had discerned our absence from Gray's building by now. I could only hope that I would never have to set foot in that place again.

The mere contemplation of becoming a means to alleviate Claire Gray's despair over the loss of her child sends a chill down my spine. It prompts me to question the nature of what truly transpired with her child. Did it meet its demise, or did it simply vanish into thin air? Departing the city became our sole recourse. We required the artifacts necessary for the higher court cards and needed to witness the outcome when they were gathered in one place. We were on the cusp of achieving that; Shadow communicated to me through our telepathic link.

The tuxedo kitten certainly possessed an innate knowledge of this place. Finally, we reached the door that led to the outside world, liberating ourselves from the nightmare within the hive. A sense of foreboding hung heavy in the air, but I let out a sigh of relief as a gentle breeze caressed my face. How long had we been trapped down there? Felix's face still lacked color, and the thought of the amount of blood Kel had drained from him ignited a surge of anger and revulsion toward that monstrous figure.

Halle directed her question to me. At this juncture, I held the unofficial title of leader within our group. Despite the void left by my missing memories, I had found a renewed sense of purpose.

"We must head to the library," I asserted, "it might contain crucial information about Kel and the Plague Doctors."

Felix pondered aloud, "It's strange, I've never encountered them before."

"They are conspicuously absent from all the literature pertaining to the Pantheons, as well as from any folklore documented before the inception of Alessia," he continued.

Elliot chimed in with a suggestion, "There must be an entry about them in the library, along with a clue to defeating them."

As we strolled along the sidewalk, I noticed a police car parked by the curb. Abruptly, a police officer issued an order, "Raise your hands where I can see them!"

I stood paralyzed by fear. We had just escaped one form of confinement, only to stumble into another—this time represented by the higher authorities tasked with protecting people from harm. Unfortunately, the police viewed us not as individuals but as commodities owned by the nobility.

The handcuffs tightened around my wrists, sending a chill down my spine. We were herded into the back of the police car, separated from the officer at the wheel by a transparent plastic partition. By noon, we had arrived at the police station, an imposing edifice crafted from white marble, embellished with a tapestry bearing the likeness of the Emperor.

An air of arrogance adorned his countenance, a smug expression that seemed to convey, "We've captured you." Despite my bound hands, a temptation welled within me—to strike that smug look from his face. It was a seditious impulse, born of desperation in the face of the dire circumstances confronting me and my companions.

Upon our arrival, we were promptly escorted to the second floor, where the office of the police chief held its position.

"Sir, I came upon a group of strays lingering on the ground floor outside the Edge," the officer reported to him. Suppressing a scoff proved challenging. "Strays," a term they had seemingly bestowed upon Halflings without owners, those conventionally referred to as "Mom and Dad." My gaze locked onto the figure seated behind the expansive desk. He was a robust individual, adorned with a dense mustache that harmonized with his dark hair, now speckled with streaks of gray. His fair skin bore subtle creases, tangible testimony to his early middle age.

The police chief donned somber trousers and a silk waistcoat over a white dress shirt. His eyes, frosty in hue, bore into me and my companions with an intensity that was hard to ignore.

"Hmmm... so you're the troublesome lot who've become a thorn in Mr. Gray's side," the police chief remarked calmly, his pronounced New York accent filling the room. None of us dared to speak.

"So, you're remaining tight-lipped, huh? Your parents must be fretting over your whereabouts," he continued, a curious blend of praise and disdain in his tone. "I must admit, it takes a certain audacity to evade the Edge."

"It's challenging to comprehend whether you're praising us or disparaging us," I retorted. "You have no idea."

The police chief's icy gaze fixated on me, and I couldn't help but feel that this man was devoid of any sense of empathy. "No idea," he mused. "Most individuals would be elated, not to mention grateful, to receive an invitation to the Edge. It's a privilege that many would kill for."

"It's not a privilege, it's a prison," Felix shot back with palpable bitterness. "Regardless, all of you will be returning to your parents." His tone was edged with defiance.

I couldn't help but flinch as the police chief reached out to snatch at a loose strand of my hair. "White hair, huh? Are you certain you're not unwell, little girl? I'm sure Gray would be delighted to exchange the reward money for your capture." My anger welled up, especially in the presence of such corrupt authority figures.

The police chief was on the verge of reaching for the telephone when the room was filled with the cacophony of shattering glass, accompanied by the wails and sobs of people. "You kids stay put," the police chief commanded, stepping toward the hallway.

However, before he could make his exit, a zombie lunged at him, sinking its teeth into his neck and extinguishing his life in an instant. Halle swiftly moved to the door, firmly closing and securing it to block the zombie's entry.

"What's happening?" Lily cried out in distress. We all converged around the observation window, affording us a view of the pandemonium unfolding in the lobby below. The sounds of shattering glass grew more pronounced as more zombies poured in through the broken windows. Chaos reigned as terrified individuals in the lobby sought to escape, only to succumb to the relentless bites of the undead.

"We must escape, and we must do it now!" Isabelle exclaimed, her voice trembling, as she sought to console her weeping sister. However, Elliot voiced a grim reality, "But we're unarmed."

"We cannot linger here indefinitely; there must be another way out of the station," I proposed urgently.

"It's official—the zombie apocalypse has begun," Trey remarked grimly.

"Kel must have realized we escaped from the facility," Halle deduced, her brow furrowing in thought.

"There has to be a way to neutralize them, but how?" Elliot demanded.

"In RPG Survival Horror, the only way is to shoot them in the brains," Trey offered with a somewhat detached tone.

"This isn't a video game, Trey; this is reality!" Isabelle screamed in exasperation.

"How on earth are we going to get our hands on firearms? We're completely surrounded!" The dire situation prompted me to ponder the possibility that someone as corrupt as the police chief might have kept a hidden stash of weapons in his office. But where could it be?

"Holy crap," Felix exclaimed, his eyes widening as he gasped at the sight of an assortment of guns and ammunition concealed within the desk drawers.

I understood the likely intent behind the police chief's possession of those firearms: probably to eliminate others and deliver me to Gray to claim the reward money. However, his intentions no longer mattered, as he was now deceased and incapable of causing harm. Holding a gun in my hands was simultaneously terrifying and exhilarating. I was not the type to be consumed by power.

"Alright, everyone, let's take action," I grinned, fully aware that it would be an exceedingly challenging day for all of us.

Chapter Thirty-Nine

The moment I exited the police chief's office, I broke into a sprint. The fear of recapture weighed heavily on our minds, though the harrowing screams from the lobby below were impossible to ignore.

"There's a fire escape on the third floor that we can use," Elliot informed us, a glint of satisfaction in his eyes. His knack for hacking into everything, from databases to the internet itself, was truly commendable.

Felix's complexion struck me as alarmingly pallid. The ordeal of having most of his blood drained had left him severely weakened. It was a wonder he was still alive. A regular pureblood would likely have perished.

"I'm starting to feel terrible," he groaned, sweat dotting his face. I spoke with determination, "You need medical attention." He shook his head. "No, that's the first place Kathy Ann would look. Regrettably, we might need to seek my father's assistance. He might be the only one who knows how to eradicate the zombies."

"Are you aware of his whereabouts?" I inquired. Before Felix could respond, Halle interjected, gesturing at the TV screen affixed to the wall.

"Attention all uninfected individuals: proceed immediately to the Grand Library for refuge. Supplies of food and medicine are available." The announcement blared from the TV, capturing our attention with its urgent message.

"It looks like we're heading back to the library," I remarked, attempting to lighten the mood. "Maybe we'll get lucky and find your dad there."

"Well, it is his favorite place beyond the Edge," Felix chuckled.

As we prepared to ascend the stairs, the eerie moans of the approaching zombies grew louder. "Let's move," Trey urged, "before they catch up."

I nodded in agreement, holding onto Felix's hand while Trey protectedively embraced Lily. Halle, Isabelle, and Elliot followed closely behind as we climbed the staircase, pushing boxes and stored furniture to barricade the door behind us. "Do you think this will hold?" Elliot asked.

"I'm not sure, but we need to get out of here quickly," I urged. Surely, the police were starting to wonder about our whereabouts by now.

I retrieved a paperclip from one of the desks and skillfully used it to pick the lock securing the window. "How did you learn to pick locks?" Isabelle asked.

"One word: observation," I replied. I had been absorbing all sorts of knowledge while on the run with the others, just in case I ended up separated from them and had to fend for myself.

The lock on the window emitted a series of clicks as I lifted it, and a refreshing breeze swept into the storage area. Freedom had never tasted so sweet. I allowed Felix to go first, followed by Trey, who was holding Lily since they needed extra assistance. Isabelle, Halle, and Elliot followed in quick succession. I brought up the rear, crawling out of the window. Descending from the fire escape proved to be a simple task; a single leap allowed me to land on my feet with the agility of a cat.

Now came the daunting challenge: navigating through the zombie-infested city en route to the library while ensuring our survival. "It's wiser to traverse the alleys," Felix suggested, "there might be a network of tunnels we can use to reach our destination."

"Why resort to tunnels?" Isabelle asked.

"These tunnels were historically used by servants for travel between locations," Felix explained. "We just need to find the right passage leading to the library's servant quarters."

"We should start now; I have a feeling our solitude won't last much longer."

"What do you mean?" I asked the straight-haired triplet, intrigued.

It was then that I sensed the texture of powdery-white snow forming at my fingertips, accompanied by frigid currents that induced shivers across my body; wendigoes were nearby.

My eyes landed on a door embedded within the brick wall of the station. It had to be the entrance that servants used for access to and from their work at the station. The chill in the air grew more intense as we huddled behind the door. Peering through the peephole, I got a clear view of the pursuing monsters, currently appearing in their human forms.

The first figure appeared to be a man with dark hair, dressed in a sleek, dark silk suit. The second was a woman, her blonde hair tightly braided, wearing a short white dress paired with gold sandals. Both shared the same vacant, ebony eyes and cast shadows that revealed their true, sinister nature.

"They must be nearby," the man uttered in an emotionless tone. "We might as well continue our search," the blonde woman responded coolly. "Master Kel requires the Frankenstein boy to remain alive for his designs to prosper."

I was left utterly shocked by this revelation.

Were the wendigoes aligned with Kel's agenda? This perplexed me. I had believed that Seneca was the only one capable of exerting control over this limited faction of monsters.

"How in the world did Kel manage to enlist the wendigoes in his service?" Halle asked, echoing the same confusion I felt.

"I have no clue, but I suspect there's more to the Plague Doctors than meets the eye," Elliot remarked.

"I concur," Halle agreed, "how is it that we've never encountered any mention of them until now?"

"We're about to find out," Felix replied, his voice weakening, likely due to the considerable blood loss he had sustained.

We needed to reach the library as quickly as possible. "How much farther do we have to go?" Isabelle inquired.

"Not much," I replied. Dread overcame me as I heard the distant, low moans emanating from the tunnel we were about to enter. How had the zombies infiltrated the tunnels? There was no escaping the relentless march of the undead.

I flinched at the sound of gunshots targeting the zombies, experiencing a mixture of discomfort and relief as the undead crumpled like discarded dolls. I felt nothing as I gazed upon the lifeless bodies I had just dispatched, not even a shred of remorse. I recognized that I was gradually succumbing to the darker aspects of my nature.

The streets offered no respite. With each block and corner, a swarm of zombies lurked, poised to seize upon the living. Some appeared human, while others seemed grotesquely altered. I could only hope that most of the city's population had been evacuated or had the foresight to fortify their residences by barring doors and windows.

"How much farther do we have to go?" I asked Elliot.

"Not much, just a few more blocks," he replied.

We were rapidly closing in on a sanctuary where we could find refuge and much-needed medical assistance, knowing that we were on the verge of facing the most significant battle of our lives.

Chapter Forty

After surmounting numerous obstacles, we finally arrived at the Grand Library. An innocent voice chimed sweetly, "What kept you all?" Glancing downward, I spotted the source of the voice—Shadow, the kitten familiar, with its golden eyes as wide as teacup saucers, staring at us. "And where have you been?" I demanded.

"This isn't the moment for an interrogation," the familiar cautioned, "especially with a zombie outbreak just a few blocks away."

I didn't entirely trust the plump little furball, but I recognized the truth in its words. It was something of a marvel that the library's doors hadn't been fortified. As we crossed the threshold into the expansive marble foyer, my eyes fell upon rows of cots arranged across the gleaming floors, populated by various groups of refugees huddled together.

Navigating among the different groups of survivors proved to be a simple task; they seemed ensconced in their own world, burdened by the weight of PTSD. Fortunately, the library offered ample space to accommodate those who hadn't fallen victim to bites.

"Felix!" a voice called out, and a woman's figure approached us. Tall and possessed of deep brown hair, reminiscent of coffee without cream, it complemented her honey-toned complexion and her eyes, shaded in a hue of blue-grey. She wore a lime green dress adorned with fuchsia ribbon accents at the sleeves and hems, tied into petite bows.

"What transpired?" she inquired.

"And hello to you as well, Mom," Felix replied, his voice feeble. So, this was Felix's mother. It was logical given their shared dark hair and skin tone.

Her gaze shifted toward me and the others. "I am Astoria Frankenstein," she introduced herself formally, a tone usually reserved for addressing non-family members.

"What sort of situation have you plunged yourself into, Felix?" Astoria queried sternly.

"It's a lengthy tale, Mrs. Frankenstein," Halle began, "but at this moment, your son and my brother's girlfriend require medical care."

"I will fetch my husband; he's in the basement. Actually, never mind—follow me."

"Seems you'll finally have a chance to meet my dad," Felix quipped with a grin.

I observed his complexion growing increasingly pallid.

"At this moment, it's imperative that we secure treatment for you and Lily if we intend to thwart Kel and find a way to eliminate the zombies," I asserted resolutely.

Felix let out a sigh. "I had a feeling we might be in for an extended stay here."

Astoria led us down a spiral staircase that descended into the library's cellar. Upon reaching the bottom step, gas lamps lining the walls illuminated the narrow passageways.

"What is this place?" I inquired.

"This is where my husband retreats to work in solitude," Astoria replied.

We followed her into a spacious room that turned out to be an office. Books were strewn across the floor, while medical equipment and prescription bottles occupied the surface of the desk. In one corner, a small TV and an unattractive white sofa were positioned. Near the desk, a man with slate grey hair and a slender build was seated, his head lowered.

"Victor, we have visitors," Astoria informed her husband gently, rousing him from his slumber. Victor gradually opened his eyes, which were framed by a pair of half-moon glasses that mirrored the same brilliant green as Felix's eyes.

"I must have dozed off inadvertently," he sighed, rubbing the sleep from his eyes.

"Hello, Dad," Felix greeted the mad scientist, whose gasp of astonishment was elicited by his son's notably pallid appearance.

"What on earth has befallen you?" Victor demanded.

"It's a convoluted story," Felix responded hoarsely.

"You have quite a bit of explaining to do, but what you require right now is a blood transfusion. It's a wonder you're still alive. Otherwise, you would have become a cadaver by now."

"I understand; I messed up. There's no need to keep pointing it out," Felix retorted.

"I have every right to, given that it's your negligence that led to the entire city being overrun by zombies after they drained you of all that blood. I'm uncertain where they originated, but your mother and I are taking you back home once this ordeal concludes."

"Wow, he seems pretty serious," Trey muttered.

"You think?" Felix shot a glare at the dark-skinned boy.

It took a moment for Victor to acknowledge my presence. "Oh, it appears we haven't been formally introduced. I'm Victor Frankenstein."

"Adelice," I replied, shaking hands with the mad scientist.

"I'm aware you're a sought-after individual, judging by your high ranking on the bounty list. It's quite miraculous that the System's agents haven't apprehended you. With my son's help, the same applies to the other fugitives."

"I didn't do it for attention. I simply saw no reason to be under the care of those who either didn't want me or intended to exploit me," I explained.

"That's quite reasonable. However, I can assure you, young lady, that your circumstances aren't as dire as you might believe."

"What do you mean?" I inquired.

"Oh, dear, I may have spoken too much. The key is, you're fortunate to have been purchased by those who desired you."

Right, I thought bitterly. The only reason my buyers wanted me was that Gray believed I was the only one capable of aiding in his wife's recovery. I struggled to comprehend how I could possibly heal the grief stemming from the loss of their missing or deceased child. As the zombie apocalypse raged on, I remained uncertain about the shape of my future.

Our immediate concern was securing treatment for Felix and Lily. "Set her down on the sofa," Astoria directed Trey. Lily continued to whimper as he gently laid her on the cushions.

"How frequently does she experience these episodes?" Victor inquired.

"Not often," Isabelle responded, "the most recent one occurred when the zombies infiltrated the police station. I suppose the most severe instance was after Kel's wendigoes abducted us and transported us to the facility where the zombies were being kept."

"A facility," Victor mused, "could you provide a description?" All of us shared what we could recall.

"Fascinating," Victor pondered.

"If I am correct in my assessment, the place you've described could be one among many that have remained dormant for decades. Not since the establishment of the Empire. Additionally, what can you tell me about this individual named Kel?"

"Not much, aside from the fact that he's one of the Plague Doctor's," I began, but I ceased upon noticing how Astoria's complexion drained of color.

"You're familiar with them, aren't you?"

"I cannot deny their existence. It's astonishing to think they've returned after all these years. Not since the Dome Colonies came into being."

"What's their connection to the colonies?" Felix inquired.

"It's not a straightforward tale. It was due to their influence that the colonies were established across the old world and the Empire was founded. When I reflect on it, Kel's actions were the impetus behind both the Colonies and the Empire."

Top of Form

Chapter Forty-One

It began much like any other narrative.

Before the Empire's inception, an era reigned in the Old World, suffused with magic, governed by those who crowned themselves royalty. They deemed themselves rightful possessors of the world's magic, an obsession that engulfed them to the extent that they sought to hoard it exclusively, igniting perpetual wars and conflicts.

Orphaned children and famine blighted the lands, followed by disease and death. Conditions deteriorated to such an extent that many resorted to selling their bodies to the highest bidder, and we were left with no alternative but to conceal ourselves, as various factions grew increasingly paranoid. Their avarice consumed them, for they were loath to share the magic with outsiders, resulting in the distorted notion of cousins marrying cousins to preserve the bloodline's purity.

Regrettably, the consequences of inbreeding rendered access to magic more elusive, as the gene became recessive and dormant within successive generations.

It was during this period that the persecution of those descended from the ancient gods of the pantheons commenced. The houses banded together in pursuit, seeking those whose lineage traced back to the era of Gaia and Uranus. Little did they grasp that these descendants possessed far greater intellect than they could fathom.

Recognizing the peril, the descendants concluded that the Old World was no longer a haven of safety. They chose to depart, establishing a new home in the New World—a realm beyond the houses' grasp, where magic was wild and untamed, resisting their control.

Not only the carriers and supernatural beings fled, but our own kind—the immortals—began their exodus as well.

All proceeded smoothly following the Empire's establishment, until the Houses dispatched assassins to eliminate the consort, along with the firstborn son and heir to the former Emperor. Thus, the mist enshrouding the Empire came into being—a measure enacted to safeguard the New World's magic from those driven by selfish motives.

It came as no shock to us that Kel harbored intentions of monopolizing the New World's magic for his own ends, yet that narrative warrants a separate telling.

It was all coming together, yet the full answer remained elusive.

"However, this still doesn't elucidate who Kel and the Plague Doctors truly are," I pointed out.

Astoria let out a sigh. "Frankly, no one possesses a comprehensive understanding of their origins. The only fragments of history we've managed to uncover position them as a cohort of demons rooted in Persian mythology. Everything beyond that leads to dead ends, as their presence isn't documented in any literature predating the Empire's establishment."

This prompted a thought. "What if the information we're seeking is concealed? Not within the library's public areas, but within the more secluded sections, perhaps even in a place where Kel would be least likely to investigate."

"Your intuition appears promising, young lady," Victor murmured.

"I believe I've discerned where you and the others should proceed," Astoria realized. "Felix and Lily should remain here, while the rest—those not afflicted by illness or injury—can accompany me." The destination she had in mind remained shrouded in mystery, poised to be unveiled.

"The tunnels will lead us directly to the shrine room," Astoria clarified. Thus far, we'd managed to avoid encountering any zombies, though we remained armed with guns and ammunition for added security.

"Where exactly are you taking us?" Isabelle inquired.

"To one of the few sanctuaries on the island," the pureblood woman responded, producing a brass key from her skirt pocket.

We observed as she unlocked the wooden door, guiding us into a windowless chamber. Metal comprised the walls, while the spiraling staircase, fashioned from glass, descended. Unpleasant memories of the hive-like facility resurfaced. Thankfully, a metal railing provided support as we descended the glass steps.

"What lies beneath?" I inquired.

"The revelation awaits you," Astoria replied enigmatically.

We trailed after her into a spacious corridor, its walls and floor fashioned from polished pink rose-quartz. I marveled at this novel experience of encountering crystal in such architectural form. The rationale behind the chamber's inaccessibility to the general populace was becoming evident.

Exiting the corridor, we were met with the sight of a grand cavern, its floor blanketed in blue sand. Driven by curiosity, I scooped some of the sand into my palm, marveling at its smooth and slightly moist texture.

"We don't have much further to go," Astoria called out.

Towards the end of the chamber, a sizable pool of turquoise water caught our gaze, accompanied by a waterfall cascading from an opening in the rocky midnight blue walls.

"How can this be?" Halle whispered in awe.

"This entire space is a product of magic," I deduced.

"That could account for the blue sand," Elliot reflected, "but I'm beginning to understand the sanctity of this place."

"In what way?" Isabelle queried her brother.

"It's straightforward; we are situated beneath what was once the state of New York," the male triplet expounded.

Stunned, we all exchanged glances, the gravity of his statement sinking in. The revelation resonated, as the city had been erected atop the island, dominated by skyscrapers and high-rise structures. This newfound understanding also clarified the island's eight-tiered design, a means of preserving the natural splendor that lay beneath the urban expanse.

I pondered who else might be privy to this hidden realm, as the caverns boasted networks of interconnected chambers hewn from diverse crystals, each paired with a blend of sand colors. Salt lamps screwed into the walls provided the sole illumination, an explanation Astoria offered as being for health benefits. To this point, this represented the sole technological presence we had encountered within the caves.

Upon contact with the pale orange globe, I detected its inviting warmth and stability. The entire environment was nothing short of remarkable, resonating with an underlying magical aura. With each step, the enchantment seemed to beckon me onward, leading us closer to the ultimate chamber where knowledge about Kel and the Plague Doctors might be found.

Within this final space, the walls were composed of polished blue geos, their surfaces smooth to the touch. Displayed within were painted canvases, silkscreens protected by glass sheets, depicting figures that transcended mere humanity—these were gods hailing from assorted pantheons. It was becoming clear why this sanctum had been shrouded from the public's awareness.

Chapter Forty-Two

In awe, I took in the wondrous beauty that enveloped the surroundings. One portrait, framed by glass, held the image of a young woman possessing creamy blonde tresses and imperial violet eyes. My attention shifted to the metal stand, supporting the glass shield, where a placard had been affixed: "Persephone, Goddess of Spring and Queen of the Underworld." A magnetic connection seemed to pull me toward her.

Yet another image caught my eye—this one portrayed a goddess with dark blonde hair accentuated by red and magenta streaks. Her eyes, the color of rose quartz, held a captivating allure. The corresponding placard identified her as "Aphrodite, Goddess of Love and Beauty."

"Incredible," Elliot breathed in reverence. It was truly astonishing to grasp that this sanctuary served as a haven for the depictions of the ancient deities.

Further within, obscured by the darkness, lay an area consumed by shadows. Here, concealed images of the Plague Doctors were likely stored, veiled in complete darkness. I needed to determine which of these entities Kel represented.

As I inquired about matches, Astoria obligingly provided them. Her gaze, however, grew more focused, a mixture of astonishment and recognition in her eyes. This reaction bewildered me—why was she observing me as though she had encountered a specter? Striking a match, I ignited a series of shivers coursing through me as the images of the Plague Doctors materialized before my eyes.

The portraits held a striking resemblance—a shared darkness of hair, pallid skin, and deep violet eyes—unifying seven boys and two girls. Among them must be Kel, but identifying him felt like searching for a needle in a haystack.

Just then, a melodic voice interjected, cautioning me against overthinking. Looking downward, I discovered the source to be none other than Shadow.

Indignation welled within me. "And where on earth have you been?" I inquired with exasperation.

"I've always been around. My natural habitat is within the shadows, after all," he replied with a hint of amusement.

Regarding my attempt to discern Kel among the images, Shadow advised, "You might be searching too hard. Focus on the one you're most fixated on—his title. Kel practically handed you the information when you and your friends linked him to the Doll murders."

"I am the one who leaves his victims defenseless," I heard his voice resound in my thoughts, as if he were present.

"The one who leaves his victims defenseless," I repeated softly, the realization dawning on me. "He gives his victims a false sense of security, manipulating them like puppets on strings. Isn't that right, Saurva?" I inadvertently spoke Kel's true name aloud, my heart racing.

To my surprise, Shadow responded, "Congratulations, you've uncovered the identity of the Plague Doctors you and your companions must confront." His tone carried an odd satisfaction.

I challenged him, "What do you mean, confront? Don't you dare deceive me, cat."

Shadow's response held gravity, "It's the purpose designated to you all by Fate. During the Scavenger event, you were chosen to be the ones to bring down Kel Mather, the Plague Doctor."

"Your task involves collecting all the court cards from the Minor Arcana," Shadow explained.

My curiosity persisted, "And what about the other Plague Doctors?"

He nonchalantly replied, "Their demise will come through alternative sources of magic present within the human factions. My sister and I have already selected individuals to confront those Plague Doctors in the future. We've orchestrated everything, even your births."

I let out a sigh, still reeling from the revelations.

With a hint of sarcasm, I retorted, "Lucky me, I suppose."

Shadow didn't seem perturbed, replying, "Consider yourself fortunate that you possess a certain charm. Otherwise, I might have left you to the wolves or doused you in ice-cold water."

"Gee, thanks," I muttered, though my mind was preoccupied with processing the newfound information. With my immediate goal accomplished, it was time to return to the surface and continue the fight against the impending apocalypse.

The pieces were starting to fit together. As Felix's health improved, we observed the growing swarm of zombies on the library's camera footage.

"It's like we're living in a real-life Resident Evil game," Felix commented, shaking his head.

I nodded in agreement, adding, "Only this time, we're the stars of this horror show."

The scale of the zombie infestation was staggering. "Kel must have been planning this for years," I mused.

"Exactly," Victor chimed in, "and the resources he needed to create zombies artificially could only come from a corporation specializing in bio weaponry."

The realization struck us collectively. "But which company?" I questioned.

Victor's eyes gleamed with recognition, "I believe I know. Among all the corporations I've interacted with, there's only one that fits the bill: the Plague Doctor Foundation."

The urgency was clear – we needed a spell that could obliterate the zombies without harming the uninfected.

"I have a few ideas," Victor began, "but we need access to the library's restricted collection."

Astoria nodded, "I have the key." With her guidance, we headed back to the secret shrine room, with its mesmerizing portraits of gods and Plague Doctors.

As we stepped into the sacred chamber, I felt the weight of the task ahead. "We'll need to find a spell that can target only the infected, without affecting the rest of the population," I explained. My eyes settled on the paintings of the Plague Doctors – Kel's face among them. I couldn't help but feel a mixture of anger and determination.

"We'll start by searching for any ancient texts or scrolls that might contain such a spell," Victor suggested.

The room felt charged with centuries of magic, and I knew that hidden within these walls were the secrets we needed to save the city from the zombie apocalypse. It was time to unravel the mysteries and harness the ancient magic that had been preserved in this sanctuary.

"The Edge," I confirmed Trey's guess. "It's his stronghold, his base of operations. We've already seen what he's capable of, and we can't let him continue this reign of terror."

As we made our way through the dimming streets, I couldn't shake the feeling that this was the climax of our journey. The final battle was on the horizon, and everything we'd experienced had led us here.

In the distance, the lights of the Edge gleamed like distant stars, a city within a city, filled with secrets and darkness. Kel awaited us there, and so did the answers to questions that had haunted us for so long. But one thing was certain – we were ready to face whatever challenges lay ahead and put an end to the nightmare that had engulfed our world.

It was a unanimous decision. With determination in our hearts, we set our sights on the Edge – the place that held the key to unraveling the mysteries, defeating Kel, and putting an end to the zombie apocalypse. As we walked towards our destiny, I couldn't help but reflect on the journey we had undertaken, the friendships that had formed, and the challenges we had overcome. The final battle awaited us, and we were prepared to face it together.

Chapter Forty-Three

We navigated the desolate streets, the sun sinking beneath the horizon, casting an eerie, dim light upon the city. The towering buildings loomed above us, empty and lifeless, once vibrant streets now rendered silent, broken only by the distant, haunting moans of the encroaching zombies. As we drew nearer to the Edge, a mixture of fear and determination intensified the pounding of my heart.

"I can't believe we're embarking on this," Isabelle murmured, her voice filled with doubt. "I mean, what if we're marching right into a meticulously laid trap?" Her apprehension held merit, yet we had no alternative. We were compelled to confront Kel and extinguish his reign of terror.

Approaching the Edge, a noticeable chill settled in the air, and the atmosphere turned increasingly oppressive. The sky above bore a deeper hue, as though the very essence of the location had been tainted by the malevolence that resided there. I stole a glance at my companions, finding their expressions mirroring my growing unease.

"Felix, are you absolutely certain about this?" Lily inquired, her face etched with concern.

Felix affirmed with a determined nod. "We have no other recourse. It's the sole means to halt him."

We crossed the threshold into the dilapidated structure, the very place we had recently fled. The corridors remained as unsettling as our previous encounter, their walls adorned with peculiar symbols and graffiti. It felt akin to stepping into a waking nightmare.

"This place sends shivers down my spine," Halle whispered.

"We must maintain our focus," I reminded them sternly. "Kel is aware of our approach. We cannot afford to be caught unprepared."

As we delved further into the heart of the Edge, our senses remained on high alert. Each creak of the floorboards and every looming shadow felt like potential threats. It was evident that Kel had meticulously readied himself for our return.

Then, a voice reverberated through the corridor, sending shivers coursing down our spines. "Welcome back, my dear friends."

We turned to find Kel standing there, his monocle gleaming in the dim light, an eerie circle of his unsettling dolls encircling him, their glassy eyes fixed intently upon us.

"It's time to indulge in some recreation," Kel declared with a malicious grin, his voice laden with malevolence.

The utopia we entered stood in stark contrast to the chaos and devastation that awaited us outside. Abundant greenery, with lush plants and trees, imbued the surroundings with a serene ambiance. Graceful fountains sprayed water in intricate, choreographed patterns, and the air was redolent with the sweet aroma of blossoming flowers. It was a surreal spectacle amidst the apocalyptic setting.

"This is utterly surreal," Halle exclaimed, her voice betraying her astonishment at the beauty that enveloped us.

"Kel must have fashioned this as his own perverted paradise," I remarked, my voice tinged with disgust. "Yet, we're not here to marvel at his landscaping prowess. Our purpose is to thwart his schemes."

We advanced cautiously through the atrium, our watchful eyes scanning for any hint of movement. The silence hung heavy, broken only by the gentle, melodic sounds of flowing water. It was an eerie stillness, the calm preceding the tempest.

As we ventured deeper into the atrium, a voice resonated through the expanse. "Ah, my cherished guests, you've at last graced us with your presence."

We turned to find Kel now standing on a balcony that overlooked the atrium. He was clad in his typical Victorian attire that was completely out of fashion, his monocle gleaming in the soft ambient light.

"Fancy stumbling upon you here," Trey muttered, his hand inching toward his holstered gun.

Kel chuckled sinisterly. "Did you truly believe you could outsmart me? My dear friends, you underestimate my cunning."

"We haven't come to partake in your twisted amusements, Kel," Felix declared, his voice resolute.

"Oh, but you have," Kel retorted with a malevolent grin. "You see, I've arranged a little test for you all—a challenge that will assess your abilities, your intellect, and your determination. If you succeed, perhaps I'll reconsider the fate of this city and my... creations."

"What sort of challenge are you talking about?" I demanded, my curiosity tinged with apprehension.

"All in good time," Kel replied cryptically. "But first, let's see how you fare in a warm-up exercise."

As if responding to an ominous cue, the ground beneath us began to tremble, and from the shadowy corners of the atrium, a horde of zombies emerged, their vacant eyes locked onto us. It was unmistakable that Kel intended to assess our capabilities in the most perilous manner imaginable. The battle was now upon us.

The zombies inched forward, their deliberate and sluggish approach sending shivers down our spines. Despite being outnumbered, our resolve remained unshaken. The group swiftly prepared their weapons, while Lily harnessed her powers to conjure small gusts of wind, attempting to push the encroaching undead back.

"Let's face this head-on," I declared, my heart racing as we braced ourselves for the impending clash.

The battle raged on, each swing of a weapon, every surge of magic, and each precise shot fired held critical significance. We moved with synchronized precision, diligently safeguarding each other's backs. Amidst the perilous fray, an inexplicable camaraderie emerged, a shared purpose that bound us together.

"Look out!" Isabelle's cry pierced the chaos as a zombie lunged toward Felix. He narrowly evaded the attack, but the zombie persisted in its assault. Before anyone could react, a searing burst of flames consumed the undead creature, reducing it to smoldering ashes. Lily stood there, her eyes aglow with the fiery intensity of her power.

"Well done," Trey commended her with a grin, acknowledging her impressive display of magic.

We battled fiercely, repelling the relentless zombie onslaught, but it felt like an unending tide, and exhaustion was beginning to take its toll. "We must devise a strategy!" I shouted above the tumult.

Felix's gaze darted about and locked onto an ornate water fountain nearby. "Lily, can you freeze the water?"

She nodded, and with a deft flourish of her hands, she solidified the water within the fountain, erecting an icy barricade. We skillfully lured the zombies toward the frozen fountain, and when they drew near, I employed my powers to shatter the ice. The shattered fragments turned into razor-sharp projectiles, effectively incapacitating the approaching undead.

"That should grant us a moment's respite," Felix remarked, his breaths coming in heavy pants.

"But it won't hold them at bay indefinitely," Halle cautioned.

Amidst the momentary respite, the snarls and growls of the undead swelled in volume, and we exchanged apprehensive looks. The cacophony emanated from the expansive, opulent atrium below us. Peering over the precipice, our gravest fears were realized: a relentless horde of zombies had breached the indoor paradise, weaving their way through the lush walkways and ornate gardens.

"How on earth did they manage to infiltrate this place?" Trey muttered, his grip on his weapon tensing with unease.

"Kel's reach must extend even into this meticulously safeguarded refuge," Felix responded with a grim tone.

Isabelle implored, "We can't linger here. We must locate an escape route."

"But how?" Halle questioned, her perplexity mirrored by us all. "This place is a labyrinth."

Lily scanned the surroundings, her expression pensive. "I can create a diversion. By manipulating the elements with my powers,

I might be able to distract the zombies long enough for us to find an exit."

"Alright, Lily, proceed with your plan," I affirmed, endorsing her strategy. "The rest of us will attempt to navigate the maze of walkways in search of an exit. Stay together and remain vigilant."

Lily closed her eyes in deep concentration, and the very air surrounding us underwent a transformation. Suddenly, gusts of wind materialized, swirling and whirling around the zombies, causing them to stagger and collide with one another. This artful diversion granted us the precious opportunity to slip away, commencing our treacherous journey through the intricate passages.

The maze proved every bit as intricate as anticipated, with labyrinthine twists and turns drawing us deeper into the heart of the Utopia. The unsettling silence was punctuated solely by the sporadic shuffling of the undead horde below. Any noise from us could prove fatal, and so we moved with utmost caution, fully cognizant that our very survival hung in the balance.

After what felt like an interminable ordeal, our eyes fell upon a glass door that beckoned to us, leading to a balcony that overlooked the open night sky. It was our means of escape, a glimmer of hope amid the zombie-infested nightmare that ensnared us. However, as we advanced toward the door, a sinister figure emerged from the shadows, obstructing our path.

It was Kel.

He wore a malevolent smirk, his violet eyes glittering with malice. "Departing so prematurely? You've hardly had the chance to savor my paradise."

"We haven't come here to indulge in your twisted fantasies," I retorted, my hand firmly gripping my weapon.

Kel's laughter sent a shiver down our spines. "Ah, my dear, you misunderstood. This isn't merely my paradise; it's the manifestation of my power—the zombies, the turmoil, the dread... they all play a part in my magnificent plan."

"We're here to bring an end to your so-called magnificent plan," Felix asserted, his voice resolute.

Kel's countenance darkened. "Do you genuinely believe you can stop me? I am the puppeteer, and you are my puppets. Your destiny was sealed the moment you set foot in my realm."

Before any of us could react, Kel raised his hand, and the air crackled with an ominous surge of dark energy. We tightened our grips on our weapons, anticipating an imminent assault. However, just as we prepared to defend ourselves, an intense, blinding light engulfed us, and the ground beneath our feet quaked.

As the brilliance of the light gradually dimmed, we discovered ourselves in an entirely different realm. It was a sprawling, desolate landscape, dominated by gnarled trees and ominous, swirling clouds overhead. Standing before us, exuding a malevolent aura, was Kel, his power radiating like a palpable force.

"Welcome to my realm of amusement," he jeered, his voice dripping with malevolence. "Let's ascertain how skillful you are in navigating my nightmares."

This turn of events confirmed our suspicions: Kel was indeed the mastermind behind the zombie outbreak. Nevertheless, the challenges that lay ahead were far from surmounted. "We must reach Kel and terminate his schemes before he can enact whatever malevolent designs he harbors," I asserted to the group, my voice brimming with determination. "We cannot permit the zombie scourge to advance any further, nor can we permit Kel to further exploit these creatures for his twisted objectives. "Indeed, the Edge is vast," Isabelle mused aloud, voicing our collective dilemma. "Locating Kel within this twisted nightmare presents a formidable challenge."

"He's likely ensconced within a heavily fortified area," Felix postulated, his brows furrowed in contemplation. "A location that affords him control over the zombies and facilitates the execution of his experiments."

"That makes sense," Halle concurred. "He would require a central hub to remotely manipulate the zombies."

Trey, deep in thought, leaned against a nearby railing. "If I were in his shoes, I'd opt for a site that offers both strategic value and exceptional concealment. A place that's challenging to infiltrate and grants him a distinct advantage."

As our collective musings converged, we recognized the magnitude of the task before us: to uncover Kel's covert stronghold within the sprawling labyrinth of the Edge.

As we pressed onward, a figure with ominous, glowing violet eyes materialized from the shadows, revealing Kel himself. His appearance had taken on an even more unsettling aspect—tall, pallid, with inky-black hair and eyes that bore into your very soul. Clad in his dark out of fashion Victorian suit that seemed to meld seamlessly with the shadows, he exuded an aura of mystery and menace.

"You've somehow managed to locate your way back to me," Kel sneered, his voice oozing with arrogance. "I must confess, I didn't anticipate your unwavering persistence."

"We haven't returned for amusement, Kel," I countered, my hand poised on the hilt of the sword I had brought along. "Our objective is to thwart your plans and terminate this zombie epidemic."

Kel chuckled, the eerie sound causing a disconcerting shiver to course down my spine. "Do you genuinely believe you possess the capability to halt me? I hold dominion over the zombies, over this city, and soon, over the entire empire."

"Cease this pointless banter," Trey snapped, his firearm aimed squarely at Kel. "We haven't come to engage in negotiations. We've arrived to bring you to justice."

Kel's smile broadened, his self-assuredness remaining unshaken. "As you wish. Let's witness your mettle."

With those words, the battle was initiated. As I battled the relentless zombies, my attention remained fixed on Kel. With a mere wave of his hand, he commanded the undead, dictating their actions and orchestrating their attacks. It was painfully apparent that defeating him would prove a formidable challenge, necessitating our collective effort and a well-conceived strategy.

"Isabelle, seek a means to disrupt his dominion over the zombies!" I called out, deflecting an assault from a skeletal undead assailant.

Isabelle acknowledged my directive and concentrated her magic on countering Kel's control over the reanimated corpses. In the meantime, Felix and Trey expertly coordinated their attacks, dispatching the zombies with meticulous precision. Lily and Elliot pooled their magical prowess to erect a protective barrier, shielding our group from the relentless assaults of the recently resurrected zombies.

The battle raged on, an intense struggle with the highest stakes. With adrenaline coursing through my veins, I harnessed every ounce of my fire-based magic. Concentrating my energy, I unleashed a searing burst of flames directly at one of the Wendigo's who joined Kel's assault unit as it grab me by its claws. The creature emitted a spine-chilling screech as the fire enveloped it. Its hold on me waned, and I stumbled backward, breaking free, while the Wendigo convulsed and thrashed in agonizing torment.

The acrid scent of burning flesh permeated the air as the Wendigo's corporeal form transformed into ash. Its eerie, fading screeches were gradually muffled until they ceased altogether. I stood there, panting heavily, as I witnessed the remnants of the creature disintegrate into nothingness. My heart raced, the pain from its claws still acute, though adrenaline managed to numb much of it for the moment.

Once that battle was over Felix, Trey, Lily, Elliot, Isabelle, Halle and I gathered, each of us taking stock of the situation and preparing for the imminent next phase of the battle. Our unity was paramount as we geared up to confront Kel and bring an end to his reign of terror. The ultimate showdown had commenced, and the destinies of the city—perhaps even the Empire—teetered precariously in the balance.

Felix rubbed his chin, lost in thought for a moment. "There's another library in the Edge, not too distant from our current location. It's reputed to house ancient texts and scrolls containing potent magic spells. If we can make our way there, we might uncover a spell capable of aiding us in defeating Kel and his zombie legion."

"That shall be our course of action," I affirmed, my determination reignited. "Our destination is the library, where we will locate that fire spell. However, we must exercise vigilance; Kel could be concealed anywhere, and he is not without allies." The gravity of our mission was unmistakable, and the imperative of time weighed heavily upon us.

Chapter Forty-Four

The library lay cloaked in darkness, a void devoid of life. Its sole source of illumination: a solitary candle, its feeble flame whispering secrets to the shadows, hinting at the presence of others.

"Who's there?" a voice, trembling with curiosity, called out from behind the weathered desk.

Drawing nearer, my gaze met a boy of kindred years, his silhouette framed by the faint candlelight. He stood, a figure of contrasts, his short stature accentuated by the unusual combination of white-blond hair, streaked ominously with inky black, and large, round glasses that concealed eyes of striking azure brilliance. An uneasy chill settled as I beheld a raven perched on his left shoulder, the bird's midnight plumage drawing focus amidst the flickering candle's glow.

"Who are you?" the boy queried, the curiosity in his voice only matched by the peculiarity of his attire—a garb of black trousers and a long-sleeved brown shirt.

"Are you like me?" he inquired, his voice carrying a hint of uncertainty. His question left me momentarily puzzled.

"Are you a Halfling?" I cautiously countered, seeking clarity. In response, he nodded affirmatively, his introduction offering some semblance of his identity. "Yes, my name is Daniel Ravenswing," he began, voice quivering with the raw emotions of recent events. "I got separated from my family when the zombies invaded the Edge. I was so scared; Stephen and I had to hide under the checkout desk. There was so much screaming; I didn't know what to do," Daniel said, his words punctuated by intermittent sobs.

"Poor kid, he's traumatized," Felix murmured sympathetically, shaking his head.

"You must think I'm a coward, don't you?" Daniel asked with a bitter edge to his tone, his self-doubt hanging heavy in the air.

I reached out to console him, placing a reassuring hand on his shoulder. "You've done nothing wrong," I assured him gently. "You got scared and didn't know what to do."

My words brought a hint of relief to his face, a fragile smile breaking through the shadows of his recent ordeal. "Thanks," Daniel replied, his voice softer, eyes reflecting the concern he had for his mother. "I'm glad my mother isn't here. Otherwise, she would have lectured the hell out of me. She must be wondering if I'm dead or alive while the evacuations to the bunkers were taking place."

"DANIEL, do you know where the sacred records are?" I inquired, my voice carrying a sense of urgency.

His inquisitive gaze met mine. "Why do you want to go there?" he questioned, curiosity intertwining with concern.

I replied firmly, "It's simple—to gather more information about the group responsible for releasing the zombies in the first place."

It was then that I felt the raven perched on my shoulder, its presence a silent, vigilant sentinel. I sensed its small head lean against my temple, a subtle reassurance of the unspoken connection we shared.

"Well, if Stephen trusts you, so will I," Daniel declared, a newfound determination in his voice. "I'm not sure where to go, but I think I know who would be willing to help with gathering the information that's off-limits."

The gang and I trailed behind Daniel, ascending the grand spiral staircase that stood as the linchpin connecting the numerous floors of the archives. Our journey concluded at the uppermost landing, where Daniel guided us into a narrow corridor, its terminus marked by a massive stone door.

"This is where the guardian spirit is housed," Daniel explained, deftly inserting a skeleton key into the aged lock. As the door creaked open, a billowing cascade of dust greeted us, testament to the passage of many dormant years.

Halle extended a small flashlight, our singular source of illumination, and the narrow beam unveiled a spacious chamber. Daniel, with a sense of purpose, chose the central door, leading us into a room reminiscent of a chapel. It boasted towering stained glass windows, enveloping the three-tiered dais in a soft, ethereal glow.

It was unmistakable that this place had been meticulously maintained.

"What is this place?" I inquired, my curiosity piqued by the reverent atmosphere.

"It's a shrine used to summon the familiars of the divine," Daniel explained, shedding light on the chamber's purpose.

And, just when I thought things couldn't become any more otherworldly, a diminutive, shadowy figure darted into the shrine. The soft clicks of its talon-clad claws resounded as it alighted gracefully. A sense of enchantment enveloped me as I beheld the tiny creature—a magnificent owl.

Its wings and body were cloaked in pristine, snow-white feathers adorned with delicate streaks of charcoal, while its bright gold eyes regarded us with inquisitive wisdom.

"Who dares enter this shrine?" the owl familiar demanded, its voice carrying an air of authority. "What do you all want?"

With unwavering resolve, I stepped forward to explain, "You may not be aware of the turmoil unfolding outside, but both the Edge and the central city of the Central Park District are under siege by a Plague Doctors who goes by the name Kel Mather."

At the utterance of that name, "Kel," the owl familiar let out a snarl of disdain. "I should have known he would be the one to instigate this full-scale assault."

"You know who he is?" Felix inquired, a hint of surprise in his voice.

"Yes," the owl familiar replied, a touch of resignation in his tone. "This wouldn't be the first time he tried to destroy the Empire. I take it using the colonists who had a hand in the murders of the late Empress Safia and Crown Prince Alexander wasn't enough for him."

A sudden realization dawned upon me. "You know what the Plague Doctors are, don't you?" I exclaimed. "You're the one we've been searching for."

"Umm…not to rain on your parade, Adelice, but how in the world is this familiar what we're looking for?" Elliot inquired, his skepticism evident.

I offered an explanation, "Think about it; owls are associated with Athena, the Greek Goddess of Wisdom."

"It's clear that the record about Kel and the other Plague Doctors isn't on a piece of paper, but rather resides within a creature that has witnessed it all. Isn't that right?" I queried, an air of certainty in my voice.

The owl familiar nodded. "Yes, I know what the Plague Doctors are. You all might want to gather 'round, for this is a tale I've safeguarded for centuries." His words carried the weight of history, a narrative that held the promise of being invaluable in the uncertain times that lay ahead—when other groups would have to confront a Plague Doctors who would rise as one sibling fell.

Chapter Forty-Five

"'The plague Doctors," the familiar began, addressing our small gathering, "are a faction of extremist drainers who harbor an intense hatred for humanity. It is this profound animosity that has brought war, famine, death, and disease upon the world." The gravity of the situation hung heavily in the air.

"Long ago, they were considered a classification of gods and spirits within the Persian Pantheon," I continued, "but, much like the evolution of many later religions, they were subsequently degraded into entities now referred to as demons. Today, they are known as drainers."

"These malevolent beings," the owl further explained, "originated from the deity Angra Mainyu, a creature of darkness and a relentless destroyer of the divine. It is his malevolence that has cast death and disease among humans, and ushered in the ever-changing seasons, ranging from the harsh frost of winter to the searing heat of summer."

As time passed, Angra Mainyu, recognizing the formidable nature of his task, came to a sobering realization that he could not singlehandedly orchestrate the downfall of humanity. To bolster his efforts, he performed a dark ritual using seven drops of his own blood, an unholy creation myth that gave rise to seven beings he would come to regard as his malevolent offspring.

The first and eldest of these Plague Doctors is Aesma, a drainer whose influence fans the flames of dark emotions—lust, anger, and vengeance. She exists as a living embodiment of war, violence, and conflict.

The second to be born from this unholy bloodline is Aka Manah, a drainer who personifies lustful desire, feeding on the darkest yearnings of the human heart.

The third in line is Ingra, a Plague Doctor who embodies apostasy, sowing the seeds of rebellion and betrayal in the hearts of those she touches.

And the fourth is Nanghaithya, who personifies discontentment, fanning the flames of insatiable craving and dissatisfaction that can consume humanity.

Next in this lineage, we have the two sisters: Tawrich, the embodiment of hunger, and Zarich, the personification of aging, their sinister influence preying upon humanity's most primal needs and the relentless march of time.

Following them is Saurva, the Plague Doctors who has the power to leave his victims utterly defenseless, his malevolence creating vulnerability in those who cross his path. And, last but far from the least, there's Kel Mather, the enigmatic force orchestrating the chaos and suffering we now face.

As the gravity of this revelation settled upon us, the room fell into a heavy silence. The weight of the knowledge that the reason I and other Halflings were brought into existence was to find the sources of magic needed to confront a specific Plague Doctors, in this case, Kel Mather, was staggering.

"So, to defeat Kel and ultimately destroy him," I finally articulated, "we must gather all the living incarnations of the tarot. But I still don't know what will happen once all the artifacts of the court cards are assembled in one place." Uncertainty mingled with determination as we grappled with the enormity of our newfound mission.

Despite the dire circumstances that loomed over the gang and me, it was imperative that we continued to press forward in our quest to thwart Kel's nefarious plans and save the Central Park District. I had unearthed fragments of history that hinted at the district's past grandeur, once a jewel among the Empire's provinces, a realm of opulence and lavish living.

Here I stood, just beyond the chapel, still plagued by the enigma of my past, a jigsaw puzzle missing pieces. My true identity remained veiled behind a shroud of forgotten memories, and the faces of my parents, obscured by the fog that clouded my mind, were inscrutable. My only certainty lay in the knowledge derived from my tarot deck—I was a being divided, part flawed and part perfect.

Returning to this place I had once fled from felt surreal, an echo of a life I had sought to escape. The sole marked difference was the desolation that now engulfed the Edge, a place once teeming with life. This desolation made me ponder the path not taken. What might have transpired had I not vanished into the forest, had I boarded that limousine with Kathy Ann?

I nodded, shaking off the futile musings of "what if," for they offered no solace. As cruel as it may seem, I had to confront the consequences of my past decisions head-on.

I was well aware of the peril associated with venturing into the archives alone, delving into relics of a world that existed before the creation of the islands. The archive predominantly housed books and films—material that I was typically discerning about when it came to what I read or watched. Still, some things within this trove of knowledge had the power to captivate me.

I couldn't help but wonder about the life that had thrived before the monumental changes swept through our world. The reverence with which these artifacts were held compelled me to resist reaching out to touch them, as if they might be sacred relics.

A voice broke through my contemplation, startling me. "What on earth are you doing here alone?" I looked up and recognized Daniel. Stephen perched on his shoulder, vigilant and watchful.

"I'm looking for something," I admitted, my voice tinged with a touch of vulnerability, "something that might help me remember who I was before."

"You mean—"

"Yes," I affirmed, understanding that it didn't take someone like Daniel long to discern my struggle with memory loss. There was an inscrutable quality about him, one I couldn't quite put my finger on.

I decided to veer the conversation onto a different path. "So, why did you name your raven, Stephen?" I asked, steering the dialogue in a new direction.

Daniel shrugged, an easygoing demeanor masking the complexity of his history. "I didn't," he confessed. "Stephen's been in my family for as long as I can remember. It was my grandad's idea to name him after this famous horror novelist from the time before the Great Change happened. Trust me when I tell you that Stephen's namesake has penned an abundance of books."

His tone hinted at the vast volume of the author's works. "So many," Daniel continued, "that it's a challenge to keep track of them all. You can imagine my shock when I learned that some of them had been adapted into movies."

"It must have been quite a surprise for you," I remarked, empathizing with his unexpected discovery.

Daniel let out a sigh. "You have no idea. So far, my favorite is 'The Shining.' I've never quite grasped why it's so terrifying. I guess I need to watch it during the evening hours to get the full horror experience." Laughter shared between us served as a momentary reprieve from the weight of our circumstances.

Yet, behind the humor, I could see the undercurrent of sadness in Daniel's brilliant blue eyes. "We'll find them, I promise," I reassured him.

"I know my family isn't gone," Daniel murmured, his gaze locking onto mine. "Are you familiar with the story of El Silbon?"

"Who is that?" I asked, slightly bewildered. It appeared that I wasn't the only one capable of swiftly changing the subject. "No, I haven't," I replied, curious about the new direction our conversation was taking.

Daniel began to weave a story, one that carried with it the flavor of his maternal grandmother's heritage, a connection to a Colombia long before the Empire's creation, where folklore and tales of the supernatural held a powerful sway. He referred to a tale known as El Silbón, the Whistling Man.

"Many years ago," he narrated, "there lived a boy who was spoiled rotten by his parents; they couldn't bring themselves to say no to his demands. One fateful day, he and his father ventured into the woods in pursuit of deer, but their hunt proved fruitless. Enraged by their failure, the boy committed a heinous act, killing his own father and eviscerating him, demanding his mother cook the entrails.

In the wake of this terrible crime, his grandfather, infuriated by the atrocity his grandson had unleashed, administered a severe punishment. He lashed the boy's back with his fury and bound him to an eternal curse—to carry a sack on his back, containing his father's bones and those of others unfortunate enough to cross his path, condemning him to wander the earth for all of eternity."

"Why share this story with me?" I questioned.

Daniel's response was laden with a sense of understanding. "It's one of the few stories that help me maintain my sanity, especially when you've been alone for hours, accompanied only by the family's familiar."

I nodded, my heart resonating with his sentiment. The sensation of isolation, with no one to share your thoughts and experiences, can be profoundly disorienting. It was this very sensation that had stayed with me from my time in the forest, running from a nameless fear. It had been the driving force behind my decision to escape my home, away from parents whose faces had blurred into obscurity due to the veil of forgotten memories.

I had reached a point where I no longer yearned to discover the family I had left behind. The specter of the past loomed, and for all I knew, they might have been the very ones I had fled from. In my second foray into the forest, I found a different kind of family—Felix, Trey, Halle, Elliot, Isabelle, and Lily. It was becoming increasingly apparent to me that family wasn't solely defined by blood; it was a tapestry woven from the bonds we shared. Through the connections we had forged, each of us had found purpose in the quest to locate all the living incarnations of the tarot.

The events of the Scavenger had introduced me to yet more individuals, forging new bonds: Aaron, Rae, Jared, and Emma. The four of them had been bound by the same purpose, set on a collision course with an adversary intent on dismantling the future we aspired to create—a future where we were not regarded as the property of the nobility, but rather as architects of our own destiny.

"So, what are you going to do about Kel?" Daniel inquired, his curiosity mirrored in the eyes that regarded me with a sense of resolve. "Find him and stop him," I replied, for this was the purpose Fate had bestowed upon my friends and me.

Chapter Forty-Six

In the depths of the night, we ventured toward one of the Edge's exclusive zones, a haunt frequented by the Elite's wives. Our path was obscured by an impenetrable darkness, the only flicker of illumination emanating from the flashlights clasped in our palms. Not a whisper of life stirred in this freshly abandoned territory, casting shadows of dread, a gnawing anxiety that a zombie or Wendigo might leap forth to seize us.

Within the wives' lounge, the sole splashes of color arrived courtesy of the furniture, a faded dusty rose, and the walls and floors dressed in rose gold marble. In my heart, I clung to the hope that others, like us, had yet to seek refuge in the bunkers, but the isolation gnawed at my soul, an insidious weight upon my shoulders.

"What exactly are we doing here?" Lily inquired, her voice trembling with uncertainty.

Isabelle cast a thoughtful gaze across the pink-infused lounge. "If I had to guess," she mused, "this is where the wives usually gather and socialize. It's all quite...pink, isn't it?"

As if life couldn't grow any more nightmarish, a slow, mocking applause echoed from the balcony above. My eyes climbed upward to behold Kel, a smug and arrogant smirk etched upon his face, while the malicious gleam in his violet eyes sent shivers down my spine. His pupils transformed from circular to menacing slits as he drawled, "Bravo. I've been waiting for your little escape act, my dear brats. It takes real guts to break free from my underground facility, where my artificial zombie army slumbers."

So, he remained oblivious to the fact that Shadow had aided our escape, I mused silently.

"We know what you are!" I called out, capturing his immediate attention. His response was laced with a warning tone, an unmistakable sign that challenging Kel was not a wise endeavor.

In this moment of vulnerability, I seized the opportunity to strike at his most sensitive nerve. "We've unraveled the truth, Kel," I declared, "about you and your siblings, the black sheep of a once-divine pantheon, transformed into demons. Why were you all kept hidden?" Kel responded with a dismissive shrug. "How should I know? The other gods cast us aside as though we were nothing."

"They sentenced us to roam the earth for all eternity, forsaken, while their legacy thrives through the descendants who dub themselves the Orita. That's why my siblings and I engineered the Dome Colonies, a means to exact our revenge on the bloodlines of the gods who cast us into the realm of mortals," Kel revealed, his words sending a chill down my spine. The revelation left me dumbfounded. The Orita, descendants of the old gods, were the catalyst behind the emergence of the Dome Colonies?

Kel's bitterness seeped into his voice as he continued, "The magic you wield is a potent weapon. It can be harnessed for good or evil, depending on the path you choose. But your kind can tap into both black and white magic without consequences. It's revolting! There can be no shades of gray in this world!"

The gravity of the situation dawned upon me. Kel was not to be trifled with; he harbored a deep-seated desire to obliterate the legacy of our divine ancestors. A burning determination.

Recalling the times when it was just Felix and me, deep in the wilderness, he had shared the basic history of the Empire's monarchy: the Emperor, the sovereign, and the Empress Consort, chosen to bear the heir to the throne.

The royal court nestled within the Starlight District, its central city crafted from platinum steel and azure glass, adorned with golden domes and silver spires.

"How can you harbor such hatred?" Felix demanded. "The colonies would've imprisoned us had we chosen their path. You can't blame us or our ancestors for seeking freedom."

"What do you know about freedom?" Kel retorted with fiery intensity, to which Felix replied, "More than you might think."

A shiver danced down my spine as Kel's violet eyes settled upon me. I harbored an uneasy feeling about the direction this was taking. "I'm offering you the opportunity to discover a spell that could obliterate all the zombies I've artificially created," Kel proposed. "But you can only undertake this task without the assistance of your companions."

Though I yearned to trust him, a nagging intuition warned me that Kel had something sinister up his sleeve. "I accept your challenge," I declared with a resolute tone. "Very well, as a reward, I'll lift the veil shrouding your memories," Kel responded. I couldn't help but scoff. "To be honest, I no longer require them. I have no intention of ever returning to the family I was born into."

"We'll see," Kel responded in a sing-song voice. As we stood amid the tense silence, Felix leaned in, whispering softly to me to ensure the drainer couldn't overhear our conversation. "Are you absolutely certain about this, Adelice?"

My determination unwavering, I whispered back, "I have to do it; it's our sole opportunity to uncover the spell and rescue the city. I don't intend to make any deals with Kel."

Felix's next question struck a nerve, but I had already made my choice. "I don't need a high IQ to piece it together, but are you really prepared to go through this alone?"

The query stung, yet I stood firm. "All I'm asking is for your trust. Do you trust me?" Felix's response was tinged with worry, "Yes, but promise me you'll return promptly?"

I understood the unspoken plea in Felix's words: "Don't let Kel claim victory, and don't let him see you lose this game." To Kel, this was all a game, a heartless manipulation of pawns without empathy or compassion.

"You've got a few hours to locate the spell. Don't waste them," Kel cautioned. I responded with a determined nod, refusing to let him glimpse my fear. I had a clear destination in mind, and I headed toward the gondola that would ferry me to the building of the company that had pursued me relentlessly from the beginning: Marvelous Radiance.

Revisiting the Edge meant stepping back into Gray's lion's den, but the comfort lay in the fact that there were no purebloods in sight to capture me. My gaze dropped to the little tuxedo kitten standing beside me on the passenger seat of the gondola.

Kel had forbidden me from bringing Felix and the others, but he hadn't stipulated anything regarding a companion with four legs. While my trust in Shadow was minimal, he represented my best chance of discovering the spell to eradicate the horde of zombies overrunning the Central Park District.

Chapter Forty-Seven

My initial impression of Marvelous Radiance was of an immaculate lobby, where everything gleamed in stark white, devoid of even a speck of dirt. It left me wondering if Gray had an aversion to germs or if the cleaning crews here were exceptionally meticulous in their work.

"How can you be certain that the spell you're seeking is within these walls?" Shadow inquired, a hint of doubt in his voice.

I replied, "I'm not certain, but something tells me this is the place I need to be." Shadow gave a small nod of understanding.

"Then you're on the right track," the tuxedo kitten assured me. "I hope so too, cat," I said, gently lifting Shadow and cradling him in my arms. His fur was warm and soft as I advanced through the doorway leading away from the pristine lobby. The room on the other side revealed itself as an art gallery, adorned with paintings and photographs gracing the walls, while statues occupied most of the floor space.

In a corner of the gallery, I stumbled upon a small library tucked away, its book spines displaying a different spectrum of colors. My gaze fixated on the warm hues of the titles. With no clear direction, I reached for a book with a brilliant red spine and declared, "This must be the right one," setting it gently on the glass coffee table. Within those pages, I hoped to uncover the essential components of the vanquishing spell.

Shadow, ever the inquisitive companion, asked, "What leads you to think that?"

"Fire," I began, "is more than just destruction; it's a wellspring of inspiration, a source of light, progress, and innovation." His curiosity piqued, Shadow urged me to elaborate, asking, "What makes you say that?"

"Progress," I explained, "is about enhancing and simplifying life, achieving results. The real journey lies in how we get there and what, or who, guides us. Then, there's the exploration of magic and technology."

"How do they fit into all of this?" Shadow probed, his curiosity undiminished.

I contemplated the question for a moment before responding, "They don't strictly adhere to either good or evil. We all possess the capacity for both. Purebloods, in particular, can either willingly choose to align with the light or the dark. For some, their decisions are matters of personal choice. However, there are others for whom the choice is not their own to make; it lies in the hands of the Committee."

"What about your kind? What role do you play in this divided society?" Shadow continued to seek answers.

"The term 'Halfling' refers to our mixed heritage: human, magic-user, immortal, and supernatural blood," I explained. "But I'm beginning to grasp that it goes deeper. It's about our parents, with one aligning with the dark and the other with the light."

"How does this connect to your current predicament?" Shadow asked.

"It's dawning on me that the reason we're called 'grey beings' is our unique ability to wield both light and dark magic without facing the usual consequences that accompany siding with one or the other," I replied. "Have you been aware of this?"

"No, but my sister and I have harbored suspicions for a while," Shadow responded. "Why else would the Elite resort to branding to claim you? Now, you understand the true essence of being in the Grey Zone; neither black nor white magic can harm or kill you."

This revelation gave me pause for thought. "If what you're saying holds true, then only someone from the Grey Zone, like me, can stand a chance against Kel and the other Plague Doctors."

Shadow's eyes sparkled with delight as he affirmed, "I knew you'd piece it together."

I carefully tore out the page containing the fire spell, stowing it in my jeans pocket. Curiosity still lingered, and I couldn't help but ask, "Why did you hide from Kel?"

Shadow replied with a hint of mischief, "Well, let's just say Kel and his kind aren't too fond of our kind."

"Is it because you're a spirit?" I inquired.

"No," Shadow explained, "he just doesn't like cats, and the same goes for his siblings." I burst into laughter, finding it rather amusing that a drainer who had once been a divine being harbored a strong aversion to and fear of cats. At least I had a backup weapon should I confront him again. As I made my way through the rooms of the gallery, a strange sensation gripped me — a feeling that I had been here before.

A throbbing ache ignited in my head as the eerie sounds of giggling reached my ears. My breath caught as I beheld the shadowy form of a ballerina, gracefully leaping within the beams of light cast upon the walls. Shadow, too, began to hiss, confirming that I wasn't hallucinating; what I saw was real, firmly anchored in the waking world.

"You're not hallucinating, Adelice," Shadow reassured me. "What you're witnessing is real. It's a ghost fragment, an energy imprint of a living person."

"A ghost?" I exclaimed.

Shadow clarified, "No, a ghost is someone who has passed on. This entity is a living fragment of a person's soul, although the person is very much alive."

Realization hit me like a lightning bolt. "I know whose energy this belongs to," I declared, striding toward the room where the shadowy ballerina had vanished. The truth unfolded before me, and I found myself face-to-face with a painting of Claire Masterson, the same image my friends and I had discovered in the hidden room within Gray's office, now preserved beneath a frosty layer of glass.

"Do you know who the woman in the painting is?" Shadow inquired.

I nodded slowly. "Not really, but I know exactly who she is; her name is Claire. She's Dorian Gray's wife. I'm starting to understand why he's so desperate to capture me, not only to cure his wife's depression but also to restore her soul."

"Is that why you're so determined to escape from him? Because you refuse to help him save the love of his life?" Shadow asked.

I sighed, attempting to convey the complexity of the situation. "It's not just that. He wants to use me as a replacement to help fill the void left by their child, who has either gone missing or is already dead. So, how do I rid myself of this?"

Shadow replied, "The only way to break free from the paranormal energy enveloping you is to confront its source. In your case, it's the portrait of Claire Gray."

"How do I go about it?" I inquired, ready to confront the source of this paranormal energy.

Shadow offered guidance, saying, "When you touch the painting, it absorbs all of its energy by immersing you in its past memories."

"Seems straightforward enough. It'll be my ticket to freedom," I replied.

Shadow pressed further, "You don't seem to hold much fondness for Claire, do you?"

I shook my head, "No, it's not that I dislike her. She hasn't harmed me in any way. Her husband is the one who's driven by a desperate desire to save her. I can't alleviate her depression, but I can help restore her soul. Here goes nothing." Determined, I touched the glass covering the painting with both hands, wincing at the cold sensation it sent through me. "Release," I whispered, and the entire sheet of glass vanished into thin air. Now, all that remained was the oil-textured surface of the painting as my mind began to soak up its memories. It wasn't long before I felt myself slipping into unconsciousness.

Top of Form

Chapter Forty-Eight

The world around me erupted in brilliant, blinding light, and it felt as if my eyes were on the verge of being seared. It wasn't unexpected, given that Claire Gray was a pureblood who had chosen to align with the light. In every direction I looked, everything, from the trees to the serene lake and the opulent mansion, bathed in a delicate pastel hue. I had entered the memory etched onto the painting—or perhaps I had ventured into Claire's very mind. Uncertain of my surroundings, I was determined to uncover my path in this spring-like realm that resembled something plucked from a Hallmark Greeting card.

"Dorian, where are we going?" a voice, angelic and full of bewilderment, inquired.

"It's a surprise, my darling," another voice teased, sending a shiver down my spine. I saw that the second voice belonged to Gray. "It's just a memory; he can't harm you," I reassured myself. I observed the two figures as they ventured into the forest, enveloped by the shadows that emanated from the surrounding trees. They made their way to a cottage nestled amidst the dense woods. It seemed to be their secret retreat. Claire, with her pale blonde curls and blue-violet eyes, appeared just as I had seen in the painting. She wore a long-sleeved, medieval-styled gown crafted from pale pink brocade, resembling a princess plucked from the pages of a fairy tale.

Gray, in this memory, appeared largely the same, save for shaggy, slightly shorter ink-black hair. Instead of a monocle, he donned half-moon spectacles perched on the bridge of his nose. He wore a dark leather coat over a violet shirt and black pants. The ever-present gloves on his hands remained a mystery.

As they reached the other side of the cottage, Claire, her curiosity piqued, asked, "What is it that you wanted to show me?" Gray's smile was enigmatic as he responded, "Allow me to introduce you to my masterpiece. I've spent weeks working on this painting, and I wanted you to be the first to see it." Claire gasped in awe, her eyes fixed on the canvas. "It's as though I'm gazing into a mirror," she whispered. "You've captured every detail, from the rose in my hair to my butterfly pendant, and you've even painted my swan. Is this why you invited me to your estate?"

"I won't deny it," Gray admitted, his voice sincere, "nor do I deny that you, young lady, have become a true muse for my art."

"More?" Claire inquired, clearly astounded. "Are you telling me there are other paintings of me?" Her naivety was somewhat startling to me. How could she not have known that he had been watching her throughout her formative years?

"Yes," Gray acknowledged, his tone smooth, though I sensed the sarcasm in it. "There are more paintings of you. Please, don't be upset. I couldn't help myself. You embody all that is good in the world, and I couldn't resist capturing your essence in your element."

Claire pressed further, her composure masking a hint of annoyance at the revelation of being semi-stalked by this peculiar artist for years. Gray sighed and confessed, "If there's one thing I can't hide from you, it's that I'd relinquish everything, even my title, just to cherish you for all eternity. Claire Masterson, I love you. I've loved you from the moment I first laid eyes on you all those years ago. I understand that you don't wish to see me again, but know that my heart belongs solely to you."

Claire appeared startled but maintained her composed demeanor.

"Thank you, Dorian, for your honesty. No man has ever given me his heart, and it would be imprudent to deny that I love you as well," Claire admitted, her voice tender.

"I will serve you faithfully for all eternity, my lady," Gray whispered, his eyes closing as he leaned in to kiss Claire, who responded with a passionate kiss of her own.

This revelation brought yet another layer of complexity to their relationship. Gray's love for Claire was unyielding, to the point where he had captured me, seemingly to shield her from the torment that had gripped her heart and soul. I found myself torn between the urge to flee and the instinct to surrender. While I couldn't cure Claire's depression, I held the power to mend her fractured soul. Without hesitation, I shut my eyes and returned to the waking world.

The first thing that met my gaze upon returning was the immense golden eyes of Shadow, peering directly into the depths of my soul.

"So, how did it go?" he inquired.

"Fine, but I believe I stayed there long enough," I replied, my body still trembling from the intensity of the memory. I had achieved my objective; it was time to reunite with Felix and the rest, my friends who had become my family.

Chapter Forty-Nine

Upon my return to the Wives' lounge, everyone remained in the same place. Kel sneered upon my arrival, but his disdain turned to visible discomfort when he noticed Shadow in my arms. The sight of the feline had clearly shaken him; it was apparent that the drainer harbored a fear of cats.

With the spell in my possession, it was time to escape from this perilous situation. I retrieved the torn page from my jeans pocket and began to chant the text. Kel demanded to know what I was doing, but I paid him no heed. "I call upon the element of fire to aid me in my defense!" I yelled, and small flames materialized out of thin air. I directed them toward Kel, who cried out in pain as the flames made contact with his worn jacket. Despite the physical agony he endured, I had a nagging feeling that it wouldn't be enough to keep him down for long. "Let's go, everyone!" I shouted, signaling for them to run.

They followed my lead, running as far away from the menacing drainer as possible. In the midst of our escape, zombies materialized out of thin air, and I unleashed the fire spell against them. I didn't spare a glance as each one succumbed to the flames and was reduced to ashes. With each step, we distanced ourselves from Kel, and the exhaustion from our frantic flight began to weigh on all of us.

"Now I see why the monster was afraid of fire," Felix whispered, eyeing the ashes strewn across the marble floor. His observation held truth—flames could reduce a corporeal being to nothing more than a pile of bones and ashes.

"Looks like the Elite will have to offer their maids some overtime when they finally emerge from their luxury bunkers," I quipped.

"I couldn't agree more," Lily chimed in, sharing a nod of understanding.

I turned my attention to the curly-haired triplet. "Kel didn't harm you or the others while I was away, did he?" I inquired, concerned that he might have done something dreadful during my absence.

Isabelle responded, "You weren't gone that long." Her observation took me by surprise. It had felt like hours to me, but I realized that time had a way of distorting in moments of intensity.

"At least you're all safe and unharmed; that's what matters," I acknowledged, relieved by their well-being.

"Kel may be a psycho, but he's not an idiot," Felix mused. "He must have figured out that our blood can serve as a potent poison, dangerous enough to be used as a weapon." This revelation shed new light on the fear that purebloods had for us; even a small drop of our blood could inflict pain akin to third-degree burns on a regular pureblood.

"We've lingered here long enough; we have zombies to vanquish, people!" Trey's booming voice broke the tension, prompting laughter from all of us, including Daniel, who had remained silent throughout the chase.

"You're absolutely right; let's go save the world," I declared with unwavering determination. It was a sentiment I never thought I'd utter, given that the world we inhabited hadn't been kind to us.

Here's something I learned about fire: it's not just a force of destruction but also one of creation. The warmth of flames has been what sustains both humanity and society throughout history. In a way, fire has played a significant role in shaping the progress of an ever-evolving community. It is from the flickering flames that people find hope.

Upon reaching one of the rooftops in the Edge, I initiated the chant for the spell, evoking a towering blaze that illuminated the night sky. The gang and I watched in awe as the fire spread across the island. It was a relief when Daniel informed me of a defense spell that would shield all the towns and villages encircling the central city from being consumed by the flames.

This brought a comforting sense of security, knowing that those who had sought refuge in bunkers or the library would have a place to return to once the night had passed.

Now, our sole remaining mission was to put an end to Kel, regardless of the time it might take. He had become the number one enemy of all Halflings, uniting us against a common threat.

"I never thought fire could be so beautiful," Felix remarked in awe.

"I completely agree," I replied. "I've come to realize that fire is not just a force of destruction; it also symbolizes hope for a brighter future filled with progress and innovation."

Felix laughed, and in that moment, we both knew that this was a night we would never forget.

After we had successfully vanquished all the zombies, we made our way to the large water fountain, surrounded by specialty shops and cafes, observing the dark and deserted surroundings. It seemed that once the night was over, everything would return to normal.

"This was the most incredible light show I've ever witnessed!" Elliot exclaimed with a beaming smile.

"At least we can finally rest easy, free from the threat of brain-seeking zombies," Isabelle remarked. Her joy was palpable, marking a rare moment of happiness since our escape from the Edge.

Just when it seemed that things were about to take a turn for the better, a slow clapping sound reached our ears. The source of the applause became apparent as I turned to see Kel on the other side of the fountain. An arrogant smirk adorned his face, while the violet gleam in his eyes betrayed the inhuman cruelty that lay within him.

"Well, isn't this a lovely gathering?" the drainer sneered in utter disgust. "All of you friends gathered in one place, how revolting. I must admit it was quite clever of you to use that fire spell to obliterate my zombie army. But, you seem to have forgotten one crucial detail: I'm the one calling the shots here! And what better way to teach you all a lesson than by taking away the one person you hold dear?"

My heart sank as he seized Felix's wrist. "No!" I shrieked, frantically trying to reach him but failing miserably. "I wouldn't advise doing that," Kel warned coldly. "I'm the one in control, and this game isn't over until someone is dead. But don't fret; I have big plans for the Frankenstein boy whose touch brings both life and death. Farewell!" I watched in despair as Kel dragged Felix into the shadows, vanishing into the unknown.

"Felix," I whimpered, collapsing to the cobblestone ground. Kel had snatched my best friend away from me, leaving a searing void in my heart. I could hardly believe the depths of my loathing for someone.

"We will find a way to get him back, Adelice," Halle consoled, kneeling beside me. "No matter what Kel has done, I doubt he would kill Felix. Alive, he holds more value than as a lifeless pawn."

I let out a weary sigh as I rose to my feet. "I hope you're right, Halle, but I have a nagging feeling that Kel won't stop until someone's life is taken."

Halle fixed me with a keen gaze. "So, what's your plan?"

"It's simple; I'm going to rescue Felix, no matter the cost. I know exactly where Kel has taken him."

"Let me guess, Marvelous Radiance?" Trey ventured.

"You got it," I confirmed with a determined nod.

Isabelle sighed, remarking, "Looks like we're heading back to the lion's den."

"No kidding, Sherlock," Lily retorted, earning a chuckle from the group.

"Man, Trey, you're a bad influence on all of us," Elliot chimed in.

Daniel laughed and shook his head, saying, "You guys are quite the bunch."

Following a brief gondola ride, we arrived at the pristine white lobby of Marvelous Radiance. To our misfortune, Kel awaited our arrival, his grip firm on Felix's wrist.

"Oh my, it seems we have some uninvited guests with the audacity to crash my evening," the drainer muttered, annoyance tainting his tone. His violet eyes zeroed in on me.

"Have you learned nothing from our last encounter, little girl? I'm the one who dictates how this game concludes. I've just about had it with you and your gang of misfits meddling in my plans. It appears you leave me with no choice but to discipline all of you."

Trey interrupted with a taunt, "Come on, man, at least have the decency to drop the illusion. That's not your real form."

I added, "What's Trey saying is right. This isn't how he truly looks. What you all see is an illusion concealing his true appearance. It's the kind of trick he uses to deceive his victims into a false sense of security."

The night had taken an increasingly bizarre turn, and I was determined not to back down. My resolve matched that of the others, and we were ready to confront whatever challenges lay ahead.

Chapter Fifty

"He's right," Kel declared with a malicious grin, "this isn't my true form. It's merely a glamour I employ to make myself more enticing to my victims." It was curious that the glamour didn't affect us completely – a fringe benefit of dwelling in the Grey Zone. However, as Kel began to peel away the illusion, things took a chilling turn.

The process was reminiscent of a snake shedding its skin, the old giving way to a new, enhanced version. A sense of dread washed over me as I witnessed Kel's true appearance. His skin was ghastly pale, with exposed, darkened blood vessels that resembled cracked porcelain. His ebony hair brought to mind the diluted, acrid coffee the others and I had sipped during our time on the run.

The once-bright violet hue of his eyes transformed into a deep and inky purple, resembling the color of a dark ink bottle. His pupils had elongated into reptilian slits, enhancing the inhumanity of his appearance. His nails, long, sharp, and jet black, seemed like menacing claws. Kel was garbed in a black and grey Victorian suit, adorned with a purple waistcoat featuring brass buttons. A matching top hat, accented with a raven feather, perched on the side of his head. He clutched a walking stick bearing maroon and forest green stripes, harmonizing with the leather dress shoes that adorned his feet. Pointed black sunglasses rested on the bridge of his nose.

"Ah, it's delightful to be back in my true form," Kel purred, exuding malevolence from his purple-black eyes.

His appearance resembled a nightmarish distortion of a Victorian gentleman, and Kel's words revealed the depth of his madness. His crazed smile was a clear indication of his insanity.

"I can't believe this is what he truly looks like," Halle remarked, her shudder reflecting her disgust.

Trey chimed in, nodding in agreement with his twin, "I'm with you on this one, sis."

Lily added, "He looks like a distant relative of the Joker," her disdain evident in her voice.

Isabelle concurred, saying, "For once, I agree with you."

As panic set in, Elliot yelled, "How in the world are we going to rescue Felix from this lunatic?" His voice held a hint of hysteria.

"I don't know," Daniel admitted with a shake of his head. I remained silent, feeling utterly helpless. We were confronting a being who had once been a god, and the gravity of the situation weighed heavily on me.

"We'll need a miracle to stop him," Daniel murmured, his head still shaking. His body language was the only sign of the fear that had gripped him.

I realized I was at a distinct disadvantage. My only source of magic was the ability to invoke the element of fire. As I pondered our predicament, a risky idea occurred to me: what if the other three factors followed the same formula? It didn't take long for the others to pick up on my thoughts, and the battle against Kel was on the verge of commencing.

The final battle was upon us. Felix broke his silence, directing a glare at Kel. "So, creating a zombie army is just one of your many plans to take down the Empire?" he inquired. It was the first time he had spoken since his abduction.

Kel let out a sigh. "Are motives all you brats care about? Let's just say I'm not fond of this Empire created from the New World. Do you want to know why the forces of the Colonies haven't tried to invade this land filled with wild magic? I willingly gave the first Emperor the spell used to create the mist surrounding the two continents that were once the Americas."

This revelation was utterly shocking. "What a nut job," I thought. It was difficult to fathom that someone as deranged as Kel Mather had played a role in the creation of the mist that encircled the Empire, protecting the wild magic of the former Americas. Just as he and his siblings had created the Dome Colonies, which served as a hidden farm for them to sustain themselves on the life force and dark emotions of humans.

Kel's vision for the future sent chills down my spine. I couldn't fathom his obsession with death and destruction, and I openly challenged him. "What kind of future could you possibly get from death and destruction?" I demanded. His close-mindedness regarding his plans was evident, and the others shared my sentiments.

"It's simple, little girl," Kel retorted, "a glorious future created from war and bloodshed. Everyone has either forgotten or wants to forget all that I've done for them. So both old and new magic wouldn't be destroyed by those who live in fear beneath the Domes of the Colonies."

His words left me speechless. Kel's twisted vision of a glorious future built upon war and bloodshed was nothing short of horrifying. I could feel the tension in the air as the final battle was about to unfold, and our determination to save Felix burned even brighter.

Kel's words shed light on his sinister plan to disrupt the peaceful existence of the Dome Colonies, which remained isolated from the outside world. He aimed to use their vulnerability to his advantage, potentially bringing harm to those living in the Colonies. His intention was to gather all the pieces for each of the aces, and he already had some pieces within his grasp.

Our determination to save Felix and stop Kel grew stronger than ever. We realized that defeating Kel was not just a personal battle but a fight to protect those in the Dome Colonies and beyond. We were prepared to do whatever it took to ensure the safety of the New World and thwart Kel's destructive agenda.

Chapter Fifty-One

This guy was seriously starting to get on my nerves. "We will put an end to your plans," I declared firmly, "my friends and I are unwavering in our resolve to collect all the scattered aces and harness their power, which will ultimately free the magic you've selfishly hoarded for decades."

Kel's response was immediate and fervent, "Not as long as I draw breath!" He bellowed, his eerie purple-black eyes fixated on the menacing Wendigo's lurking behind him. In a moment of realization, it hit me — he must have stealthily conjured them without our knowledge.

"Seize those brats," Kel commanded the monstrous creatures. I sighed deeply. As the final battle loomed before us, a sense of impending chaos enveloped the air. The eerie, animalistic wails of the Wendigo's were becoming increasingly grating.

"What's your strategy, Adelice?" Trey's voice cut through the cacophony, intermingling with Halle's agile dodges to evade a Wendigo's vicious claws. My cheek stung as a scratch drew a thin line of blood.

From that moment, the Wendigo that had inflicted the scratch began to howl in agony as if its claws had come into contact with a corrosive acid. It appeared our blood could indeed be a formidable weapon.

"Adelice!" Elliot's panicked cry pierced the chaos as he unleashed a combustion spell that detonated the monster's body. He sprinted toward me, eyes wide with shock at the sight of the minor scratch on my cheek. "I'm fine, it's just a surface wound, and I can handle it," I reassured him.

"Girl, you look like you're on death's doorstep!" Trey exclaimed, his expression a mixture of shock and concern.

He was making it sound as if I were at death's door. "Don't concern yourselves with us! Focus on getting Felix out of Kel's clutches," Halle urged urgently. I nodded and began to discreetly navigate the shadowy recesses of the lobby. To my surprise, I spotted Felix crawling on the floor. Evidently, he'd managed to escape while Kel was engrossed in directing the Wendigo attack.

"Are you okay?" I inquired as I closed the distance between us, noting that he was a few feet away from the drainer who was preoccupied with commanding the Wendigo's to eliminate us.

"I'm fine, Adelice; I've endured far worse than being held captive by a drainer," Felix replied with a nonchalant tone.

"None of you will escape with your lives!" Kel's proclamation rang out as he snapped his fingers with grim determination. An agonizing groan escaped my lips as a searing headache gripped my mind.

"What in the world is happening!?" Lily demanded, her voice laced with frustration.

"I possess the power to manipulate the human psyche," Kel stated with eerie calm. The throbbing pain in my head intensified, resembling the sensation of a blade being driven into the back of my skull.

"It's through this power that I influenced individuals responsible for some of the most heinous crimes in history: John Wayne Gacy, Ed Gein, Ted Bundy, the Night Stalker Richard Ramirez, and Jeffrey Dahmer. I even incited some of the darkest events in history, such as the Salem Witch Trials and the St. Valentine's Day Massacre."

"It's through my influence that these ominous figures and events have been etched into the annals of history. I feed on the discord and thrive on the chaos and suffering of humanity," Kel boasted with a chilling pride. Even from our vantage point, Felix and I could observe the sinister transformation of Kel's nails, which had assumed the appearance of obsidian daggers. Their razor-sharp tips oozed a noxious green liquid, undoubtedly a deadly poison where a minuscule dose the size of a fingernail could prove fatal. I found myself in a precarious position.

The mere touch of Kel's poison would be a death sentence for me. "Feeling the fear yet?" Kel taunted, his voice dripping with scorn. "You ought to be, considering that even a tiny drop of my venom can be lethal."

"Make sure none of his venom touches your exposed skin," Felix cautioned. I nodded, fully aware that there was one spell capable of neutralizing the poison before it could come into contact with us.

"I invoke the power of ice!" I cried out, my voice resonating with urgency, as sheets of frost materialized and were directed straight at Kel's deadly, venomous nails. A look of sheer astonishment crossed the drainer's face as he beheld his most potent defense transformed into a glacial array of icicles.

"Curses," he spat, his voice laced with frustration, "this isn't the end! I'll make every moment of your lives a relentless nightmare!

As long as I draw breath, you should brace yourselves for the pain and torment I shall unleash!"

"Coward!" I bellowed in response as he and his monstrous cohorts made a hasty retreat from the lobby. No, he couldn't be allowed to escape!

I couldn't allow him to escape, not after all the havoc he'd caused. Acting on pure instinct, I made the decision to pursue Kel, tracking him out of the building. The moment I stepped into the open, I noticed a vivid red stain on the left side of my shirt.

Blood, my mind registered with a jolt. The injuries inflicted by the Wendigo had been more severe than I initially realized. It wasn't just my cheek; my hip had been grazed as well. "Someone, call an ambulance; that girl's bleeding!" A panicked voice resounded, and I blinked as I became aware of several purebloods who were looking at me, their expressions a mix of astonishment and genuine concern.

They must have escaped from the bunkers, I surmised, feeling a sinking dread that things were taking a turn for the worse. Just when I believed the situation couldn't deteriorate further, Kathy Ann dashed to my side, gathering her skirts to facilitate her hurried movement. The plump woman gasped, her eyes widening in horror as they fell upon my injuries. "Good Lord, child, what have those monsters done to you?" she inquired, her voice resonating with the same genuine concern that the other purebloods exhibited outside the building.

"Ma'am, I spotted some Wendigo's in the lobby!" a man's voice echoed, recognizing Daryl's distinct tone. Panic surged within me; the others were still inside, and I needed to reach them. I attempted to move, but my body felt feeble, weakened by the blood I was steadily losing.

"It's okay, Adelice, you're safe now," Kathy Ann reassured me. I stood there, taken aback. I had heard frightening tales about this woman, and it was astonishing to see her showing kindness to me after weeks of attempting to elude her.

The cacophonous wail of approaching ambulance sirens reached my ears, growing louder with each passing moment. My strength was waning rapidly, and the only desire I harbored was to surrender to the embrace of sleep. My vision blurred, and I sensed the presence of something sharp being inserted into the center of my arm, delivering a potent sedative that caused my eyelids to droop heavily, sealing me in a peaceful darkness.

Chapter Fifty-Two

I couldn't discern the passage of time during my slumber; days blended together in a hazy, uncounted sequence. Upon waking, I was enveloped by an overwhelming expanse of stark white, and for a fleeting moment, I questioned if I had entered the realm of the afterlife. As my vision gradually sharpened, I realized I was reclining on a sterile hospital bed, an intravenous line snaking into my arm. My attire consisted of a simple white nightdress.

A surge of anxiety coursed through me as I comprehended my hospital surroundings. A pressing thought intruded: Where were the others? Panic began to set in, driving my frantic thoughts. In my haste to ascertain my condition, I attempted to shift, only to be met with a sharp jolt of pain. Without hesitation, I lifted the hem of my nightdress, revealing a swath of thick gauze bandages concealing the wound on my hip. A solitary Band-Aid adorned the scratch on my cheek.

The hospital room I found myself in held an oddity I couldn't ignore—luxurious flower arrangements and baskets of delectable baked goods festooned the table adjacent to the television, while a collection of sophisticated get-well cards graced the windowsill.

What in the world was happening here!? My thoughts raced with hysteria; I needed to escape and locate the others.

The situation took an even more bewildering turn when Kathy Ann entered the room, her face adorned with a broad, cheerful smile upon seeing me ensconced in the bed. "Marvelous, you're awake!" she exclaimed with evident delight. "The doctor predicted you'd regain consciousness soon, and he was absolutely right!"

"What's all of this?" I inquired, pointing at the abundance of flowers, baskets filled with baked treats, and the array of get-well cards. "These are expressions of sympathy from the aristocracy," the System agent elucidated, her smile still in place.

"You're quite the sensation in elite circles," she beamed. I scoffed. "It's not as though I've achieved anything remarkable; all I did was evade being captured by you and your agents."

Kathy Ann let out a somber sigh. "Why did you choose to run away?" she inquired, her curiosity appearing sincere. Despite the many ominous tales surrounding this woman, she seemed to exhibit genuine concern and an amiable demeanor.

"I failed to see the purpose in staying where I wasn't wanted," I responded candidly, offering my honest explanation.

"Oh, dear, you've got it all wrong. The moment they saw your profile, they were eager to welcome you back as soon as you were fit for travel. Your benefactors never stopped searching for you after you ran away." My inner thoughts couldn't help but add, "By hiring a private investigator, I presume." However, a more pressing question gnawed at me. "Where are my friends?" I pressed urgently.

"They're in a secure location," Kathy Ann assured me, her tone soothing. What she meant, however, was that they were confined in separate cells at the local System Center, awaiting the arrival of their birth families. My heart sank, and it dawned on me—my life and my freedom were officially over.

"Now that you're awake, it's time to consider traveling to your benefactors' residence," Kathy Ann suggested gently, "but it's essential to take it easy given your injuries."

A woman clad in blue scrubs, unmistakably a nurse, wheeled in a serving cart. "You should have a meal first," Kathy Ann advised. "There are clothes for you in the closet to change into. We can't keep your benefactors waiting," the agent chimed in with an ear-piercing sing-song tone, causing my ears to sting as she exited the room. While Kathy Ann's effervescent demeanor grated on my nerves, I had to admit she wasn't a sadist.

I contemplated the array of food on the tray: angel hair pasta smothered in a rich, creamy sauce crafted from butter and cheese, embellished with green onions, breadcrumbs, and two meaty chunks that my discerning eye identified as swordfish. My stomach recoiled. After subsisting on popcorn and beef jerky for weeks, I wasn't sure if my system could handle such indulgent, gourmet fare. Nevertheless, I took a few tentative bites of the pasta, and to my surprise, it didn't taste as bad as I had initially feared. Perhaps it was the hunger talking, having gone hours without a proper meal.

I couldn't resist the temptation and nibbled on a few of the baked goods from their respective baskets: chocolate chip cookies and yellow cupcakes adorned with strawberry buttercream frosting. If I were on death row, this would certainly be my ideal last meal.

As I stepped into the closet, I was taken aback by the sight of my jeans and t-shirt, now immaculately clean and devoid of the bloodstains from my injuries. After I changed out of the nightdress, I found my attention drawn to the largest flower arrangement in the room: a resplendent display of red roses with small stuffed ravens artfully nestled into the foam supporting the stems at the base of the vase.

These tokens of gratitude, I realized, must have been a gift from Daniel's parents, their way of expressing appreciation for my care of their son. It provided me with a small comfort, knowing that I had garnered an ally within one of the Elite families. As for the others, my confidence waned, given that I had essentially ridiculed their superior. Nevertheless, the presence of the get-well cards and baskets seemed to indicate that they didn't harbor significant ill will towards me.

With a resigned sigh, I accepted the inevitable and braced myself to meet the family who had purchased me. Though I knew little about them, save for their affiliation with Gray's inner circle, there remained the possibility that they would be as relentlessly cheerful as Kathy Ann.

The gondola ride was a somber journey, each passing minute drawing me closer to an ominous fate. It wouldn't be long before I met the individuals who had acquired me, and the commencement of my life sentence.

As Kathy Ann and I disembarked from the gondola and set foot onto the private sky deck, a palpable sense of foreboding washed over me. "Is it her? I rushed here as soon as I heard she was awake. Claire will be ecstatic when I deliver the news." The voice sent an instant wave of fear coursing through my veins. I recognized that voice; it was the same voice I had heard during the talk show interview, a lifetime ago. Dread and repulsion engulfed me as Dorian Gray came into view, confirming my darkest suspicions. The reality was far grimmer than I had ever imagined – the individual who had purchased me was not merely a member of Gray's inner circle; it was Dorian Gray himself.

Dorian Gray's appearance remained unchanged since my friends and I had last encountered him. Clad in his customary regal purple attire, from waistcoat to suit jacket, he exuded an air of timeless elegance. His dark, flowing hair was tied with a satin ribbon, a few loose strands cascading gracefully on one side, an apparent nod to the latest fashion trends. His left eye was adorned with a gold-framed monocle, lending an air of refinement to his enigmatic demeanor.

As I inhaled the lilac cologne that enveloped him, an overwhelming sense of revulsion washed over me. I stood motionless, gripped by terror, as he scrutinized me with his piercing cornflower blue eyes. The situation took an even stranger turn as he meticulously removed one of his silk gloves, revealing sharp black stiletto nails beneath. I couldn't help but think, "I'm done for." I braced for an imminent retribution for my audacious escape, but instead, his exposed fingers tenderly traced the locks of my hair in a manner that defied all expectations.

"An uncommon hair color for someone of mixed heritage, but I find it rather becoming," Gray remarked, his smile returning as he gracefully slid his glove back into place. It suddenly became clear why he concealed his hands in gloves; they shielded the visible trait that marked him as a Flawed Pureblood.

"What are your intentions with me?" I questioned, striving to conceal my fear. This man, after all, was notorious for striking a Faustian deal to maintain his youth while his portrait bore the ravages of time.

Gray peered down at me, an expression of mild surprise coloring his features in response to my query. "Do you know who I am, my dear?" he inquired with an overly saccharine tone.

"Yes," I responded, bracing for whatever scheme he had in store for me.

"Pray, enlighten me," Gray purred, clearly entertained and sporting a malevolent grin. It was the only opportunity to put down this vain, superficial, narcissistic, purple-obsessed individual.

"I understand your reason for acquiring me, to alleviate the despair that afflicts your wife," I declared. It wasn't a direct insult, but it was sufficiently pointed to elicit a sharp, disapproving glare from Gray. At last, his true nature began to reveal itself.

"So, my suspicions were correct. You and those other young ruffians were the ones who invaded my office and personal sanctum, and dared to peruse my diary," he responded, his voice taking on a menacing tone.

It was abundantly evident how infuriated he was upon discovering that my friends and I had violated his privacy – not that I cared in the least.

"Can you really blame me? I'd rather endure the hardships of the slums than be utilized as a mere pawn in your wife's recovery, meant to fill the void left by your absent or deceased child," I retorted. Gray regarded me with astonishment.

It was confirmed; my fate was sealed, and I was now on death row. After a few moments of eerie silence, he burst into laughter. His mirth was unsettling, as if my words were nothing more than a jest to him. Once he had wiped away the tears of laughter and his smirk returned, he delivered a revelation that sent shockwaves through my very being.

"Oh, sweetheart, there appears to be a colossal misunderstanding," he began, his tone dripping with condescension. "I didn't purchase you to take the place of my child; it's because you are my child."

My vision began to blur as Gray's words echoed in my mind. It couldn't be true. I yearned to protest, to vehemently deny his audacious claim.

"Adelice is the name Claire and I favored the most," Gray prattled on, seemingly oblivious to the turmoil roiling within me. "It not only means noble and good in the Germanic tongue but is also a fusion of her name and that of my mother. The name we bestowed upon you, Adelice Marie Gray."

"No," I managed to whisper before the overwhelming shock and exhaustion overcame me. I felt myself slipping into the comforting embrace of unconsciousness.

Chapter Fifty-Three

I had slumbered for hours, and the world outside the window now bathed in morning light greeted my awakening. After ridding my eyes of sleep, I discovered myself in an unfamiliar, opulent bedroom. My initial instinct was to flee, to make a swift escape without falling into captivity once more. A sharp wince shot through me as my bare feet met the chill of the marble floor. One thing was certain: I had awakened in Dorian Gray's penthouse.

Silently, I exited the room, stepping into a narrow corridor adorned with lilac walls. Along one side stood a long, rectangular table, bearing elegantly framed photographs. Most of them depicted Gray and Claire, radiating happiness in each image. In one particular photograph, Gray was clad in an exquisite tuxedo, his arms enveloping Claire, who wore an ivory silk gown adorned with delicate white lace and intricate glass beading.

Wedding photographs, I speculated, initially thinking of leaving when a specific image seized my attention. It depicted Gray and Claire in a hospital room, the fair-haired girl reclining gracefully in a hospital bed with a weary but contented smile, while the dark-haired narcissist sat nearby in a chair, cradling a small, swaddled bundle in his arms.

My eyes widened as the realization hit me – a baby. The infant had pale olive skin and a luxuriant crown of moonlit white hair, bearing an uncanny resemblance to my own features. I gingerly lifted the photograph and noticed writing on the back of the frame. The words etched on the label jolted me: "Me and Claire after the birth of our daughter, Adelice Marie Gray."

"No, this can't be real," I whispered, feeling a sharp pain in my head as memories hidden beneath layers of fog began to gradually unravel.

The sound of approaching footsteps broke my reverie. "Good morning, Miss Gray. I trust you had a restful night?" I glanced up and observed that the voice belonged to a pureblood woman. She was tall, with ash-blond hair, fair skin, and brown eyes peering out from behind a pair of half-moon glasses perched on the bridge of her nose. Her attire, a black schoolmarm's dress, suited her well. I opted for a white lie, responding, "I slept quite soundly." The woman smiled warmly. "I'll inform our guest that you're awake," she said before departing.

As the woman departed, a strange, sticky sensation trickled down my cheeks, causing a sudden surge of fear. I was horrified to see the tears streaming down my face and staining my cheeks with crimson. Blood, I realized, I was crying tears of blood. First, the gruesome nightmare of being sutured on my back, and now this unsettling occurrence of blood-soaked tears.

"Is everything all right, Miss Gray?" the woman inquired upon her return from the living room area. I replied with a false assurance, "I'm fine," only to abruptly recognize that I wasn't actually shedding blood from my eyes.

"Our guest is prepared to meet with you now," she relayed. I needed to escape this place and locate my friends, but I harbored an unsettling premonition that Gray and his wife wouldn't let me depart so easily. The revelation of my true parentage had left me in shock, and the cryptic second calling loomed ominously in my thoughts.

For the time being, I needed to be patient and devise a plan for my escape from the penthouse and the Edge for the second time. I had to discover the whereabouts of Trey, Halle, Elliot, Isabelle, Lily, and Felix, and ensure their safe return with me to the island housing the artifacts of the higher court cards.

"Right this way," the woman with the half-moon glasses guided me out of the hallway and into the living room. She proffered a white satin robe for me to don, a clear indication that the Grays and their enigmatic guest were eager to meet with me. Calling them Mom and Dad was going to be quite the challenge after everything I had experienced. In a way, I had come to accept that I wasn't the same person I had been when Sera and her family discovered me wandering alone in the forest near the Slums of the Garden District.

She had perished the moment she lost her memories, embarking on a once-in-a-lifetime adventure alongside a boy who had, over time, become her dearest friend. On this journey, she had encountered five others who had similarly grown into cherished companions. Later, she added four more friends to her circle during the events of the Scavenger. Over time, the eleven of us had transformed into something more profound than mere friends, becoming a family not linked by blood but by the strength of our bonds. I pledged never to cease my search until I reunited with my family.

"Don't fret, my dear friends, I'm on my way," I vowed, ignorant of what awaited me in the uncertain present.

www.ingramcontent.com/pod-product-compliance
Lightning Source LLC
Chambersburg PA
CBHW070526310726
48976CB00002BA/552